THE FRANKENSTEIN REVELATION

Kevin Schultz

ISBN-13: 979-8-8691-1182-1 (paperback)
ISBN-13: 979-8-8691-1183-8 (ebook)

For Kaylee, always

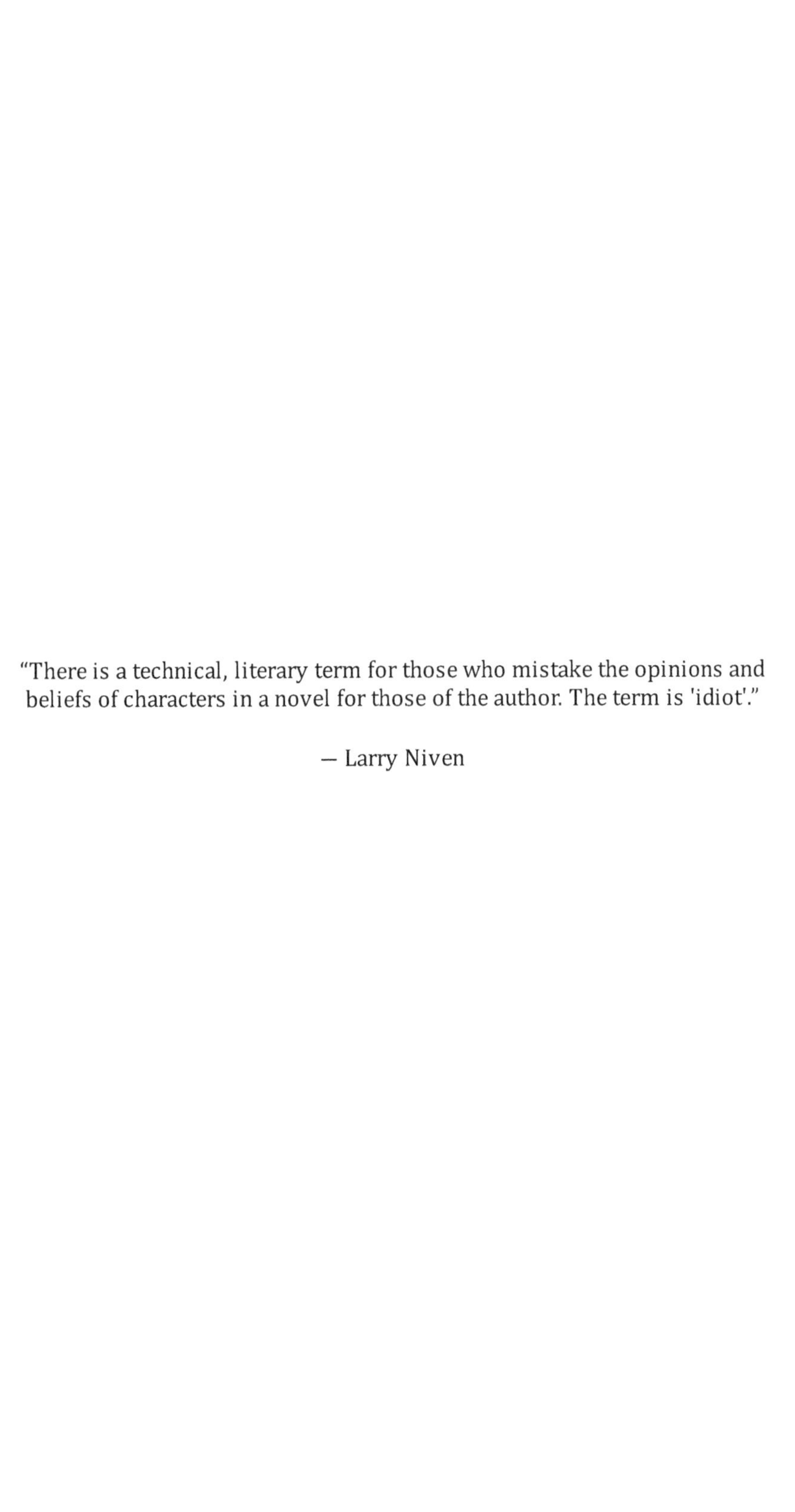

"There is a technical, literary term for those who mistake the opinions and beliefs of characters in a novel for those of the author. The term is 'idiot'."

— Larry Niven

CHAPTER ONE

In the Forest of the Night

It was just after sunset. The only remaining source of illumination, apart from my flashlight and the one held by the fire chief who stood beside me, was the glow of the forest fire still some distance off to the southeast. The light from the blaze was visible to us as we stood on the shore of the Pacific Ocean, facing away from the waves and discussing the fire. The forest itself ended at the crest of a line of cliffs, about one hundred yards away from where the two of us stood. The drop from the clifftop to the ground was about fifty feet, in my estimation.

As the fire chief spoke proudly of the job he and the men from his department, along with the region's stalwart smokejumper crews, had done to successfully keep the fire at bay, at least for now, I saw something. Up where the forest ended, a figure appeared from out of the woods. Backlit by the glow of the blaze, we could not make out any features on the face of the person. For it definitely was a person, that much we could tell. But... was there something about the figure, something... familiar?

The man, at least we guessed it was a man, from his shape and staggering movements, charged uncertainly out of the trees and came to an abrupt halt just short of the edge of the cliff, then turned and seemed to look back the way he'd come. Immediately concerned, the fire chief leapt into action, running towards the base of the cliffs below the figure, shouting out a warning to the man above. Unfortunately, the warning seemed to produce the opposite effect, as the stranger spun back around, lost his balance, wobbled, then toppled forward and plummeted over the edge, landing with a hard thump on the rocks at the base of the cliff.

I ran to catch up with the fire chief. As I neared the fallen figure I could see he wasn't moving. He did, however, appear to still be breathing. That was something, at least, I thought.

The chief hurriedly knelt beside the man, paused ever-so-briefly, almost as if surprised at something, then immediately began his emergency medical ministrations. Pulse check, airway check, various other procedures I once knew long ago from first-aid classes but had since sadly forgotten.

As I played my flashlight over the unconscious man, giving the chief light for his work, I finally caught sight of the man's face. I gasped. I knew then why the chief had paused just that little bit.

Lying there before us, unconscious, was the Frankenstein Monster.

*****

At this point, you may be asking yourself, as a great man once (well, many times) said, "What? What?! WHAT?!?"

Yes, there will be many more *Doctor Who* references before we're done here. Brace yourself.

My name is Harrison Edwards. But you probably knew that, being my daughter Katie. What am I doing? I'm telling you a story. An important story. But we'll get to that. First, let me set the scene, so you know what, where, when, etc. I guess when, especially, as this was a while ago, now.

It was the space year 2011. Moonbases, flying cars, teleportation, all that we dreamed of for our future when I was a child… never came true. At least, not yet. Maybe by the time you're old enough and read this. One can hope. Sadly, 2015 came and went, and no flying DeLoreans. Though the Cubs did win the World Series in 2016. *So* close!

So, I'm in my… let's say mid-to-late thirties. I'm a senior staff reporter for the *Arbor Harbor Coast Post* (yeah, that name makes me wanna vomit, too), the daily newspaper that still serves our little village of Arbor Harbor, as well as its neighboring towns north of us along the coast of the Pacific Ocean.

Arbor Harbor. A peaceful, quaint, old-fashioned maritime seaside village in Northern California, USA, Earth. (Hey, you never know, might need to specify that sometime in the future.) A small natural bay off the Pacific gives the village half of its name, while the other half derives from the forest which surrounds the town on its other sides. Yeah, the name's a bit of a stretch, but that's what the town is called, so we have to live with it.

We're small-ish, but with plenty of modernity, such as our newspaper, a hospital, a police department, fire department (mostly volunteers), and even a little community college. We even have the internet. However, so far we have resisted each and every attempt by fast food chain restaurants and big-box stores to invade our little hamlet. Mon-and-pop stores are more our style. We're a bit of a distance off the main highway which is to our east, and that distance contributes somewhat to our relative seclusion and spirit of independence. And perhaps all of these features are what continually draw tourists every summer. That's just fine with us, we love the tourists, they have such good taste. And we love the money they leave behind.

As to why I'm telling you this story, well, my reasons will become clear as we go on.

***

A few hours before the shock at the base of the cliffs, Chief Hank Brewer of the Arbor Harbor Fire Department called me up and suggested we meet in order for him to update me on the progress being made against the distant but bright forest fire. Yes, we could have done that over the phone, but it was a beautiful night, and I felt like getting some fresh oceanside air. So we met at the public beach area of Theodore P. Judah County Forest, which bordered Arbor Harbor to its south. I left my house, a nice two-bedroom one-story home not far from the newspaper offices, hopped in my car with my sweet, goofy black-and-white English Springer Spaniel named Sonny, and headed for the park which was named after a prominent mover-and-shaker on the Trans-Continental Railroad saga in California, way back in the late 1800s.

I parked my car and cracked the windows for Sonny so he could enjoy the smells and feel the breeze. And breathe, of course. True to form, however, Sonny stuck his nose out briefly, then withdrew and settled himself against the back of the rear bench seat. Oh, well. That's my little chicken-dog, sweet and loving but not very brave.

I got out and told Sonny I'd be back in a jiffy. Of course, he didn't know what a "jiffy" was. Come to think of it, neither do I. Anyway, he thumped his tail against the seat and watched quietly as I headed off. I found Chief Brewer and began the interview, asking him about the efforts being made against the fire.

It had sprung up a few days earlier, and its exact cause had yet to be determined. Its origin had apparently been in the far southeast corner of the large county forest area, and its slow but inexorable spread to the north had begun to worry the residents of Arbor Harbor. Chief Brewer was confident the blaze would not approach anywhere near the town itself, and so far the efforts to contain it were succeeding. But in a town close enough to see the glow of the fire after sunset, one learned to stay constantly alert to shifting winds, the smell of burning wood, the clouds of smoke. And Chief Brewer had always been very good about keeping the media and the general public fully informed and updated on any potential fire threats.

And then we encountered the Frankenstein Monster.

Now, like any sane, reasonable person, I knew *Frankenstein* was a fiction book, a brilliant story written by Mary Wollstonecraft Shelley in 1818, and most famously presented to the world in the form of the 1931 Universal movie, starring Boris Karloff as the "Creature", as he was billed in the credits. (Well, strictly speaking, in the end credits; he was listed only as "?" in the brief opening cast list in order to sustain the mystery.) The man before us couldn't possibly be the actual Frankenstein Monster, because there was no such thing in the real world.

So how, why did he look just like the Karloff Creature? And I mean just like it, *exactly* as if Boris himself, in full makeup, had walked off the set from eighty years ago, hopped in a time machine, and landed nearby just a few minutes earlier and a short distance away from us. But that was impossible. Yet the details were exactly right, uncannily, eerily, inexplicably exactly right. The black hair was perhaps a bit longer and shaggier than the classic iconic image, but the flat-topped skull, the pronounced forehead and brow, the sunken eyes, the nose, the jaw, even the goddamn bolts in the sides of his neck were damn near perfect. And to my admittedly inexpert eyes, it did not appear to be a mask or prosthetics or makeup, no, sir. It looked like the real deal.

And it gave me the chills.

Meanwhile, Chief Brewer had radioed for an ambulance, which duly arrived just a few short minutes later. The paramedics brought a stretcher and gear, and, after determining the patient was stable enough, shifted the man carefully onto the stretcher and brought him to the waiting ambulance.

"Will he be alright?" I asked Chief Brewer, both of us still somewhat in disbelief, as we followed the medics to the parking area.

"For now, I'd say," Brewer said as the ambulance was loaded and driven off. The chief opened the door of his Land Rover and looked at me. He knew we were both just as unnerved by the face of the stranger. "The doctors will know more after they've examined him, of course."

I hopped in my car and followed the chief and the ambulance to Sacred Family Memorial Hospital, where I parked and told Sonny to be just a bit more patient. He thumped his tail on the seat, which, as always, brought a smile to my face, even in these weird circumstances.

CHAPTER TWO

Survival

Once inside the Emergency entrance of the hospital, I found two young women sitting behind the admissions counter, chatting quietly amongst themselves. They looked up as I approached.

"Can I help you, sir?" the taller one said.

"Yes," I said politely, "I'm Harrison Edwards, I'm with the *Post*." I often shortened the name of the paper to "the *Post*" to spare myself the embarrassment and usual snickering. "Would someone be available to talk with me about the man that was just brought in?"

The two women looked at each other. Oddly enough, neither of them seemed familiar to me. Not that I visit the Emergency Room often, but in my line of work I do visit the hospital on occasion. Also, the relatively small population of Arbor Harbor tended to make acquaintances of nearly everyone. The taller woman, whose little plastic name badge read "Stacy R." said "I'm not sure we can talk about patients..."

I sighed inwardly. "Then perhaps you could tell me if Dr. David Ashraf is on duty tonight?" I asked patiently. Dr. Ashraf was one of the doctors on staff with whom I had developed a good working relationship.

The two women again looked at each other. Stacy R. whispered something to the other, who I saw was named "Jolene W." Jolene W.

shrugged. Stacy R. turned back to me and nodded. "Yes, he's here."

"Could you please tell him that Harrison Edwards from the *Post* is here and would like a word, please?"

"I can try," said Stacy R., scribbling on a Post-It, "but it's been, like, super busy tonight."

I nodded as she headed off. I politely ignored the fact that no one else had been in the waiting area when I'd arrived, and no one had come in since. Maybe the "busy" was behind the double doors that separated the waiting area from the actual working area of the ER. "Well, when you can, please, thanks," I said flatly.

I went and sat down in one of the not-very-comfortable chairs that seem to be ubiquitous to hospital waiting rooms everywhere. After a few minutes of glancing at the magazines on offer, I got up again and went back to the counter. Stacy R. had returned, told me it would be a little while before Dr. Ashraf would be available. Then the two women were chatting again. Stacy R. was twirling and clicking a retractable pen in a very annoying manner. "Super busy" indeed.

"I'll be right back," I told them, then headed outside.

Those two sure didn't seem like traditional, regular Arbor Harbor residents to me, I thought. Was the job pool for the hospital drying up so they had to hire from further afield outside of town than usual now? That was a bit sad, if that was the case. This community loved its self-sufficiency and its spirit of togetherness. Maybe the two women were just still too young and not yet fully in cheerful Arbor Harbor mode. Maybe I was just too cynical. Maybe I was just getting old.

I collected Sonny from my car and took him for a short walk to do his business. When he was finished I took him on a leisurely stroll around the hospital grounds. Partly it was killing time, giving Dr. Ashraf a chance to get free, and partly it was to clear my head regarding the strange man we'd discovered earlier that evening.

Who the heck was he? Why did he look like Boris Karloff as the Frankenstein Monster? Where had he come from? Why had he been in the forest that night, running from the fire? It quickly became obvious I had plenty of questions but zero answers. Still, it was a nice, clear, crisp March evening, and I was walking my dog, and that wasn't so bad.

***

After dropping Sonny off at the car, I headed back inside the hospital. The inner set of sliding doors opened as I came in, revealing the thin, rumple-haired figure of Dr. David Ashraf standing at the check-in counter talking with Stacy R. and Jolene W. Dr. Ashraf turned at the sound of the doors, then gave me a tired smile, running a hand through his thick black thatch of hair. It didn't help. He led me over to a corner of the still-deserted waiting area, and we sat down.

"I understand you're interested in the John Doe that just came in," Dr. Ashraf said in his smooth, cultured, slightly accented voice.

"Yeah," I said, "I was there when he fell off the cliff."

"Well," the doctor went on, "he's currently stable, we think, but he is comatose. He had multiple contusions and small lacerations all over his body, most particularly on the head. None of these wounds appear to be life-threatening. However..." He hesitated, frowning in obvious puzzlement and frustration.

"Yes?" I prodded.

"Well, many of his vital signs do appear to be stable, but... they're very... odd. Some of the numbers we're seeing would typically indicate a severe reaction to some trauma or other, completely apart from his fall and the injuries to his head. From what I can gather, it appears his vitals are generally all at standard, nominal levels for him. His systems in general appear to be in good condition, it's just that they're running very... strange."

"How so?"

Dr. Ashraf shook his head. "His pulse is more than double that of an average adult male, and the sheer strength behind each beat is incredible. Blood pressure is severely abnormal as well, breathing is extremely deep and powerful. Just about the only 'normal' reading on him, as compared to average adult human male standards is his EEG, which shows his brain activity to be on a par with what would be expected of the typical comatose patient. Frankly, this is like nothing I've ever seen, or even read about, not even remotely."

I considered for a moment. "You're sure about those readings?"

Dr. Ashraf looked at me with a raised eyebrow and a tired smile.

"Of course you are, I'm sorry," I said.

"I checked them all, multiple times. Always the same." He sighed and shook his head. "Do you know who he is?"

"No," I said. I hesitated, then added cautiously, "Though he did look familiar..."

The doctor blew out a huge sigh. "That's the other crazy thing about him. And before you ask, that is his actual face and skull. Flat head, enlarged brow, sunken cheeks, bolts in the neck... They're all real. Not makeup, not prosthetics, nothing like that. There are a number of very faint scars which lead me to believe he may have had plastic surgery at some point, and quite a while ago at that. There was even a faint trace of an autopsy scar, you know, the Y-shaped incision on the torso. Again, like the other scars, it had to have been a very long time ago."

An autopsy scar? I thought, puzzled, to myself, feeling more and more lost. "How long ago, would you estimate?"

"Difficult to say with any precision, especially with his abnormal metabolism." Dr. Ashraf sighed again wearily. "All in all, his similarity to Boris Karloff as Frankenstein is... I'd almost say 'impossible', were it not for the fact that it's right in front of my face."

I almost spoke up and corrected the doctor about Karloff actually playing the Monster (as he was billed in the end credits, the opening cast list just had "?" for the Monster, as we've already discussed), whereas Colin Clive played Dr. Frankenstein, but I figured it was not the time to nitpick just then. I have a tendency to do that, to nitpick, I admit. I've tried to control it, to behave myself better. But I don't do it to show off, or as some kind of oneupmanship against anybody. For me, it always stemmed from a rather OCD-type desire for absolute clarity, neatness and accuracy. Though I'm sure an ex of mine would probably beg to differ.

"There was no identification on him," Dr. Ashraf continued, "absolutely nothing on him at all, so I had hoped you knew something about him. Chief Brewer had no clue who he was either. I've contacted the police department to have someone sent over to fingerprint him. Maybe that will tell us who we've got here."

"If he's in the system," I said.

Dr. Ashraf looked at me. "Do you plan on printing this?"

"I don't know yet," I answered honestly. "I don't know if anyone would believe the whole Frankenstein thing, even if we ran pictures or uploaded video. I'm thinking I might just log a basic John Doe blurb, just a few innocuous sentences, something careful like that."

"That might be for the best, for now at least. I really don't want to tell you how to do your job, and you know I wholeheartedly support freedom of the press, but... well, you can probably imagine what a zoo this place would be if this got out."

"I know," I said quietly. "Believe me, I'm just as reluctant to become a laughing stock."

Dr. Ashraf chuckled. "I hear that."

"Can I see him?"

"Not right now," the doctor said with a shake of his head. "I'm keeping him isolated at least overnight as a precaution while we monitor him. Tomorrow, possibly, it might be all right. I plan on keeping the number of people that have access to him to the absolute minimum necessary for his proper care. Hopefully that will help prevent the spread of any gossip or rumors."

"Let's hope," I said, knowing not to push the doctor for the moment. Didn't want to harm the working relationship we had just to take a quick peek of someone I'd be able to see more fully in just a few hours anyway. "Well, you know best. I'll let you get back to your work. Thank you for taking a few minutes to talk with me. If I find out anything that might be relevant or helpful to you—"

"Same here," Dr. Ashraf said, nodding.

"Thanks, Doctor," I said.

We shook hands, then I headed outside to my car. Before starting the engine, I sat for a moment and thought about the strange man lying unconscious in the hospital right there in Arbor Harbor. Would anyone believe such a crazy thing? Frankenstein's Monster? Seriously? I needed more, I needed something, anything solid and factual, before I dared publish anything so sensational or career-damaging.

I turned to look at Sonny in the back seat. He fixed his sweet, big brown eyes on mine. "I think I need to sleep on this," I said. "What do you think?"

Sonny wagged his tail and leaned forward to give me slobbering doggy kisses.

"I'll take that as a 'yes'," I chuckled, giving him a pet on the top of his head.

CHAPTER THREE

Mission to the Unknown

The following day was Sunday, so I woke up and did my usual Sunday morning routine. I let Sonny out into the back yard, filled up his bowl, filled up the bowl for my black cat, Sam, let Sonny back in, had myself some breakfast (Froot Loops, so sue me), showered, went to church, then headed over to the office.

The *Arbor Harbor Coast Post* (ugh) took up the entirety of a one-story building just a few blocks from the actual harbor itself. The building is not fancy, in keeping with most of the structures in what constitutes the small "downtown" area of our village, nothing elaborate or overwrought. Just a nice, pleasant facade with a modest identification sign with the newspaper's logo above the main entrance.

Once inside, I headed straight for my cubicle in the open-plan central area, glancing at the Editor-in-Chief's office along the way. As I had suspected, her door was shut and through the large window beside it I could see the lights were off and no one was inside. Lisa Takagi usually arrived in the afternoon on Sundays, in time for the daily bullpen session with all of the writers and editors to start putting the next issue of the paper together. The timing worked out for me, as I wanted to try to get more information on the mystery man before I talked with Lisa.

First things first, however. I wrote up my interview with Fire

Chief Brewer. Fortunately, we'd pretty much wrapped everything up regarding the fire before the arrival of the stranger. I left that particular part out of my article. When I had gone over the article again a few times, tightened some things up and so forth, I was finally satisfied with the writeup. I submitted it to Lisa's email and then moved on to what I really wanted to work on.

My boss still had not arrived, so I decided to head over to the police station, which was only a few blocks north of the *Post*. Outside it was a wonderful chilly day, hazy sun filtering through the clouds and the haze of smoke from the nearby forest fire. As I walked the short distance, the bracing coolness was very refreshing to my still-tired body. A good walk can do wonders.

***

I found Police Chief Raymond Packer in the lobby of the station talking with Mrs. Zucker, one of our long-time residents, so I waited patiently for the two of them to finish their business. Chief Parker shook my hand firmly, then led me through several doors and corridors until we reached his cramped office. We sat down and faced each other across his cluttered desk, surrounded by papers and boxes of files.

"So, what brings you out on a Sunday?" Chief Packer asked in his cheery voice.

"I'm looking into that John Doe that was brought to the hospital last night," I explained.

A slight frown creased the chief's face. "Yeah, I heard about that. No ID, doesn't match any outstanding persons..."

"Exactly," I said, trying to sound casual. "I think we would have heard about it if the Frankenstein Monster had been reported missing."

Packer grimaced. "I really could have done without that part. Can you imagine the media circus we'd have around here if—" He broke off, realizing what he'd been saying. "I mean—"

"Hey, it's fine, I'm kinda worried about that myself."

Nodding, the chief continued. "Looking like... like he does, you'd think it'd be a slam dunk to ID the guy. But since I'd rather not make that public at the moment, we're left with trying to identify him from his fingerprints. Unfortunately, the set of prints we took off of him last night didn't seem to turn up any match."

"None at all?"

"Well…" He hesitated.

"Well, what?"

Chief Packer frowned again. "Well, the fingerprint check we ran through the system did turn up a match this morning, from an older database. But it's an error, obviously."

"Why do you say that?"

"Because according to the data from the file, if the fingerprints are indeed a match, then this guy is over one hundred and twenty years old." He laughed. "I mean, come on, seriously? The officer who took the prints showed me the photo he'd taken of our John Doe, and he ain't no hundred-and-twenty years old."

It did seem extremely ludicrous, but… I slid my iPad out of my trusty shoulder-bag and launched my note-taking app. "I see," I said carefully as I began typing. "So whose prints did he match?"

Packer flicked through some papers on his messy desktop. "Here it is," he said, picking up a sheet. "Carlsen, Broderick Bishop," he read off. "Born March 1, 1887, Los Angeles, California. 1887. Ha! No way is this our guy, our guy is maybe sixty or seventy at most."

"Where exactly did the prints come from?"

"From his fingers," Packer quipped. Nice to see he could still maintain an air of humor at such a strange time.

"Walked into that one, I guess," I said with a good-natured smile. "I mean, where was the matching record from?"

Packer handed over the sheet he'd been reading from. I didn't recognize all of the police jargon or abbreviations, but I could see that it was a copy of part of a Los Angeles Police Department file from 1925, specifically pertaining to a charge of aggravated assault. Aside from that, along with Carlsen's inked fingerprints, his name, birth date, and the case number, there wasn't much more on the sheet that appeared to be of any use to me at the moment. But you never know.

"Did anything else come with this?" I asked.

Packer shook his head. "I'm guessing all they had was a fingerprint card or somesuch, no further info attached. We ran a search on Carlsen this morning through all the systems and databases we have access to. Came up empty. Most likely if it's an eighty-something year old record the LAPD may not have gotten around to scanning it or entering the data, apart from the fingerprints. Things tend to pile up, you know, especially with damn budget cuts and whatnot."

"Can I have a copy of this?" I asked.

"You can keep that one," Packer sighed.

I was starting to get a rough idea of a plan together, but I needed just one more thing from the chief. "And could I also maybe get a copy of the prints your officer took last night?"

Packer nodded and printed off another sheet from his computer. After passing me the fresh sheet, he suddenly narrowed his eyes at me. "Don't tell me you actually believe this John Doe of ours could actually be a one-hundred-twenty-year-old Broderick Carlsen?"

Treading lightly, I said, "Well, it's a possibility I think I need to run down, if only to eliminate it."

"It's bullshit, I'm telling you," he said, shaking his head. "A mistake! A records fuck-up! They happen all the time, sad to say. Don't waste your time on it, kid."

It was very possible he could be right, but I really felt I needed to at least check into it. And I never really liked being called "kid".

"We ran the prints multiple times," Packer continued. "Always the same result. But that doesn't mean it's correct, it just proves there's a mix-up in the system somewhere."

"You're probably right," I said diplomatically. "But I think I want to just follow up on it anyway."

Chief Packer threw his hands up in defeat. "All right, kid, go for it. See if you get anywhere. As far as the AHPD is concerned, that John Doe over at Sacred Family stays a John Doe, until either he wakes up and talks to us, or someone comes forward and positively identifies him."

"Logical thinking, that's fine by me," I said calmly. My final request, now I'd set myself on course to investigate the matter more deeply, might prove somewhat tricky with a now-grumpy Chief Ray Packer. Careful treading was called for, though sometimes that was not a very strong suit of mine. "Could I just ask one small favor, please?"

"I am all ears," he said with a smirk.

"Could you possibly give the Los Angeles Police Department a heads-up that I'd like to look into their records, in particular those pertaining to Broderick Bishop Carlsen?"

Packer sighed again and considered me for a moment. Then, making up his mind, and clearly not sure he should be doing so, he said "You're probably gonna have to go down there and look into it in person. I doubt they'd assign anyone to dig through dusty decades-old files for some wild goose chase."

I didn't bother to point out that the LAPD wouldn't actually know it was a wild goose chase, unless he told them it was when he contacted them. But I felt sure, from working with him for several years now, that he wouldn't do something unprofessional like that. So I just said, "That'd be fine. I'll probably get a flight for tomorrow morning."

Packer chuckled. "All right," he said, his grumpiness easing somewhat. "If it makes you happy. But you do know you and your story will be laughingstocks, right? I mean, come on, a hundred-and-twenty-year-old guy who looks just like Frankenstein?"

Encouraged by the chief's improved mood, I could not resist saying, "It's the Frankenstein Monster, actually. Frankenstein was the name of the scientist who created the Monster." Old habits die hard, sometimes.

"Whatever," Packer said, shaking his head. "I'll give LAPD a call after lunch and let them know you're coming."

"Thank you." I stood and collected my things.

"Hey, it's your funeral." He smiled as we shook hands. A generally decent man, Chief Packer. And a good policeman. Just not a very open mind, on occasion.

***

I stopped at Ricky-Lou's Bar-B-Q for an early lunch, a tiny 1950s-vintage diner that specialized in charcoal-broiled burgers, the most delicious burgers I have ever tasted in my life, and believe me, I've tasted plenty of burgers over the years. After polishing off four hamburgers (the burgers they make aren't huge, so four isn't quite as gluttonous as it sounds), I dropped by my house to let Sonny out and check my mail. After glancing briefly through the latest issue of *Doctor Who Magazine*, which I'd been collecting since about 1986 when I first learned there was actually an official magazine devoted entirely to my favorite (or favourite, keep reading) British (there it is) science fiction TV show, my favorite TV show ever, come to that, I then drove over to Sacred Family Memorial.

Dr. Ashraf happened to be available when they paged him to reception. He looked even more tired and haggard than when I'd left him the night before.

"Did you even get to go home last night?" I asked him as we got on the elevator for the short ride up to the second floor.

"No," he answered, "but I did catch a few winks in one of the supply closets, so that's something."

"I don't know how doctors and nurses can survive, much less do such critical work, on such crazy schedules."

"I'm not too sure either," Dr. Ashraf replied, "but it is the life we lead."

The doctor showed me into a room along a quiet hallway, in view of the nurses' station near the elevator. It was a basic, plain hospital room, this one with only one bed. And on that bed was our John Doe. Or should I start thinking of him as Broderick Carlsen? Maybe not just yet.

As I stepped quietly to the unconscious man's side, Dr. Ashraf said softly, "He's still comatose, but we're more confident that he's stabilized now. Difficult to say for sure with his abnormal readings, but we believe he's past the worst of it now."

I shivered as I beheld once more that surreally familiar face. Damn, it was creepy, being right there next to a person that to all intents and purposes seemed to be the Karloff Frankenstein Monster. Even unconscious, in a hospital bed, under blankets, attached to various pieces of medical equipment, in totally modern twenty-first century surroundings. It was incredible. It *was* the Monster. I'd almost swear to it.

Almost.

In better lighting than I'd had the previous night, I could see a faint greenish tinge to the man's skin, just at the edge of perception. Jesus, who the hell was this guy? No way could this have happened naturally, the odds against it were astronomical. Weren't they? This had to have been done deliberately, and done by another person. Dr. Ashraf had to have been right about the indications of probable plastic surgery that he'd detected. But why would someone do that to themselves? Himself? I was so thrown I was uncertain of my grammar.

"For now," the doctor continued, "we're still keeping him isolated. I've brought in only one other doctor and a minimal amount of nurses and swore them all to secrecy."

"Can you be sure no one will talk?"

Dr. Ashraf shrugged. "They're all good people. I trust them. When I spoke with them we all agreed it would be best if we could prevent any crazy rumors or gossip or unwanted media attention. Present company excepted, of course," he added hurriedly.

"Thanks for that," I said graciously. Even though I'd been on the scene when the stranger had been discovered, the doctor could have easily put a lid on the entire thing and issued nothing but a "No comment". But Dr. Ashraf had let me in and trusted me, and that meant a lot. Especially in both our lines of work. And it demonstrated the strength of our mutual professional respect. "I'd like to take a picture of him, if that's OK with you…?"

Dr. Ashraf hesitated.

"Not for publication, I promise," I said. "I'm planning to head to Los Angeles to look into a possible lead on his identity, and a picture would be useful if a question of verification happened to come up. Please?"

Finally the doctor nodded. "All right. Just one, though. And please use it with discretion, OK?"

"Agreed. Thank you." I pulled out my iPad and snapped a pic.

"Los Angeles, huh? So the cops were able to ID him after all?"

Now it was my turn to hesitate. Did I really think the fingerprint match was correct? Was the John Doe before me actually Broderick Carlsen? Aged one-hundred-and-twenty? It seemed impossible, incredible. And yet, a teeny tiny voice at the far back of my mind said ever so quietly, "Maybe." Over the years I'd learned to listen to that little voice, as it was right far more often than it was wrong.

"Maybe," I said. ("Good boy", said my inner voice.) "They did a match on his prints, but the match was supposedly a man named Broderick Carlsen, who was apparently born in 1887. Which would make this guy—"

"A hundred and twenty-four." Dr. Ashraf frowned. "That does seem pretty unlikely."

"I know," I nodded, "but right now it's all we've got, so I want to check it out. Especially since the police apparently have no interest in doing so."

"Chief Packer's a nice enough person, but he's not exactly a 'think outside the box' type of person, is he?"

"No, he is not," I said, chuckling quietly as I put away my iPad and brought out the printouts the police chief had given me earlier, the fingerprints his officer had taken the previous night here in the hospital, and the prints from the 1925 LAPD file. I crouched down beside the bed to take a close look at John Doe's right hand. It was palm down, so I asked, "Mind if I just visually double-check his fingers against these records? Just to make sure for myself that they all really do match up?"

"No problem," Dr. Ashraf said.

With the doctor lifting up the hand gently for me, I checked each digit, comparing each one with both the Arbor Harbor PD set and the LAPD set from 1925. Then we did the same with the patient's left hand. To my admittedly untrained eye, they all looked identical, without question. Both hands. "Looks like they're all a match, as far as I can tell."

"I would agree," Dr. Ashraf said as he eased John Doe's hand back to the bed. "Amazing." He looked over at me. "Now what?"

And there could really only be one answer. "Looks like I'm going to Los Angeles to investigate our Broderick Carlsen here."

***

My boss Lisa was in her office when I got back to the *Post*. I knocked on her open door and sat myself down across the desk from her. She didn't look at me, instead kept focused on her monitor screen while she typed frantically at her keyboard. "Nice work on the Chief Brewer piece," she said.

"Thanks."

"Seemed a bit short," Lisa added.

I paused. I knew I had to bring up the John Doe thing, but I wasn't sure how best to go about it. Lisa Takagi could be… prickly. "We were, uh, interrupted."

Still not looking up at me from her work, Lisa repeated, "Interrupted?"

"Yeah," I said. Here goes. "A man ran out of the forest and fell off that cliff at the south end of the beach. You know, where the trees end and it's right at the edge of the sand with that rocky—"

"I know the place," Lisa said brusquely. She could tell I was stalling. "Why wasn't this in the article? Sounds like something noteworthy. Perhaps even *newsworthy*…?"

I didn't speak. Instead I got out my iPad, brought up the photo of John Doe I'd taken a short time before, and handed it across to Lisa, who finally pulled her attention from her computer.

"What the hell is this?" Lisa said quietly. Lisa didn't get quiet very often.

"That's the guy," I said, "the man who fell off the cliff. He was unconscious by the time Hank and I got to him. He's in a coma over at Sacred Family right now, but apparently stable."

"He looks just like fucking Frankenstein."

"The Frankenstein Monster, technically," I said, earning a harsh glare from Lisa. I hurried on. "And yes, he does. It's not makeup or anything like that. The doctor believes he may have been surgically altered to look like that."

"So who the hell is he?"

"No ID on him. The police ran his prints, but…"

Lisa looked at me again. "What?"

"Well, if the fingerprint match they got is correct, then this guy is a hundred and twenty-four years old."

She looked down at the photo again. "What the hell…? There's gotta be some mistake."

"Probably," I said to keep things smooth. "I don't quite get it either. But that's what the fingerprint match came up with. Broderick Carlsen, born 1887 in Los Angeles. The match comes from a 1925 case file down there."

Lisa was still staring at the picture. "Why would someone purposely make himself look like Frankenstein?"

I bit my tongue, saying instead, "I don't know. For a movie? But that would be stupid, to do all that for just one movie. And even if someone did remake *Frankenstein,* which I would have to assume would be what the surgery was for, you'd think they'd create and design their own look for the Monster, not just have a Boris Karloff clone. Or whatever this guy is."

"True," Lisa said.

"I'd really like to dig into this further," I said carefully. "I think there's something here that merits looking into. My first step would be to head down to LA to see what exactly they have on this Broderick Carlsen."

"Who may or may not be our John Doe."

"Exactly."

Lisa was silent as she thought for a moment. Then she nodded. "Okay," she said. "But I'm not running this story unless you can give me a solid and concrete explanation for all this crap. I'm not risking this newspaper's reputation on a crazy story like this, not unless all of our 'i's are dotted and our 't's crossed to the frickin' nth degree, you hear me?"

I nodded. "Understood. Thank you."

Back at my desk I booked a flight that was leaving early the next morning, as well as a hotel and a rental car. Ah, the joys of having a company credit card. I finished up in time for that day's bullpen session in the conference room. Lisa and the writers and editors worked out assignments for the following day's edition of the paper. Lisa briefly mentioned I would be "on assignment" for the next few days or so.

*****

On my way home, I called up a few of my friends to see if they wanted to hang out a bit that night before I headed out of town for a while. I needed to wind down somewhat after a rather strange twenty-four hours, so I was grateful when we agreed to meet up at another of my favorite Arbor Harbor haunts.

Ah, the Earl of Essex. Inside its rather nondescript exterior down near the docks in the harbor was a lively British-themed old-fashioned pub. The walls were festooned with British flags, soccer— I mean, football banners, photos and prints of famous British personages, landmarks, scenery, and so forth. Around the place several flat-screen TVs often showed football matches from across the pond via satellite TV, as they were doing that evening when I walked it. It was warm and comfortable after a chilly March day.

I quickly spotted my friends seated in my favorite booth, the one that had photos of all eleven (so far) Doctors from *Doctor Who* framed on the wall beside it. There was even a small picture of Peter Cushing as "Dr. Who" from two non-canon Dalek movies from the 1960s. He wasn't a "proper" Doctor, and I cringed at the use of "Dr. Who" as his character's name, when in the TV series he is only ever "the Doctor". Apart from the couple of times when "Who" was mistakenly used as his last name. Also, the first eighteen seasons of the Classic Series listed him in the credits as "Doctor Who", but that doesn't count, because the credits are outside the "fiction" of the *Doctor Who* universe. But never mind that, there goes my nitpicking side again. Anyway, it was still cool to include Peter Cushing, as the Dalek movies were generally entertaining, regardless of canonicity, and to have an actor of the caliber of Mr. Cushing was quite a nifty thing.

"Harry!" Jerry Willems enthused as I sat down. He grinned at me from behind his round John Lennon glasses. I never quite thought his long, flowing prematurely-white hair, which he usually kept in a ponytail, really suited him, but what did I know? Jerry's bright gusto helped keep him as the top real estate agent in the county. We'd met at UC-Sacramento, where he went on to earn a Bachelor's in English, which I'm not sure has ever been of use in his chosen career as realtor and property developer. We stayed friends after graduation, and when he moved to Arbor Harbor he joined me in the local community college's wind ensemble in the brass section, Jerry on French horn, me on trumpet.

"Harrison," Johnny Goldschmidt, the serene, somewhat balding, bearded man across from Jerry said evenly with a polite smile and a nod. Johnny was more reserved than either Jerry or myself. I'd known Johnny since grade school, then had gone to high school together, and on to college, where we'd met Jerry. The three of us were nearly inseparable for a time, even marching together in the Velvet Knights Drum and Bugle Corps during our summer breaks from school (Jerry and I on soprano horn, Johnny playing percussion in "the pit" up front) until we aged out at 21. Johnny had gotten his MBA after I'd gotten my journalism degree, and shortly thereafter he'd bought the Folio Bookshop in our native Arbor Harbor. He'd been at the downtown bookstore ever since, dealing in rare books, book repairs, and the like, as always in his calm, straightforward manner.

My two best friends were great sounding boards for me, their decidedly different but often complementary takes on various issues serving me well on many occasions. They'd helped me through my painful breakup with Sarah, for one thing. My current conundrum wasn't quite the same, of course, but I figured I'd be able to count on Jerry and Johnny for support if nothing else.

I ordered my usual fish and chips, along with a nice thick dark brown British stout.

"So, you seeing anyone yet?" Jerry asked brightly.

"Jerry," Johnny said quietly but warningly.

"What?" said Jerry. "A guy can't as his buddy if he's seeing someone?"

"Yes, he can," Johnny replied patiently, "but you do it so incessantly."

"It's fine," I said with a small, weak smile. "He means well. And, no, I'm not."

"I still say," Jerry continued happily, "you should let me set you up with this one gal I know —"

"Thanks, but no thanks, Jerry."

Jerry sighed. "Still expect it to just 'happen', huh?"

"Yeah," I said firmly. "What's wrong with that?"

Shaking his head, Jerry said, "Nothing's just gonna 'happen' unless you *make* it happen. Or let someone else, for instance me, make it happen *for* you."

"Jerry," Johnny interjected softly, "just let it go for now, all right?"

Jerry shrugged and took a gulp of his beer. I nodded a silent "thank you" to Johnny. I really didn't feel like discussing relationships just then.

"Anything interesting at work lately?" Johnny asked to refocus the conversation.

And of course I hesitated. I'd wanted to hang out with my buddies to talk about what I was investigating, among other things, but now the moment had come I suddenly felt unsure.

"What's wrong?" Johnny asked. I guess my pause and whatever look I had on my face had betrayed me.

Looking at my two best friends, I said to them, "Not a word of this to anyone, all right?"

"As usual," Jerry said as they both nodded seriously. And from past experience, I knew I could trust them both.

So I proceeded to tell them the story of the mysterious John Doe, and the possibility of him being a one-hundred-and-twenty-four-year-old man from Los Angeles.

"That *is* weird," Jerry said when I'd finally finished.

"Indeed," added Johnny. "What's your plan?"

"Heading to LA tomorrow," I said. "Which reminds me. Johnny, would you mind watching Sonny and Sam while I'm gone? I'm hoping it'll just be a couple of days."

Johnny smiled. "Sure. You know how much Rachel and I love those little guys."

"Thank you. Normally I'd ask Mom and Dad but they're still on their Alaskan cruise."

"It's not a problem," Johnny reassured me.

"Need a ride to the airport?" Jerry asked. "I'm headed that way for work tomorrow morning."

"That'd be great, thank you."

"What've you got planned for LA?" Jerry continued.

"Nothing too definite. Gonna check into that fingerprint record, try to look at the police files on Carlsen. If it's even him."

"It does seem rather far-fetched," said Johnny.

"Yeah. I'm not convinced one way or the other yet. This could just be some clerical error, or… Hell, I don't know. Part of me says just to chuck it and say 'T'ell with it', as my grandpa used to say and move on. But I just don't like unanswered questions."

Johnny chuckled. "You never did."

"And you never will," Jerry chimed in. "It's what makes you such a good reporter."

"Oh, shut up," I said as I felt my face redden. I was never good at accepting compliments.

"No, it is," Jerry continued. "Just look at that award you got a few years ago. That didn't come from just giving up and moving on. Did it?"

"No," I admitted as I took another sip of my drink.

"No," Jerry went on. "You don't give up. Not when your instincts tell you something's there. Like I think it's telling you now in this case. Right?"

I shrugged. "Yeah."

"Well, then," Jerry said with a triumphant grin. "Get your ass to LA and go crack this story."

He was right. My gut almost never led me astray, as my Northern California Press Association Award for Excellence demonstrated. Though I had had a gut instinct about Sarah, which did not turn out to be true at all. So I was not infallible. I did have some doubts about the John Doe story before me, but deep down inside I knew there was *something* there, something to get to the bottom of. "Thanks, guys," I said. "I appreciate the help."

"What help?" Johnny asked with a twinkle in his eye.

I chuckled, and we spent the rest of the evening enjoying our food and drinks while being amused by a table of Manchester United fans get overemotional about the match being show on the pub's main TV.

***

The next morning arrived pretty dang early for my liking. I woke up, got ready, let Sonny out, fed him and Sam, then waited for my ride. When I spied Jerry's car coming down the street, I gave Sam a big hug, which he didn't seem to care much for, as usual. Cats. I set him down again and he strolled away with a typical feline "Yeah, whatever, I've got better things to do" attitude, hopped up on the sofa in the living room and curled up in a corner of the cushions. Sonny also got a big hug from me, which he really didn't understand, as usual, but my sweet doggy gave me a few anxious kisses and wagged his tail excitedly. I told them both to behave for Johnny and Rachel while I was gone, then headed out the door.

As we rolled out of town in Jerry's car, the cloudy sky was just beginning to lighten. It was that early pre-dawn twilight which always felt to me like the day was just waking up itself, bleary-eyed, taking a huge yawning stretch. A while later, after the sun had risen above the horizon, Jerry dropped me off at the airport in Eureka, and a short time after that I was airborne for the not-too-long flight to Los Angeles International Airport.

When we reached the point at which it was safe to use our electronics (as if me writing up an article on my laptop or iPad would actually bring down a huge airplane like this, I mean, come on) I brought out my laptop and put in my DVD of the original 1931 *Frankenstein* which I'd packed the previous night. I wasn't quite sure why I'd grabbed it, apart from the fact of John Doe's resemblance to Karloff as the Monster in that particular movie, of course. I really didn't know if it would somehow provide any clues or leads or anything like that which might be relevant to my current assignment, but at the very least, it would kill some time on my flight.

Frankenstein was my all-time favorite horror movie, ever since I was a boy. I never really went for the more modern type of horror film, I didn't care for the Freddy or Jason style of slasher movies, nor the recent crop of dumb style-over-substance jumpscare shockfests or gorefests. No, give me a classic Universal monster movie any day. And *Frankenstein* in particular.

It wasn't that I found the 1931 film all that scary, really. Rather it was more the feel of it, the mood, the tone, the essence, the atmosphere of it. The stark black-and-white cinematography, the wonderfully impressive sets, the evocative direction, it all just *worked*. Even such detail as the obviously fake skies in the background of the "outdoor" scenes clearly filmed indoors on a soundstage, such as the opening graveyard scene, simply added to the fantastical eeriness of the thing. The director, James Whale, had done one hell of a fine job on the movie.

Take the introduction of the Monster, for example. The scene of his first full appearance, not counting his undead form or the reanimation scene, is a masterpiece of tense anticipation. The slow shuffling steps approaching from off-camera. The door to the room slowly, slowly opening. The Monster backing into the scene — *backing* into it! Slowly turning around. The quick jump-cuts from almost full-length on the Monster to the close-up right on Karloff's face. Just wonderful. Then the play of emotions from Karloff as the Monster is shown the sunlight far above him, then the sunlight is taken away from him. His reaching out for what was taken away, his joy replaced by sad confusion. Such a powerful display of technical and artistic mastery, both in front of and behind the camera, in just a few moments on screen. Simply breathtaking.

By the time the windmill was destroyed and the Monster defeated at last (…or was he?), my flight was on approach to LAX. I stowed away my laptop and tried to prepare myself for the completely unique world that is Los Angeles, California.

CHAPTER FOUR

The Search

I had been to Los Angeles before, numerous times. Back in my youth my parents would take me to Disneyland every Easter as a treat, at least until life got more complicated once I reached high school. Other non-Disney trips over the years, both with my parents and without, broadened my familiarity with the city, as did my more recent and usually work-related visits. However, none of that prevented the sprawling metropolis from seeming ridiculously crazy, especially to a motorist. Or anyone, for that matter.

My rental car turned out to be, as improbable as it sounds, a sweet black Corvette with all the trimmings. I'd requested a standard compact car, but when I got to the counter at LAX the very nice clerk offered me the 'Vette at the compact rate. Well, how could I say "no" to that? I didn't ask the reason for the upgrade, just took the keys with a poorly concealed stupid grin on my face and went out to the lot to find my new ride.

And it was so cool. I've never been a big car buff or gearhead or whatever the current "official" term is for an automobile enthusiast. But I do know a few things about cool (yes, I do, shut up back there), and that car most definitely was. The sleek black shape looked like a predator ready to pounce, and I couldn't wait to drive it. Even in LA. I threw my luggage in back, got settled behind the wheel, plugged in the

GPS unit I'd programmed the night before, started the engine, and hit the road, making my way to my first port of call, the headquarters of the Los Angeles Police Department.

The car handled spectacularly well, even in the ridiculously busy traffic that is customary to LA. The sun was shining through a cloudless yet somewhat smoggy day, and I left the top up until I felt more used to handling the car. Oh, did I not mention the Corvette was a convertible? Heck, yeah, it was. But I didn't want to get carried away joyriding with the top down until I was sure I knew just what the car was capable of. I'd never driven a Corvette before (unless you count the die-cast model of the Corellian Corvette starship from the beginning of the first *Star Wars* movie I had as a kid) and I didn't want anything disastrous to happen, least of all on the first day.

***

Almost everyone is familiar with Los Angeles City Hall from countless appearances in TV shows and movies, perhaps most famously from the Jack Webb TV series *Dragnet*. And also the 1980s *Dragnet* movie startting a pre-super-mega-stardom Tom Hanks and a post-mediocre-stardom Dan Aykroyd. Call me crazy, but I've always gotten a kick out of that silly movie. Anyway, after a drive through the traditionally insane streets, I found a parking ramp a few blocks from the iconic City Hall landmark, parked, got out my shoulderbag, and walked the short distance to my destination in the bright, warm, slightly breezy Southern California morning.

I've never been a fan of heat, so I appreciated the breeze as it kept me moderately comfortable as I walked. I know what you're probably thinking. If you don't like hot weather, why do you live in California? Easy. I live in the more temperate northern part of the state. It makes a huge difference, let me tell you. Also, Arbor Harbor itself benefited from being right on the ocean which helped keep temperatures more moderate and much more to my liking.

By the time I climbed the steps and entered the hallways of City Hall, my shirt was starting to cling to my back. It was a bit warmer out than I'd been expecting, and the walk had been a bit longer than I'd estimated. The air-conditioned interior of the building felt like heaven to me. I started to hope that this trip to LA would be over sooner rather than later, if March was going to be this inordinately warm, even for down south.

I arrived at the police department and asked at the main reception desk for Lieutenant Stephanie Llewellyn, the contact name Chief Packer had emailed to me the night before. I was led a short distance to a small windowless office.

Lt. Stephanie Llewellyn reminded me strongly of a beautiful actress named Francesca Hunt, who had, among other projects in her career, portrayed Secret Agent Rebecca Fogg on the short-lived cult steampunk sci-fi TV series *The Secret Adventures of Jules Verne*, a quirky little show I'd stumbled onto late one night and fallen in love with. And more particularly in love with the dynamic character of Rebecca Fogg. This Lieutenant Llewellyn was very similar in appearance, from the attractive figure to her pretty face and her luxurious red hair. She smiled at me politely as I sat in the chair opposite her.

"I'm Harrison Edwards with the *Arbor Harbor Coast Post*,' I said, proffering my ID and press credentials. "I believe our town's Police Chief Packer spoke to you about me…?"

Lt. Llewellyn nodded. "Yes, he did," she said, with sadly zero trace of an English accent. "He said you were looking into some old records from a case from the Twenties?"

"Well, sort of," I said. "I'm wondering what you might have on a Broderick Carlsen, born in 1887, I believe."

The pretty officer picked up a sheet of paper from her desk. "Yes, that *is* old," she said as she scanned the sheet. "This is all I was able to find when I ran a search on the name this morning. Just a list of charges and case numbers, I'm afraid." She handed me the printout.

It was exactly what she'd said it was, simply a printed list of various criminal charges and their respective case numbers, all attached to one Broderick Carlsen. The counts ranged from burglary, assault, battery, and theft to disorderly conduct, disturbing the peace, and so on. The dates ran from 1905 through to 1931.

"And this is all there is on him?" I asked.

"In our computer system, yes," Llewellyn said. "The related files and records themselves are stored down in the archives. We used to have more of these older cases digitized, but we had a server crash a short while back, and we just haven't had the time or personnel to rescan everything back in yet."

"Ouch," I said. "I've lost a few articles myself thanks to computer crashes. It really sucks."

Llewellyn chuckled. "It does indeed."

"Is it possible to access the original hard-copy records, by any chance?" I asked with a hopeful smile.

"Certainly," the lieutenant answered with a small smile of her own. Oh, yes, I thought, very much like Ms. Hunt. "Barring anything sealed or classified and so on, of course. Nothing involving national security or juvenile records and the like."

"I don't think my research should go anywhere near anything like that."

"Excellent," Llewellyn said as she stood. "Shall we head down there now?"

I followed the alluring figure of the lieutenant as she led me from her office and through a maze of hallways and doorways. I couldn't be sure, and I'd never actually looked into it, but as the chaotic layout was typical of police stations everywhere, it almost felt like the layout had originally been intended to confuse and frustrate intruders. Might look into that. Another time.

"I'm afraid our rescanning hasn't gotten anywhere near as far back as the 1920s or '30s," Lt. Llewellyn said as we walked.

"That's alright," I said amiably, "as long as the originals are still around. And legible."

"They should be," my attractive guide said. She opened a final door, this one with "Archives" neatly etched on a little nameplate beside it.

Inside was another windowless room, though considerably larger than the lieutenant's office we'd just left. To the right of us was a service counter beside a closed Dutch door, to our left were several very-uncomfortable-looking chairs and a few tiny end tables, while directly opposite the entrance to the room was a row of computer workstations, currently empty. Apart from myself and the lieutenant, only one other person was present, a young man seated in one of the chairs off to the side, taking notes from a file folder which rested on the table beside him.

Llewellyn went over to the glass-fronted service counter and pressed a small doorbell-like button affixed to the counter. It must have made some sort of sound somewhere, though we heard nothing, because a few seconds later an older, gray-haired woman appeared behind the counter and smiled at the lieutenant.

"Lieutenant Llewellyn," the woman said cheerily, "what brings you down here today?"

"Mrs. Stansfield," Llewellyn said, then nodded in my direction. "This is Harrison Edwards, he's a reporter working on a story and needs to look at some of our older records. Standard media access rules." I took that last to mean the national security and such she'd mentioned earlier.

"Certainly," Mrs. Stansfield said. She smiled at me with the kind of smile that made you feel like it was a really nice day and you were among good friends. "Please call me Holly, Mr. Ahrens."

"Only if you call me Harry," I said as I grinned back.

"I'll be in my office if you need anything further," Lt. Lewellyn said curtly, then she spun on her heel and headed out the door, closing it behind her.

"So, what can I do for you, Roger?" Holly asked.

I gave her the case number from the 1925 record from which the fingerprint match had been made. She went off out of sight amongst the rows and rows of storage racks which were the only things visible from my side of the counter. A few moments later Holly returned with a slim file folder which she passed across to me through the gap below the glass window.

"Thank you," I said as I took the file. I went over and sat down in one of the chairs. I had unfortunately been correct in my earlier assessment. These chairs were indeed extremely uncomfortable. Nevertheless, I tried to ignore it and concentrate on my work, pulling out my iPad and my pocket notebook, the kind that flips open like a communicator from the Original Series of *Star Trek*. Which is probably the reason I use that type of notepad, but I can neither confirm nor deny this.

Opening the manila file folder Holly had given me revealed a black-and-white mugshort on the top of a slim pile of papers.

It was him. It was John Doe.

He didn't look like the Frankenstein Monster in the old mugshot. That would have been ridiculous. Instead he looked like an ordinary person. No flattop skull, no bolts in the neck. Just a normal human being. Albeit a human being that vaguely resembled Boris Karloff.

Rather like Zachary Quinto looks somewhat like Eli Roth. (Go ahead, Google it, I'll be right here.)

I pulled out my iPad and compared the photo I'd taken the day before in the hospital side-by-side with the 1925 mugshot. John Doe's jawline and cheekbones were different, and the hair was also different. But a lot of things were quite similar, in fact identical in many instances. The ears, for one, the ears and the earlobes were exactly the same in both pictures. The nose matched. I stared at the mugshot. I stared at my iPad photo. Finally, I was convinced. As different as the two images appeared to be, there was enough there to conclusively persuade me that John Doe truly was Broderick Carlsen. My gut told me so as well, and I always listened to my gut.

It was against all common sense. And a glance at the two photos wouldn't have made things at all obvious. Yet I knew that the man who was lying in a coma at Sacred Family Hospital back home in Arbor Harbor really was a one-hundred-twenty-four-year-old criminal from Los Angeles named Broderick Carlsen.

I also knew that the mugshot itself wasn't proof enough of that fact. I needed more, and more solid, to back up what I knew would be a story that would be mocked and ridiculed if it were only based on such circumstantial and admittedly flimsy proof as the mugshot and the fingerprint match. Those would be a start, but I needed more. A lot more.

So I went through the rest of the file. It was a case of aggravated assault from July 7, 1925. Carlsen had beat up a man in a grocery store. The incident report didn't include too many details of the assault itself, as apparently neither Carlsen nor his victim had felt inclined to discuss it all that much with the authorities. An argument had led to a fight, and that seemed to be it. Supposedly. The file included a reference to a Los Angeles County Court case number. There was also a very familiar-looking fingerprint card.

I looked up at Holly, who was still at the counter, typing at a keyboard and gazing at a monitor which was just out of view. I went over and asked, "Am I able to get photocopies of any of this?"

"Anything I give you," Holly said, "you are permitted to copy."

"Digital imaging, too?" I asked, holding up my iPad.

"Sure," Holly smiled.

I imaged the mugshot and the incident report papers, then slid the file back over to Holly. Feeling a bit more certain I was on the right track, I asked her for several more records from the list Lt. Llewellyn had provided me, including the latest record listed chronologically. The helpful Holly returned with several manila folders, which I accepted with a "Thank you!" for the kind woman.

I sat down in a different chair, but it was just as uncomfortable. Sighing, I opened one of the files. And then several more files. They all contained similar mugshots and identical fingerprints. Idly I wondered why only one of Carlsen's fingerprint records had come up on the search done by the Arbor Harbor PD. Most likely, I thought, only one of the records, the one from 1925 I'd first looked at, happened to have been scanned back into the computer system after the crash. Or maybe somehow it had been left intact and had never been lost. Whatever the case, I could see that over many years of criminal activity, the same man had been photographed and fingerprinted under the name of Broderick Carlsen.

Finally I turned to the file on an incident from August 24, 1931, the latest date on the case list printout from Lt. Llewellyn. My trivia-obsessed brain gave me a little nudge which said, "Hey, don't forget, *Frankenstein* came out in 1931." I politely thanked that part of my brain and told it to hush up for now as I was working.

An incident report summary gave a description of the events of the early morning of August 24, 1931. At 1:13 a.m., the LAPD received a phone call reporting an attempted burglary at Robinson Jewelers. The caller, identifying himself as the shop's owner, Daniel Robinson, requested police and an ambulance. Police arrived a few minutes later and found three subjects inside the shop. One was Daniel Robinson, the reporting owner, who was holding a gun on the other two men, both of whom were wearing nondescript black jumpsuits. One of the two men in black was seated on the floor with his hands on his head. The other man was lying on his back on the floor amongst broken jagged shards of glass.

The owner explained he'd heard noises coming from the shop below his apartment on the second floor. He went downstairs and found the two strangers struggling with each other. Robinson spotted a gun lying on the ground a short distance from the two men. He picked up the gun and shouted at the intruders, whereupon one of the men, who'd had his hands around the other man's throat, put up his hands in surrender. The other man fell to the floor.

The ambulance arrived, and the man on the floor was quickly declared dead. Subsequent questioning of the surviving intruder fingered the deceased as Broderick Carlsen. Several police officers also positively identified the deceased, thanks to numerous past dealings with Carlsen.

Shit.

Well, so much for the theory of the hundred-plus-year-old coma patient.

If Broderick Carlsen died in 1931, as the report indicated, then obviously he wasn't the man who'd run out of the forest, fallen off a cliff, and ended up in the hospital just a few days ago.

And yet…

I was so sure the mugshots were of the same man from the hospital back home. I was sure of it! Could the police have misidentified the deceased man back in 1931? Maybe mixed up the names of the two intruders? I paged through the file before me until I came across some photos from the crime scene. I peered closely at the shot of the dead body on the floor of the jewelry store. The man's eyes were wide open, staring out at nothing with a frozen mixture of shock and fury.

It was him. It was definitely Broderick Carlsen. The same man from all of the other mugshots, including the one from 1925 tied to the fingerprint record that had sent me here. Broderick Carlsen was dead.

Now what? I didn't quite know how to proceed. My one lead, albeit a slim and unlikely lead, had just been shot down pretty dang conclusively.

I decided to keep investigating Carlsen, to make sure he was really, truly, honestly and positively dead, that the police hadn't misidentified him or screwed up the paperwork or something. Anything. So I read through the rest of the file on the Robinson Jewelers break-in.

The surviving intruder, Albert Lawrence, cooperated with the police and confessed to partnering with Broderick Carlsen, as he'd done several times before, this time to break into the jewelry store and make off with "the goods". As per their usual arrangement, they had agreed to split everything 50-50. However, according to Lawrence, as they were about to leave the store with their stolen treasure, Carlsen pulled a gun on Lawrence and reneged on their agreement. Lawrence jumped Carlsen, knocked the gun loose, and started strangling Carlsen. He then heard a shout, turned and saw a man pointing Carlsen's gun at them. Lawrence let go of Carlsen, who fell to the floor.

The file also included some cross-reference numbers, specifically to the court case involving Lawrence, as well as a record number for the coroner's report on Carlsen. I imaged these, as well as the rest of the documents in the Robinson Jewelry case file, not entirely sure why, as my investigation seemed to have reached a solid dead end. Then, closing the folder, I took my stack of records back to Holly and slid them over to her.

"What else can I do for you?" Holly asked.

"I don't suppose you have access to court files here, do you?"

"Sorry, no, those would all be filed over at the court offices."

"That's kind of what I thought," I said with a small frown.

"I could call over there for you, if you'd like," Holly suggested smilingly.

"Would you, please? That'd be great, thank you!"

"Not a problem, just give me a few minutes." Holly stepped away from the counter and out of sight.

While I waited, I pondered just what to do next. I had the apparent fact of Broderick Carlsen's death in 1931 to tell me he was not my John Doe. I also had the apparent face of the matching fingerprints to tell me he *was* my John Doe. Then there was my gut, my trusty, ever-reliable gut, which told me that the man in the old mugshots and the man in the hospital back home were one and the same.

Maybe there had been a bunch of documentation screw-ups between Carlsen's day and today which had completely screwed the pooch in terms of getting any definitive, positive identification in this case. But that wouldn't explain away the match between my visual inspection of John Doe's actual fingers and prints and the Broderick Carlsen fingerprints in the records.

All things considered, I decided to follow my gut, as I'd done many times before. And which had yet to let me down. (Well, apart from Sarah...) So I decided to keep following up on this Carlsen business. Maybe if nothing else I could at the very least figure out all the potentially confusing and conflicting documentation issues which I was pretty sure I hadn't seen the last of. Great, doing the PD's work for them. Yay.

Holly reappeared at her counter. "I'm afraid I was right," she said. "You'll have to go there in person to look at their records."

"That's no problem," I said.

"I let them know you'd probably be stopping by yet today."

"You read my mind," I grinned.

Holly slid a business card over to me. "Here's my card, and I wrote the location and phone number for their records department on the back."

"Thank you so much," I said as I picked up the card.

"Is there anything else?" Holly asked with her bright smile.

"Actually," I said, checking my watch to see it was nearing midday, "do you know of any good eateries nearby?"

"There's a very nice deli a few blocks west," Holly said. "It's usually not too busy, the food is good and so is the service."

"Sounds perfect, thank you." I slid the business card into my wallet and slung my shoulderbag over my shoulder.

"Well, if anything does come up, feel free to give me a call here," Holly said.

"I will," I said. I paused, then added, "Thank you for all your help. It makes a nice change to get some real help and have it offered and given gladly by a government worker. Unfortunately that's pretty rare outside my home town, in my experience."

"Oh, I'm sorry to hear that," Holly said. "I just try to do my best."

"And an excellent best it is," I said gallantly.

With a twinkle in her eye, Holly whispered, "Just don't go to the finance department here if you're looking for good customer service." She winked.

I laughed, and with a cheery wave I left the records room. Fortunately there was helpful signage in the hallways, and soon I was back at the main entrance, and back in the bright hazy sunshine.

***

Holly had been right. The Reuben sandwich I had at Martello's was fantastic, and the small cozy deli itself was a pleasant air-conditioned break after the busy and frustrating morning I'd had.

I headed back to my car, considering my next step. The interior of the rented vehicle was piping hot, so I sat for a few minutes waiting for the air conditioning to cool things down enough before heading out. By the time I pulled back out into traffic, I'd decided to start by checking into the records for Carlsen's partner, Albert Lawrence. Maybe Lawrence had revealed some further information during questioning that might be relevant to my story. Or my theory, I should probably say. "Story" seemed a bit too solid at the moment for what I was working on. And a bit too fiction-y. Maybe I could also look at the coroner's report on Carlsen, see if there was anything of relevance there, too. Overall, the plan I had wasn't much, but at least it was a plan.

***

Using the address for the LA County Courthouse which I'd plugged into my GPS unit, I found my traffic-snarled way to my next destination. Another parking spot, another uncomfortably hot walk from car to building, and at last I was inside the blessedly cool interior of the Courthouse, a.k.a. the Hall of Justice, apparently, though I saw no superheroes the entire time I was there. Of the comic book type, anyway. At least, as far as I knew.

The directional signage on the walls quickly led me to the main records department. The room was larger than LAPD's set-up, and the service counter, which ran along almost one entire side of the room, had no glass window, instead opening on a work area with several employees at individual desks working dutifully away. The customer area held several chairs and tables, as well as a wall comprised of cubicled workstations.

As I approached the counter, a man of average size with an average face stepped over from the desk area to greet me. "Can I help you?"

I flashed my credentials and began, "I'm Harrison Edwards from the Arbor Harbor—"

"Oh, yes," the dark-haired man said with a smile, "Holly called over earlier and said you might stop in. I'm Ken, what can I help you with?"

I pulled out my notes and gave the man the court case number for the Robinson Jewelers break-in, figuring I might as well finish up that line of inquiry before going any further.

"Yes, we should have that," Ken said. "Are you familiar with our computer system here?"

I shook my head. "No, sorry."

"No problem," Ken said. He stepped over to a door near the end of the counter, came through to my side, and led me over to one of the unoccupied mini-cubicles in the room. He sat me down and showed me the basics of the actually very user-friendly operating system of the database. Within minutes I was ready to go, and Ken left me to myself with a cheery, "Call me if you need me!"

I settled into the surprisingly comfortable chair and got to work.

The court case documents came up on my screen, and I started digging through them. There was a copy of the original police report from August 24, 1931, the one I'd seen earlier. But the bulk of the documents in the file were numerous court documents, transcripts, hearings, motions, and various other legal paperwork. It took a while to work my way through everything, but certain things eventually became clear.

Albert Lawrence had readily confessed to the attempted jewelry store burglary, but he had vehemently denied any premeditation in regards to murdering his partner Broderick Carlsen. From day one he adamantly stuck to his story of how Carlsen had pulled a gun on him and demanded the whole haul from the burglary. Lawrence stood by his claim that he'd only been defending himself by attacking Carlsen, knocking the gun away and trying to choke him. There were, of course, no witnesses to corroborate his claims, as the jewelry store owner only arrived in time to see Carlsen being strangled by Lawrence.

Lawrence pled guilty to the burglary charge, but refused to plead guilty or even no contest to the charge of murder. He also refused to consider any sort of plea deal offered by the prosecution if it involved any kind of admission of guilt on the murder charge.

The state, knowing their case for murder was shaky, dropped the murder charge to manslaughter and prosecuted the case on those terms. They had Daniel Robinson's eyewitness testimony of the strangulation, as well as Lawrence's prints on Carlsen's throat. Yet he continued to protest it had been done in self-defense, and his attorney argued from that angle as best he could. In the end, it took the jury only two hours to find Albert Lawrence guilty of manslaughter. Appeals followed, but Lawrence died of a heart attack in prison in 1933 before anything had been settled.

Nowhere in the file was there any further information about Broderick Carlsen beyond the fact of his strangulation and death at the hands of his partner-in-crime Albert Lawrence. There was no sudden shock appearance of a living Carlsen. There was no revelation from Lawrence of knowledge of unusual recuperative or regenerative powers possessed by Carlsen. There was nothing at all to suggest Carlsen hadn't, in fact, died that early morning in August of 1931.

Well, so much for that, I thought resignedly to myself.

I printed off a few documents that I thought I might need to use as background if I ever did end up writing up a story about this whole crazy business some day, and I jotted down a few notes. Then I turned to the other main reason I was there: the coroner's report on Broderick Carlsen.

The autopsy report on Carlsen was one of the most detailed and descriptive post-mortems I had ever encountered. The Los Angeles County Coroner of 1931 went into almost mind-numbing thoroughness of technical details, using many obscure medical terms, phrases and jargon that I was completely unfamiliar with, even with my journalistic experiences of other autopsies in the past. But Google can be your friend.

I won't bore you with the nitty gritty details here. Suffice to say, the main result was a definitive conclusion on the part of the coroner. Broderick Carlsen was dead. The report included a few black-and-white photos, one of which featured a straight-on view of the deceased's face. It was the very same face I'd seen earlier that day in the old mugshots from the police reports I'd reviewed. It was Broderick Carlsen, no doubt about it. Albeit without any Frankenstein Monster alterations, that is.

So, clearly, Carlsen could not be my comatose John Doe.

And yet…

I was still feeling that nagging doubt, that persistent pestering from my gut that kept whispering to me that Carlsen *was* my John Doe.

Then again, I'd thought Sarah was The One. How wrong can a

person be?

God damn it, this thing was really frustrating the piss out of me.

I printed out some more pages and took some more notes as I skimmed through the rest of the coroner's file. The very last document was a disposition form, giving the final fate of Carlsen's body.

"The remains were turned over to the deceased's family via the Heavenly Rest Funeral Parlor, Los Angeles, Calif.," it read. Below that simple statement were two signatures, one being the coroner's with his name typed below, the other being an indecipherable scribble I could make neither head nor tail of. And with no typed name below it. The form was dated August 25, 1931.

The deceased's family? This was the first mention of possible relatives of Broderick Carlsen that I'd run into. Admittedly I hadn't been digging too long or too deep by that point, but it still jumped out at me that relatives had been mentioned at all. I had perhaps made a biased assumption about Carlsen, the on-the-run criminal with no ties to his past or his family. Guess I was wrong there. I made a mental note to search for potential family members later, then printed off the disposition form.

I put away all my notes and the papers I'd printed, then returned to the counter.

"Anything else?" Ken asked.

I thought for a moment. I didn't really think there was anything just then, but I did have one question. "Do you know if there is a Heavenly Rest Funeral Parlor still in existence in LA?" I asked.

Ken handled this seemingly out-of-left-field query admirably. "I don't think I know the place, sorry, sir," he said with an apologetic frown-smile. Frile? Smown?

"That's okay," I said, "it was a shot in the dark anyway. Thank you for your help."

***

On the walk back to my car, I noticed a coffee shop offering free wi-fi, and since the interior looked nice and cool I ducked inside to escape the LA heat. (*LA Heat*, tonight at 8 on NBC!) I ordered an iced mocha frappuccino and took a seat in one of the overstuffed super-comfy easy chairs scattered throughout the shop. It felt so much better than the government-provided chairs I'd been dealing with all day.

I pulled out my iPad, jumped on the shop's wi-fi, and ran a search for the Heavenly Rest Funeral Parlor. As I mentioned earlier, Google can be your friend. Usually. But I had learned by that point not to pass up a chance to ask actual people for local knowledge of the area. Sometimes you get lucky, other times, like I'd just had with Ken, not so much.

Eventually I found a listing and website for the Heavenly Rest Funeral Home, a local Los Angeles business which the website stated had been established in 1891. Since I could find no current listing for a "Parlor", I had a feeling the place had undergone a minor name change at some point in the last eighty years. Either that, or it was not the place I was looking for after all, and I was probably S.O.L. (And I don't mean Satellite of Love, *MST3K* fans.)

A glance at my watch told me it was still well before the 5pm closing time given on the funeral home's website, so I put my things away, grabbed my frapp, and ventured back outside into the sweltering streets. My car seemed to cool down a lot quicker this time than it had earlier, perhaps because I was still nursing my iced beverage, I don't know. In any event, I was ready to go once I'd entered my next destination into the GPS.

It may be a cliche to complain about the traffic in LA, a cliche I've clearly been guilty of, perhaps too often by this point, but it really, truly is terrible. Too many people wanting the freedom to drive themselves around too congested an area in too many cars. It certainly made Arbor Harbor seem like a pleasant, idyllic, quiet place in comparison. Which it pretty much is anyway, but the contrast between the two places was extraordinary.

***

Despite the horrible traffic problems, I did eventually reach the funeral home, which was located in a nice, well-kept commercial district. The building itself was set back somewhat from the street, allowing for a short driveway which led past the main entrance to an adjacent parking lot. The structure itself was a solid-looking two-story mansion, painted a tasteful pinkish-cream tone. Numerous antique-looking lighting fixtures across the front facade made me think the building probably looked quite pretty at night. But I wasn't there to judge aesthetics, so I parked in the lot and headed to the entrance.

The wave of cool air that washed over me as I entered was a relief from the still-hot late afternoon sun, even after the relatively short walk from the parking lot. I looked around the entrance, noting a staircase to my left leading up, and a hallway leading directly away from the main doors. Several other doors led from the hallway on either side. My eyes also noted a few modest pieces of abstract art dotted about the walls, as well as various potted plants set here and there. As I looked about for someone to talk to, a short, portly, balding man with wire-rim glasses ambled out of a door down the hall and shuffled toward me.

"Hello, I'm Rick Elson," the man said with the patented smile of funeral home directors everywhere that said, "So sorry for your loss, we'll take care of everything for you." Out loud, the man continued, "I'm one of the directors here, how may I be of assistance?"

"Harrison Edwards," I said, "with the *Arbor Harbor Post*." I'd found it was less uncomfortable using a slightly shortened name for my newspaper, especially when dealing with non-police figures. "I'm looking into an old case and your company's name came up."

"Ah, this way," Rick smiled politely. If I'd unnerved him at all, it didn't show. He led me into a small conference room just off the main hallway. The little room consisted of a round table with four chairs around it, a neat little two-shelf bookcase, a telephone, and a TV/DVD combo player on a stand.

"At least I think it's your company," I continued as we sat at the table. "It was actually the Heavenly Rest Funeral Parlor in the paperwork I saw."

"Yes, that's us," Rick said. "That was our name until 1941, when we moved into this location from a few blocks north of here."

"Well, that would explain it. The document was from 1931."

"Yes, that would fit."

"You wouldn't happen to still have records from back then, would you?"

"We should," Rick said. "Most of them, anyway. We've tried our best, but things do happen after so many years sometimes."

"Understandable."

"And I'm afraid we only have the original records themselves," Rick went on. "We haven't been able to afford to digitize everything. Not really at the top of our priority list, you see."

I nodded.

"You must understand, however," Rick continued, his smile slipping ever so slightly, "that I am hesitant to just give free access to our records to just anyone who asks. Our clients presume upon our discretion and privacy to a great extent."

"I do understand," I replied politely. "I don't want to cause any problems. But like I said, it is a very old case I'm looking into, and by all accounts any persons connected to the, um… deceased person in question… have most likely all passed on by now as well. So I don't believe anyone would still be around to be offended if I were to discuss this in an article. Which, to be honest, is looking more and more unlikely as I go on. I have a feeling this visit is more a matter of tying up a loose end on a wrong-turn dead end than actually discovering any relevant and noteworthy details. But I must pursue the leads where they go. It is my job, after all."

Rick hesitated, and when he spoke there was still a bit of caution in his voice. "All right." He took out a business card and a pen. "Do you have the name of the deceased, or…"

"I have a name and a date as well," I said, consulting my little notebook. "Broderick Bishop Carlsen, and the date he was apparently released to Heavenly Rest was August 25, 1931."

Rick scratched on his card with his pen. "All right, let me go look. Please wait here."

"Okay," I said as I watched him leave the room. As I waited, my eyes drifted around the nice but rather bland room, eventually falling on my notepad. The thought occurred to me that Paramount Pictures should market a line of flip-up notebooks designed to look like old-school *Star Trek* communicators. I started to wonder who to contact with that idea, remembering another idea I'd had when I was a kid and had seen *The Empire Strikes Back*. It seemed the most natural idea in the world to have Yoda backpacks. A backpack for schoolbooks and whatnot but with the figure of Yoda clinging to the wearer's shoulders, as if he were actually riding in the backpack, just like when the little Jedi Master was training Luke Skywalker on Dagobah. I never did anything about that particular idea of mine. Years later I discovered online that such a backpack had actually been created and offered for sale. Then I learned that someone else had had an even cooler *Empire*-related invention. The dead Tauntaun sleeping bag, where the outside is designed to look like the beasts of burden the Rebels used on Hoth, the zipper in the shape of a miniature lightsaber, and the inside of the bag is designed to look like the guts of the Tauntaun. Sheer genius.

Rick returned to the little room clutching a large old-fashioned ledger book. "I think I must have written something down wrong," he said with a puzzled frown.

"What do you mean?" I asked with a sinking feeling developing in my stomach.

"Well, I couldn't find any listing for the name or date I wrote down," Rick said as he sat down next to me at the table. He set down the ledger then looked at the card he'd made his notes on. "Can I see the form where you got your information?"

I gave the printed copy to him. He looked at it and his frown deepened.

"That is weird. I did write it down right. I guess there just is no listing for a Broderick Carlsen having been received by us on that date."

"What?" I said. "That can't be right."

"Well, let's take a look here," Rick said as he slid the ledger over.

Embossed on the cover of the volume was "1931". I opened it to find page after page of meticulous details regarding the receipt and ultimate fate of each deceased subject handled by Heavenly Rest. I skimmed through to August and found August 25.

There was no record of Broderick Carlsen.

I looked again. No Carlsen. I looked further, through August 26th, 27th, then back to August 24th and August 23rd. Then the whole of August. And July. And September.

Nothing.

"Could he maybe have been added later, after the fact?" I asked Rick as I continued paging through the ledger.

"He shouldn't have been," Rick said, "that isn't how the processing is supposed to be done. The arrivals are supposed to be logged into the record as soon as they're received here."

I kept looking through the ledger, but at no time during the whole of 1931, as far as I could tell, was a Broderick Carlsen ever received at Heavenly Rest. At least according to the official log.

"Did the coroner's office get the year wrong?" I wondered aloud. Rick shrugged. "No, that wouldn't account for it. All the other documents clearly refer to 1931. And he wouldn't have been delivered to you a year after his death, would he?"

Rick shook his head. "No chance."

"So I guess that means... that Broderick Carlsen never made it here." Or, strictly speaking, to Heavenly Rest's previous location, but Rick understood what I meant.

"I don't know what to say, I'm sorry," the funeral director said quietly.

"But why would the coroner's paperwork specify Heavenly Rest as the ones that picked up the body?"

"Could I see that form again, please?" Rick asked. I slid it over to him again. "Hmmm," he said as he peered closely at the sheet of paper. "I recognize the coroner's signature, but not the other one, the one supposedly of one of our employees who received the body."

"It is pretty hard to make out," I said. I looked at the form with him. "Well, I think that first letter is maybe an I? Or a J?"

"I thought maybe a P or an R," said Rick.

I began jotting down our guesses in my notepad. "Maybe an F? Man, it's hard to say for sure."

"Yeah."

"Okay," I said, "what about this one here? I think it looks like possibly the first letter of a last name."

"A U?" Rick suggested with a shrug.

"Or a V. Maybe a W?"

"Could be a very bad L."

I wrote down our guesses. "I don't suppose you happen to still have any old paperwork listing all your previous employees and with their signatures, would you?" I asked, not feeling very hopeful.

"Well..." Rick said, clearly uncertain. Finally whatever question he had on his mind was apparently resolved, as he stood and said, "Follow me."

"Lay on, Macduff," I said as I followed Rick into the hall.

"I think it's actually, 'Lead on, Macduff'," Rick said as we walked.

"No, I think that's the common misquote."

"I thought 'Lay on' was the misquote," Rick said as we started down a staircase.

"Hang on," I said. I pulled out my iPad and fired up my favorite Shakespeare app. A few seconds later I said, "Yep," and showed the screen to Rick.

"I stand corrected," he said good-naturedly as he led me down the stairs.

The landing at the bottom of the staircase had three doors, one directly opposite the stairs, one to the left, and one to the right. Rick leg me through the door to the right.

We entered a dank, cool, dark basement room that wasn't made very much less dank, cool or dark when Rick flipped on the overhead fluorescent lights. It looked like a basic catch-all storage room, with stacks of boxes, racks of metal shelving, a few tables and chairs and other miscellaneous furniture all jumbled together and presumably cast off from use in the rooms upstairs.

After rummaging around for a bit, Rick said, "A-ha!" and walked over to a four-drawer steel filing cabinet. He fished out a set of keys, unlocked the bottom drawer, and pulled it noisily open. Withdrawing a thick file folder, he moved over to a steel-surfaced table which had been shoved into a corner of the room. Boxes and papers and assorted office supplies covered one end of the table, while on the other end there was a sizable space clear of any objects. Rick set the folder down on the cleared surface and looked at me as I joined him.

"I'll look through these files," Rick explained, "but they're confidential so I'm afraid you're not allowed to see them. However…" He dashed over to a nearby shelf and pulled down another large ledger book similar to the one he'd brought to the conference room. He gave it to me and said, "You can look through these payroll statements for a name that might fit our guesses for the signature."

We began searching through our respective documents. It was after I was a few pages into the company's payroll records ledger from the early 1930s that the peculiarity of the table we were using struck me. It was cold steel, with a raised lip around all four sides. The surface appeared to be slanted somewhat towards the end at which we stood. And at the center of our end, at the base of the raised rim, was what looked like a sink drain.

"Uh… Rick?" I said, not really sure I wanted to hear the answer to the question I was about to ask. "What kind of table is this, exactly?"

"Hmm?" Rick looked up at me, then glanced back down at the table. "Oh, it's an examination table."

Exactly the answer I'd not wanted to hear. I wasn't squeamish about blood or death or corpses, per se, but the fact was I was not thrilled to be working at a table that had been used for such… uncomfortable purposes.

"Oh, we've never actually used this one," Rick said, apparently having noted my discomfort. "Well, only a few times, until we discovered the drainage system wasn't working right."

Which completely failed to put me at my ease. I tried to shove the matter from my mind and instead concentrated on the ledger, the pages of which I turned a lot more carefully from that point on.

And so Rick and I continued to look through our documents. And looked. And looked. A while later, we finished. Rick had not found any name or signature to match that of the mysterious body-picker-upper of 1931, and I hadn't found anything plausible either that might fit our guesses as to the mystery man's name or initials.

"I'm sorry, I can't think of anything else," Rick said as we headed back upstairs. "I don't know what to say."

"It's alright," I said. "I think I already knew this was just another dead end in an investigation full of dead ends. Uh, no pun intended," I added hurriedly.

Rick just smiled kindly, as funeral directors throughout time must do, and said, "I wish we could have been of more help to you."

"You've been a big help, believe me," I said. "Thank you."

As I walked to the parking lot, I felt my frustration start to slide into resignation. Maybe this was all just a big mix-up after all, I thought to myself. Maybe my John Doe isn't Broderick Carlsen. Maybe Broderick Carlsen really is dead. Maybe the fingerprint records really were screwed up. Maybe all of this, the apparently disappearing body I'd been trying to track down, had nothing to do with the man in the coma back in Arbor Harbor. Maybe I shouldn't worry about someone possibly posing as a funeral home representative eighty years ago to steal the dead body of a two-bit criminal.

Yeah, right. I had a story, and it, and Broderick Carlsen, wouldn't let me go.

***

Once back in my rental car, I didn't feel like heading to my hotel just yet. It was late in the afternoon, and the sun was on its slow fall into the ocean to the west. Well, strictly speaking, the sun wasn't actually falling, of course, it just looked that way from our viewpoint here on Earth as our planet rotated in orbit around the sun at the center of our solar system. And the sun isn't fixed in place, either, is it? It's part of the Milky Way Galaxy, which is itself... Dang it, there I go again. Well, you get the picture. Now, where was I?

The sun appeared to be heading downwards in the sky as I struggled through the busy streets one more and made my way to one of the numerous beaches along the coast. I needed a quick break, a refresh, a recharge, away from archives and records and files. And funeral home examination tables.

Upon arrival at the beach, I didn't feel like dragging my swim trunks out of my luggage and dealing with changing and all that. So I just grabbed a towel and strolled out onto the sand. I found a nice, peaceful spot with a lovely view of the Pacific Ocean in front of me, and a lovely view of some bikini-clad young women playing beach volleyball a little distance off to my left. Ah, Southern California. I laid my towel out on the sand, slipped off my shoes and socks, unbuttoned my shirt, and laid back on the towel. And didn't give one single thought to John Doe, or Broderick Carlsen, or whoever the hell he was.

I didn't doze, I didn't think about anything. I just kicked back and breathed and relaxed. I felt the frustrations of the day drifting away from me on the cool ocean breeze as I just chilled. It was wonderful.

About an hour or so later, I felt ready to soldier on. I put myself back together, folded up my towel after shaking the sand off it, and, with a cheery wave to the oblivious volleyball beauties (obliviousness being the standard response of beautiful women to me, after all), I walked back across the beach to my car.

The parking lot was busy with after-work surfers heading out to the water for a surfin' safari. Or maybe some skeet surfing. Whichever, I chuckled to myself, recalling the few times I'd tried surfing and the subsequent failures thereof. Oh, well. More power to those who could actually do it, though.

***

I drove to my hotel in the darkening late late afternoon, parked, checked in, and went up to my eighth-floor room. Single king-size bed, non-smoking, flatscreen TV. The basics, but nice basics. I started feeling hungry again just then, but really didn't feel like going out anymore that night. So I went downstairs and enjoyed a wonderful filet mignon in the hotel restaurant.

Returning to my room, I unpacked a bit, not sure I'd be staying more than just the one night. And then my eye fell on my *Frankenstein* DVD case. I took it out and stared at it. What the heck was it about this movie? I thought frustratedly to myself. Why would someone have physically altered himself to look like Frankenstein's Monster? Why was that someone apparently recorded to have died in 1931, the same year *Frankenstein* was filmed and released? Was there a connection? Or did it all just come down to massive coincidence? Was there something to be learned at Universal Studios itself, perhaps? I sure didn't have many, or frankly any, other leads at the moment.

You'll note that I was leaning towards the assumption that Broderick Carlsen was my John Doe. I still wasn't quite ready to give up on that just yet, however difficult it was for my brain to wrap itself around that possibility.

Will all of that in mind, I fired up my laptop and found a phone number for Universal Studios. It was after 5pm, but I still got through to the general switchboard. Does anyone still use actual switchboards anymore? Probably not. Anyway, I told the operator I was looking for the records or archive department, if they had one.

"Just a moment, sir," I heard. After some dreadful Muzak, another voice came on the line.

"Universal Archives, this is Maria," said a tired-sounding voice.

"Yes, I'm sorry to call so late, but I'm hoping you can help me," I said. "I'm a reporter with the *Arbor Harbor*, uh, *Post*, and I was hoping I could take a look at some of your old records."

There was a pause, and then, "Well, we're actually closed for the day."

"That's fine, I understand, could I stop in tomorrow?"

Another pause, then a weary sigh. "Hang on." I heard some keyboard action, then the voice was back. "We have an opening for tomorrow at 8 a.m., if that works for you."

"That actually sounds great!"

"Name?"

"Harrison Edwards."

"Contact number?"

I gave my cell number to her.

"Right," Maria said finally. "8 a.m. tomorrow. Your name will be on the list at the main gate, bring photo ID and your press credentials."

"Thank you very much."

I wasn't quite sure what, if anything, I hoped to find at Universal. Some kind of connection to Broderick Carlsen, obviously, but what sort of connection that might be I had no idea. Not the best plan I'd ever come up with, but after all the dead ends I seemed to keep running into, at least it was something.

There was, however, one other dangling thread that I wanted to undangle. The body of Broderick Carlsen had supposedly been turned over to "the deceased's family" via Heavenly Rest, according to the disposition form in the County's files. I wondered if there might be a chance I could find a relative of Carlsen's. The likelihood of any relatives who'd been alive in 1931 and still around today was almost zero, but maybe I could track down a descendant who'd been told the story. If there was a story.

I surfed over to my favorite genealogy site and entered "Broderick Carlsen", birth year 1887, and Los Angeles, California as search parameters. Oodles of results turned up, as usual, but, as usual, only a very few were directly relevant to my inquiry. Using the censuses (censi?) from 1890 through 1930, as well as other varied sources available, a skeleton picture began to form.

According to the 1890 census, a three-year-old Broderick Carlsen was living with his father Lewis, aged 30, and his mother Ethel, aged 25. Louis was listed as a grocer. By 1900, thirteen-year-old Broderick was still at home with Lewis and Ethel, working as a grocery clerk. Not a student, I noted. Not a rare thing in those days, but interesting.

In 1910, Ethel was listed as a widow, with her apparently only child Broderick, now a twenty-three-year-old house painter, still living at home with her. I could not find Broderick in the 1920 census, at least nothing I could be certain of, for by that time Ethel had died and Broderick would be living alone. However, the 1930 census showed a forty-three-year-old Broderick Carlsen still in Los Angeles but working as a janitor. I felt reasonably certain that was my Broderick Carlsen.

Other non-census sources told me Lewis had died in 1909, Ethel in 1912. In neither case could I find a cause of death.

I ran down what few siblings and cousins of Lewis and Ethel I could reasonably link to the family, but after a few generations their trails all went cold.

The upshot appeared to be that Broderick Carlsen had been an only child who apparently had never married nor had any children of his own.

I did a search for any obituary record for Broderick Carlsen, but found nothing. I also tried an online search of cemetery records for Carlsen. Again I found nothing.

Well, so much for that.

I decided to call my boss to check in.

"Hey Lisa, it's Harry," I said when she picked up.

"Harry," Lisa Takagi said. "What've you got?"

"I've been looking into a bunch of records down here, LAPD, County, and so on. Broderick Carlsen was born in 1887 and died in 1931."

"1931? Then he's not our John Doe."

"Weeellllll…"

I heard Lisa heave a resigned what-have-I-gotten-into-now sigh. "Well, what?"

"Well, I think he might still be our John Doe."

"How can he be, if he died in 1931?" Lisa asked, understandably enough.

"I'm still trying to figure that out," I said. "But all of the police records prior to his death in '31, the mugshots all look like him, the fingerprints all match, everything is consistent."

"Those mugshots of Carlsen look like Frankenstein?" Another

reasonable question.

I bit back my nitpicky correction. "Well, no, but I can see it's him, I can tell it's the same guy we have in the hospital. I'm sure of it."

"You're sure," Lisa said. "How sure would the average person or reader be?"

"They… might not be as convinced," I admitted reluctantly.

I heard Lisa sigh again. I knew she wasn't sold on the Carlsen-is-John-Doe theory, but I knew from past experience that she trusted my gut, almost as much as I did. "Alright," she said finally. "I'll give you a little more time to come up with convincing proof Carlsen is our John Doe. Or convincing proof he isn't, I don't care. Either way, get me something soon, or get yourself back here." And she clicked off.

Well, that could've gone worse, I thought wryly.

My next phone call did go worse. I called Arbor Harbor Police Chief Raymond Packer to update him on my progress. I needn't have bothered. Chief Packer was even less impressed with the little that I'd come up with so far. Packer growled at me to not bother him again unless I was able to prove something definitively, or even better if it was an entirely different story. Then he hung up.

Oh, well.

The final call I made that night was much more agreeable. I phoned my house-sitting friend Johnny Goldschmidt to see how everything was going at home.

"Oh, everything's fine, fine," Johnny said calmly. "Sonny and Sam have both been extremely well-behaved."

"They better be," I joked.

"Rachel and I took Sonny for a walk earlier, and now he's lying next to us on the sofa with his head on my leg. He had to nose Sam out of the way to get there…"

"Jealous little doggy," I chuckled.

"Sam just got out of the way, and now he's curled up behind me on the back of the sofa, right up against my shoulders."

"That sounds about right."

"We can tell Sonny misses you," I heard Rachel call out in the background.

"Hi, Rache," I said.

"Roger says 'Hi'," Johnny dutifully reported to his wife.

"Hi, Roger!" I heard Rachel say.

"Rachel says 'Hi'," Johnny dutifully reported to me. He never quite got the fact that I could always hear Rachel just fine when she spoke off-phone, as it were. "Sonny went to the back door a few times this afternoon. I think he was waiting for you to come home. I opened the door to let him out in case he needed to go, but he just looked outside, sniffed, then backed away from the door once he figured out you weren't there, I think."

"Aww, poor Sonny," I said. My dog sure had an attachment to me. And vice versa. He'd been my buddy for several years, and had helped me get through some tough times, especially my break-up with Sarah Fisher, my almost-fiancée. When your dog sees you crying and starts licking your face to wipe away your tears, you know you've got a special animal there. "And I bet Sam couldn't care less," I added.

"Pretty much," Johnny answered. "As long as we feed and water him and change his box, that's all he seems to need."

"Thanks again for doing this, you guys. I can't thank you both enough."

"It's not a problem, Harry, don't worry about it. That's what friends are for, right?"

"Well, it means a lot to me."

"How's it going down there?" Johnny asked. "Getting anywhere?"

I sighed. "Hard to tell. Maybe and maybe not. Some of the... evidence, I guess you could call it, is telling me what I thought was the case apparently isn't. But some of it is telling me I'm actually on the right track. I think. It's pretty frustrating, I'll say that much."

"Keep at it," Johnny said. "Trust your instincts. Your gut's always been right so far, hasn't it? So keep using it, keep following it. You'll get there, I know you will."

"Thanks, Johnny."

"I believe in you too, Roger!" Rachel called out in the background.

"Thanks!"

"Roger says 'Thanks'," Johnny reported.

I heard Sonny give his goofy guttural bark-growl and laughed.

"Sonny believes in you, too," Johnny said with a light chuckle.

"Awww," I said. "Could you give him a hug for me?"

"Sure," said Johnny. I heard some rustling through the phone and then Johnny's muffled voice saying, "That's from Daddy." A few squeaks from Sonny told me he knew who Johnny meant, and that he missed me, too. Another rustle, then a muffled purring told me Sam got a hug, too, as Johnny told him, "Daddy says 'Hi'."

"Thanks," I told my friend when he was back on the line.

"Of course. They're good boys. Do you know when you'll be coming back yet?"

"I was hoping I'd be back tomorrow, but it's not looking likely. Probably just a few days, I think."

"Well, however long you need, we're here."

"I really appreciate it."

"Harry," Johnny said sternly, "quit saying that or you'll start to annoy me."

I'd never seen an annoyed Johnny Goldschmidt, and had a hard time imagining it. But I took his meaning. We said our goodbyes and hung up.

It was getting late, I was tired, there was nobody interesting on Letterman or Kimmel or Conan, so I hit the sack. I had a nasty suspicion that tomorrow was going to be just as frustrating a day as the one I'd finally finished.

CHAPTER FIVE

The Awakening

The next morning dawned cool and cloudy, much more my kind of weather. I made my way over to Universal Studios and pulled up to the main gate. After going through the security rigamarole with the guard, a kind, older gentleman named Arthur, and receiving a lanyard pass to wear, a parking pass for my car, and a map showing the location of Warehouse 1-B, temporary site of the Archives, as the regular housing for the Archives was undergoing major repairs at the time, I drove onto the lot of Universal Studios, Hollywood, California.

Though I think technically it's in the municipality of Universal City, but "Hollywood, California" sounds so much more showbizzy, doesn't it?

Even though I was a California native, and though I'd visited Los Angeles on numerous occasions, I'd never actually been on a movie studio lot before. Then again, on second thought, maybe I hadn't been on a movie studio lot *because* I was a native Californian. In any case, I was duly impressed by the massive scale of the property. I felt dwarfed among the giant soundstages, the towing office buildings, the numerous huge warehouses. The occasional maintenance buildings and bungalows made me feel a bit more my normal size.

Interestingly, the place was all relatively sane and business-like. There were actors, but clad mostly in modern-day garb or near enough. Assistant directors wearing headsets and clutching clipboards or tables hustled from place to place. There were golf carts, little mini-trucks, and even a few Segways tooling around (sadly no sign of GOB Bluth, though). There were numerous expensive-looking cars parked in places that to my mind couldn't possibly be actual parking spaces. I saw down a few alleyways that I drove past collections of movie star trailers tantalizingly close yet disappointingly quiet.

I did not see the usual "behind-the-scenes at a movie studio" cliches. No groups of actors costumed as Romans, or Nazis, or cowboys, or spacemen. No horribly fake scenery which would never pass muster on an actual film being carted around. No over-sized mirrors or plate-glass windows being precariously moved and just itching to be shattered. And I did not see any actors or directors that I recognized, unfortunately.

I followed the map Arthur the guard had given me and soon pulled up in front of a roughly two-story tall building that stretched on for what had to be at least the length of a football field. A sign above the main entrance marked it as Warehouse 1-B. I heeded Arthur's warning and avoided picking in any of the nearby stalls that were either marked with a specific name or the more general "Reserved". That meant I had a bit of a walk to get back to the front door of the warehouse, past plenty of empty stalls, but it was thankfully a cool day so I didn't mind.

Inside I found a very no-frills reception area, seemingly recently constructed, probably for the recent move of the Archives to this temporary repository. Across from the main door was another doorway leading deeper into the building. Nearby was a desk with a pretty blonde woman, over by one wall was a set of chairs, an end table with some magazines, and a lone potted palm.

The woman at the desk, whose name, according to the neat nameplate on her desk, was Taylor Newman, looked up at me as I came in. "Hello, sir," she said with a warm smile.

I introduced myself, and explained I had an 8 a.m. appointment. I flashed my ID.

"Welcome, yes, come on in," Taylor said brightly. "Let's get you squared away. If you'd care to follow me, please?"

Taylor led me through the door by her desk into what was

basically the corner of a long, backwards capital "L", a shorter hall running off to the left and a much longer hall, seemingly reaching all the way to the far end of the warehouse building itself, leading directly away from us.

"Sorry for the rough-and-ready nature of the place," Taylor said as she led me down the long corridor. I saw a few people off in the distance.

"It's fine," I said. "The guard at the gate said your regular building was under repair?"

"Yeah," Taylor said. "One of the corners of the old building started to collapse. The inspectors shut down the whole building until it gets fixed because they said it showed signs of spreading out from that one corner. I'm just glad no one got hurt while they were allowed to transfer everything over here."

"How long will it take to fix?"

"About another year or so, I've been hearing."

"Was anything lost or damaged?" I asked, very slightly worried. It'd be just my luck if what I came to look for was gone forever.

"No, we managed to get everything out of there pretty quickly."

"That's good," I said, relieved.

"I've put you in Research Room 3," Taylor said as we reached a door on our right with that very name printed on a sheet of paper taped to the door. It turned out to be a small conference room, with an oval table, four chairs, and another potted palm. They sure liked their potted palms here, I thought. On the table itself were some legal pads and a handful of pens, along with a silver tray upon which sat a pitcher of iced water and several glasses. "Miss Perry has been assigned as your Archivist today," Taylor went on. "I'll go let her know you're here." With a smile, she left me alone in the room.

I set my shoulder bag on the table and took a seat.

Miss Perry, I mused. The mental picture that name immediately conjured up was that of the actress Nicola Bryant, who had played a character named Peri on *Doctor Who* in the mid-1980s, right when I was about the age when major crushes on pretty actresses tended to develop rather quickly. I'd always thought that Miss Bryant was an extraordinarily beautiful woman, a very pretty brunette with a gorgeous curvaceous figure. I'd even met Miss Bryant in person a few years back at a *Doctor Who* convention, and she was still stunningly beautiful, perhaps even more so. I'd always had a thing for Peri.

There was a polite but firm knock on the door to the room, then in walked the most devastatingly beautiful woman I had ever seen in my entire life.

I hadn't been far off in my mental image of Nicola Bryant. Miss Perry, or at least the person I assumed was Miss Perry, was a bit taller than the actress but had similar medium-long-ish straight hair, styled in a sort of modern version of what I think was called a "bob", a kind of 1920s flapper hairstyle, curling inwards just below the jawline. Beautiful, lively brown eyes behind a small pair of black-framed glasses; slim, cute nose; pretty, smooth lips. Her teal-colored blouse was rather snug against her ample bust which pressed against the fabric quite nicely, in my opinion. A simple yet professional dark gray skirt hugged her hips wonderfully, ending just above her knees so as to show off a sexy pair of spectacularly gorgeous legs. I guessed her to be a few years younger than myself, but I've always been horrible at guessing ages so I could have been way off.

The goddess was speaking. To me, apparently. "Mr. Edwards," her sweet voice was saying, "I'm Alison Perry. Please call me Alison. No need to call me 'Miss Perry', I'm not super-famous like Katy Perry, you know, the singer?" Though when she mentioned the beautiful and sexy pop singer, I realized that was the other person Miss Perry — Alison — reminded me of. A cross between Nicola Bryant and Katy Perry, with perhaps a dash of actress Alison Brie from *Community*, was not a bad thing at all, not by a long shot. Alison was still speaking. "Though I do love her music, she's really talented and a lot of fun, don't you think?"

Belatedly I realized she was holding out her hand. I pulled myself together, shook her delicate hand and said, "Well, yes, actually do like her, as a matter of fact." I hadn't even noticed I'd stood up when Alison had come in, so distracted was I. We sat down next to each other at the table. I noticed she held a small, slim leather-bound portfolio.

"Ever since 'I Kissed a Girl' I've been a big fan," Alison went on. It took me a second to realize she'd referenced the Katy Perry song, and wasn't talking about something she'd done herself. It struck me that Alison seemed rather excited, going on like she was about a pop singer. Was she nervous? Why would *she* be nervous? She was the beautiful goddess, I was just a poor schlub from up north. "Every album of hers is great," Alison continued, "she's had so many great hit songs." She stopped abruptly, apparently realizing she'd been babbling somewhat. "I'm sorry," she said, fiddling with her glasses, "I get carried away sometimes."

"I've been known to do the same thing," I said with what I hoped was a charming, encouraging smile, recalling all the times I'd gotten carried away myself talking about *Doctor Who*.

"Anyway," Alison said, smiling back nervously, "it's just Alison."

"Call me Harry," I said.

"Thank you," Alison said, her smile brightening. Oh, Lord, what a radiant smile. "I'm your Archivist for today. Here's how we usually do things, it's a little different than when we're in our regular place, so please bear with us. You just let me know what file or record or whatever you're interested, and I'll go retrieve what we have from storage and bring it back here for you. I can look things up by movie title, TV show title, actor, actress, writer, director, producer, composer, contractor, subcontractor, key grip, best boy, and so on. You do get to look through anything I retrieve for you, but if anything goes missing, you do need to know what whatever gets pulled for you is logged in our system by requester so we can track whoever last accessed the missing records or what have you. Not that I'm saying you'll do anything like that, but we do want you to know."

"Understood," I said. "Am I allowed to make copies or take pics of anything you bring me?"

"Yes, I can go run copies off for you, or you can take our own image scans with your phone or tablet or whatever. You just need to sign a brief legal release form." She pulled a sheet from her portfolio. It was a standard archival access agreement, so I signed it. "So," Alison said brightly as she took the form and put it away again, "what can I do for you today?"

I felt myself starting to drown in her lovely brown eyes, but somehow managed to pull myself free. "I'm working on a story for my paper that appears to reach back to the 1930s," I explained. "What have you got on the original 1931 *Frankenstein* movie?"

"Oooh," Alison said, "I love that movie, so spooky!" A woman after my own heart. "We probably have quite a bit of material, I would think."

"What should I start with?"

"How about I get, say, three boxes for you to start with, and we see how that goes, okay?"

"Sounds good to me," I said, as I really had no specific idea of what I should begin my research with.

Alison nodded, jotting a note in her portfolio. She stood up and headed for the door. "I'll be back," she said with a smile as she left.

Alison's departure was just as lovely as her arrival, I mused dreamily.

Hey, quit looking at women as objects, I told myself.

I know, I'm sorry, myself told I.

Show them more respect, they're human beings, I continued.

I'm sorry, I'll do better, myself replied.

Besides, it's not like you're the relationship type, are you? said I. Didn't you prove that with Sarah?

Myself was too stung to answer.

Realizing that I'd stood up once again as Alison had left, I sat back down and waited for her to return, grabbing one of the provided legal pads and a free pen, pulling out my iPad, and getting comfortable in the really quite nice chair.

A short time later, Alison returned, wheeling in a small cart about the size of a hotel room service trolley. On the cart were three bulging bankers' boxes, brimming with papers. Together Alison and I transferred the boxes to the conference table, which fortunately was sturdy enough to bear the weight.

"Thank you," I said to Alison as I dusted off my hands.

"No problem," she said as she wheeled the little cart to one corner of the room. "Is there anything else I can do for you?"

"Not that I can think of at the moment," I said as I faced the boxes that awaited my digging.

"No specific search parameters I could run through our database for you while you're working here?"

"Unfortunately I won't really know what exactly it is I'm looking for until I find it."

"Ah," Alison said, her smile turning a bit wistful, "one of those kinds of problems."

"Exactly."

"Wel, if you do think of anything, anything at all," Alison said as she headed for the doorway, "I'll be in my office just down the hall, 106. Well, I call it an office, it's more a sort of glorified closet, really. But I like calling it an office. Anyway, it's down the hall to the right, second door on the left, number 106, my name's on the sign next to the door with the room number. I'll leave my door open. So if you need me you can find me there."

"Okay, thank you," I smiled at her.

Alison smiled a glowing smile back at me, paused in the doorway, then turned and hurried off down the hallway.

Sweet woman, I thought to myself. Very helpful. Must remember to compliment her to her boss if I can.

I sat down again, pulled the box labeled *"Frankenstein - 1931 - Archive Materials - Box 1"* closer, removed the lid, and pulled out a handful of the somewhat crackly, yellowing paperwork.

I will spare you most of the boring details of the following few hours. There was a particular sketch on *Monty Python's Flying Circus* where an accountant, played by Michael Palin, goes to see a vocational guidance counselor, played by John Cleese, in hopes of finding a new career. At one point, when the counselor suggests that accounting was an exciting job, the exasperated response is, "No, it's not, it's dull, dull, DULL!" And he goes on a bit about how mind-crushingly boring it is being an accountant. Well, that's what my initial research into the *Frankenstein* Archives at Universal Studios was like.

Scripts, script revisions, actor contracts, crew contracts, subcontractor agreements, bills, receipts, invoices, pre-production sketches, hair and make-up concepts, set design sketches, costume development, shooting schedules, call sheets, details on how, when and where each print of the finished film was distributed, agreements with distributors, box office receipt tracking, reviews clippings... all jumbled together in apparently random order. Anything and everything.

And nothing.

Nothing at all that was seemingly of any help to me in my investigation. No mention of Broderick Carlsen, no connection to him at all, as far as I could tell, no connection or reference to the Heavenly Rest Funeral Parlor. No sign of anything that could in any possible way tie in to my John Doe back home. The nearest thing to a link of any kind was the fact that principal photography on *Frankenstein* commenced on August 24, 1931, the very same day that Broderick Carlsen was killed by his partner. And even that told me pretty much nothing. It could just be a mere coincidence, especially since that one tiny fact seemed to be the only "connection" to Carlsen.

I was getting extremely frustrated after several hours of fruitless digging when there was a tap on the conference room door. I looked up to see Alison Perry standing in the doorway.

"It's getting close to noon," Alison said, "and I usually take my lunch break at noon. I usually go to the studio commissary. It's actually pretty good, they have a nice big selection to choose from, and it's all very good, so I usually just go there for lunch…"

As she paused, I realized I was indeed hungry myself. I didn't feel like eating in a loud, crowded public commissary, even if there was a good chance of bumping into a celebrity or two there. I'd noticed a pizza joint near the main gate of the studio on my way in. That sounded good to me.

"Am I allowed to leave the property and come back?" I asked.

"Oh," Alison said, seemingly taken aback for some reason. "Uh, yes, just make sure this door is locked when you leave the room, we'll let you back in when you get back. The main gate will let you out and back in."

"Thanks," I said as I gathered up my shoulder bag and headed out, shutting the door behind us. "Have a good lunch."

"You, too," Alison said quietly as she turned and walked slowly away.

***

On my way out I had Taylor book me for another appointment on the following day. There was no way I'd be finished with all three of the boxes Alison had brought me by the end of the day, much less the rest of however many more boxes there still were in storage. I didn't want to give up after just one day, however hopeless it was seeming, and despite the fact that I still didn't really know what I was looking for.

Gino's Pizzeria was a small, crowded place filled with the intoxicating aromas of, well, pizza. As busy as the cramped place was,

I didn't feel like hogging a whole table or booth just for myself, so I ordered my pizza to go.

Back at the gate I offered Arthur a slice, which he politely declined, patting his belly. Taylor also politely turned down my offer of some pizza as she let me back into Research Room 3.

So I set the pizza box down on the table to my left, arranged the archive boxes to my right, set my pen and paper and iPad in front of me, and went back to work, eating with my left hand while going through documents with my right. I was extremely careful not to let the old papers get dirty at all. Gino's had provided a big handful of napkins, and good quality napkins, too, not the cheap kind that shreds instantly and leaves bits stuck to your fingers. And thus I returned to the dull slog I'd begun that morning. At least now, though, I had the boost of the delicious pizza. And excellent pizza it was, not quite as delicious as the thin crust, sausage and extra cheese pizzas from Frankie's Pizza Palace back home in Arbor Harbor, but still damn good.

A few minutes after I set to work, Alison stopped by. "Hi," she said as she entered the room. "Just checking to make sure you got back okay, and to see if there was anything else you needed, and is that from Gino's?"

"It is indeed," I said. "Care for a slice?"

"Thank you!" Alison gushed. She sat across the table from me, grabbed some napkins, and took a slice from the box. "Gino's is *the* best, I *love* their pizza! I probably shouldn't have any but that salad just didn't do it for me today. Thank you again." She somehow managed to say all of that in between bites. She quickly finished her slice, then wiped her hands and lips with the napkins. "That was delicious, thank you so much. Are you sure there isn't anything else I can do for you? Anything?" She looked at me, eyes wide. She had very pretty eyes.

"No, not that I can —" I broke off. You idiot! I said to myself with a mental *NCIS* Gibbs-to-DiNozzo slap to the back of the head. Why didn't I think of it earlier? It was so obvious. "You said you could search your database by name?"

"Yes," Alison said as she flipped open her trusty portfolio. "By name or just about anything else."

"Okay, if you could please search for a man named Broderick

Bishop Carlsen, that'd be great. 'Broderick' as in Matthew Broderick, 'Bishop' like the church office, and 'Carlsen' like…" I couldn't think of a Carlsen right off the bat.

"Oh, I know," Alison said chirpily. "Like Mr. Carlsen from *WKRP in Cincinnati?*"

"Yes, thank you! Though I can't remember if it's spelled the same."

"That's alright, I can try by various spellings."

"This particular Carlsen is spelled C-a-r-l-s-e-n," I explained.

Alison scribbled it down and looked up at me. "Anything else?"

With an "Oh, what the hell, why not?" shrug I said, "Maybe also the Heavenly Rest Funeral Parlor. Or Funeral Home, either one." Worth a shot, I though.

"Got it," Alison said as she stood and went to the doorway. She paused to look back at me again. "I'll be back," she said brightly, then turned and headed away down the hall.

I resumed my paperwork drudgery and soon was mired once again in the seemingly fruitless frustration of my search.

Not too much later, Alison was back. "Hello again," she said rather quietly as she came in.

"Hi," I said glumly, ticked off somewhat at my lack of success so far. "Any luck?"

"Nothing," Alison said with a shake of her head. "I'm sorry."

I sat back, not in disbelief but still feeling defeated. I hadn't really expected there to be any mention of Carlsen in the archive database, but I'd held out a tiny bit of hope nonetheless. Now that hope was gone.

"I tried every alternate spelling of each name I could think of," Alison went on sympathetically. "Still nothing. Zero results. And nothing on the funeral parlor, either."

"Dammit," I grumbled, running my (non-pizza) hand through my hair.

"I'm really sorry," Alison said softly, gently resting a hand on my shoulder. I hadn't realized she'd moved that close to me. I barely knew this woman, and she barely knew me. I was touched by her gesture. Perhaps it wasn't entirely professional on her part, but I sure appreciated it at that moment.

"It's okay," I mumbled, them summoned up a tired smile to offer her. "It was a long shot anyway. Well, it looks like I've still got a bunch of boxes to get through today and tomorrow, doesn't it?"

"Tomorrow?" Alison said, withdrawing her hand.

"Yeah, I booked another session. Didn't want to give up too quickly."

"So you'll be back tomorrow," Alison said, a smile starting to brighten her face again. "Great! I mean, I'm glad you'll have more time to keep working at your story. I'm just sorry I couldn't be more of a help."

"Alison," I said, clasping her hand with a quick, gentle squeeze before releasing it, "you've been a great help to me today."

I wasn't quite sure, but I think she blushed just then. I couldn't be certain because she headed for the door, chattering as she went. "Oh, you're too kind, I'm just doing my job. So anyway, if you do think of anything else you need, I'm just down the hall, remember. Good luck!" Her shoes clacked on the concrete floor as she hurried away.

Dammit, I thought, what the hell was I thinking, grabbing her hand like that? No wonder she rushed out of the room, she probably doesn't want some strange man touching her like that. Why the hell did I do that? Then again, I thought, she *had* touched my shoulder.

Ah, forget it, Harry. Just be more careful and more professional. And get back to work.

I got back to work. And it was more of the same, a dull, frustrating search through seemingly endless frail, yellowing documents. But I kept at it, hoping to find at least one piece of evidence that would vindicate my decision to follow my gut on this latest wild investigation of mine. Was I wrong in this case? I could not shake the doubt that whispered in my mind. But I was determined to keep going.

Some time later, as I was skimming towards the end of Box 3, I was startled by a sudden voice from the doorway. The deep, bass rumble that said, "Harrison Edwards?" was most definitely *not* Alison Perry's voice. In fact, this voice was pretty much the complete opposite of Miss Perry's sweet musical tones.

When I looked up, what I saw was a figure that was also pretty much a complete opposite of Alison. The man in the doorway was big, bald and beefy, and encased in a very tight dark gray suit that seemed to emphasize the huge muscles underneath. His narrowed, glaring eyes were staring straight at me.

CHAPTER SIX

A Battle of Wits

"Harrison Edwards?" the big man repeated in his deep rumble.

"Who's asking?" I said calmly.

"Harrison Edwards?" the man said for a third time.

"Nice to meet you, Mr. Edwards," I said cheekily. I probably shouldn't have gotten so snarky, but I get that way sometimes, especially if something I hadn't expected suddenly cropped up out of nowhere to rattle my usually well-ordered world. I like to tell myself it's a defense mechanism. Also, in this particular instance, I'm pretty sure the long and seemingly wasted day of research had put me in a generally pissy mood, and that didn't help at all.

Whatever excuses for my snarkiness, the big man in the fancy suit did not want to play along. "Please come with me, Mr. Edwards," the man said with a weary sigh.

So much for trying to pretend I wasn't me. "Where?" I said, still hoping to stall.

"Just come with me," the man said. "Please." The word sounded forced out.

"Well, since you put it that way," I said as I stood. "Mind if I bring my things?" I had a feeling that wherever it was I was being taken, I probably wouldn't be coming back to the research room that day, especially since a glance at my watch told me it was almost closing time for the Archive.

Mr. Suit (I had decided to call the man "Mr. Suit", since I really didn't think he was named Harrison Edwards, too, after all) nodded slowly, his eyes narrowing, probably in impatience, I guessed.

I gathered up my things and slung my bag over my shoulder. "I'm sorry there's no pizza left or I would've offered you some," I said cheekily.

Mr. Suit backed out of the doorway to let me exit the room. As I paused out in the hallway, I glanced to my right. Heads were sticking out of doorways all along the corridor, and I quickly spotted Alison, looking worried. I gave her a quick discreet wave of my hand and a brief smile, hopefully conveying an "I'm okay" signal to her.

Mr. Suit cleared his throat noisily and pointed towards the door to the reception area. I shrugged nonchalantly, still feeling snarky and defensive, and did as he instructed. Passing through reception, I couldn't help but notice Taylor at her desk doing everything she could to studiously ignore me and Mr. Suit as we walked past her.

Outside, I blinked in the sudden onslaught of sunlight breaking through the cloud cover. A shiny white golf cart was parked right by the entrance.

"Get in," Mr. Suit grumbled.

I hopped in, settling myself behind the steering wheel. Mr. Suit gently but firmly pushed me over to the passenger side. "Hey, careful!" I protested.

Mr. Suit got behind the wheel. "I didn't say in the driver's seat."

"You didn't specify." Defense mechanism still fully active.

Mr. Suit started the engine and drove us away from the Archive warehouse. I must admit he was a very safe and conscientious driver, obeying all the posted speed limits and yielding right-of-way to any pedestrians. I probably could have safely jumped out of the cart at any point and gotten away, but I was definitely curious about who this guy was, why he'd come for me, and where I was being taken. So I just sat back and observed my surroundings as Mr. Suit drove on. We passed from the busier areas with their bustle and commotion, on to quieter and quieter areas, down alleys and roads and pathways, until finally, with one last turn down a narrow alley, Mr. Suit pulled up in front of a neat-looking little white bungalow in a corner of a deserted clearing surrounded by tall buildings.

Mr. Suit got out first and directed me inside the little building. He led me down a short hall, then stopped, pointing through a doorway off to the left. "In there," he said.

I smiled at him. "Thank you, my good man," I said. He did not react.

What struck me most about the sitting room as I walked in was the palpable sense of abandonment which hung over it. Which is not to say it was dirty, dusty, full of cobwebs or any of that. Instead it was very clean, very tidy, and very comfortable-looking. Two of the walls were mostly window, giving the room a nice airy feel. There was a sofa, some chairs, a coffee table, and a desk with an office chair before it. The desk was placed against one of the windowed walls so that a person seated at it had a good view of the alleyway and parking spot in front of the bungalow. Overall, one felt that this place had been used regularly, and then everyone seemingly just up and left and never came back, while the room waited patiently, frozen in time, for someone to return.

Oh, and there was also a man in the room. Well, apart from myself, of course.

He was seated in an easy chair in the corner farthest from the doorway I had just passed through. He appeared to be in his late fifties, give or take on account of my notoriously bad guessing of ages. In general he reminded me somewhat of Michael Gambon, the British actor who played Professor Dumbledore in the *Harry Potter* films after the great Richard Harris had died. And who had once guest-starred on *Doctor Who,* I might add. And, in fact, do add. Obviously. Anyway, he looked rather like Mr. Gambon but with a fuller head of gray hair, no facial hair, and also more jowly. Which is saying something.

"Have a seat," the man in the chair said, not unkindly. And with no trace of a British accent, dang it.

Still in full snark mode, I sat myself down in the office chair at the desk and gazed happily at the view outside, my back to the man in the corner.

"I'm really not in the mood for jokes," the man said, the change in the tone of his voice backing up his words.

I swiveled around until I faced him. Still feeling like being cheeky, I stretched out my legs, crossed them, leaned back, and laced my fingers behind my head, still smiling.

"Did you know," the main said, apparently choosing to ignore my attitude for the moment, "that at that very desk, in this very room, Orson Welles wrote the first draft of *Citizen Kane*?"

"Really?" I said.

"Indeed," the man said with what I can only guess he assumed was a charming smile.

"No, I didn't know that," I said. "Probably because it isn't true. For one thing, *Kane* was an RKO picture, not Universal. For another—"

"Yes, yes, yes, alright," the man barked grumpily. He heaved a sigh. "Dammit. I used to be better at impressing non-movie people. I guess I'm losing my touch." His face fell slightly, and I felt a teeny-tiny bit of sympathy for the man. Before I could say anything, however, he went on. "I'm Roger Ahrens, I'm the CEO of Universal Studios, and I've had you brought here to tell me everything you know about Broderick Carlsen."

I hadn't been sure of why I'd been taken to meet this man before me, but I certainly hadn't expected to hear him say *that*. Even though, perhaps, I maybe should have. I really didn't know what to think anymore. So, this guy knew about Broderick Carlsen, eh? What did that tell me? And just what did he know about Carlsen? And how did he know it? And how could I get him to tell me what he knew? And how did he know I was investigating Carlsen? Surely Alison wouldn't have — ah, of course, I thought. The computer search.

"Why do you ask?" I said, still stalling while my mind raced.

"Because I want to know, obviously," Ahrens said, impatience beginning to color his tone of voice now. "And I don't want to play any games. Just tell me what you know about Broderick Carlsen."

I figured it wouldn't hurt to tell him the basic facts I'd learned so far about Carlsen's early life. Or first life. Or whatever you want to call it, up until the point where he supposedly died. Ish. "Alright," I said. "He was a habitual criminal back in the 1920s and '30s who was killed by his partner in 1931." I didn't dare say anything about Carlsen's possible reappearance a few days ago, and especially not his resemblance to the Frankenstein Monster. I didn't trust this guy, especially not after how he and his goon had been treating me.

"What else?" Ahrens pressed, leaning forward slightly in his chair.

I shrugged. "That's it. He did a bunch of criminal stuff, then he died in 1931."

Ahrens frowned. "Why are you investigating him?"

Hoo-boy, well, that was a good question, wasn't it? But Roger Ahrens was not going to get the complete truth about that from me, nosirreebob. "My newspaper is doing a series of articles looking into interesting old cases, to see if any new evidence or material has turned up in the years since. Carlsen's case came up, and I got assigned to it." Which was mostly sort of true. From a certain point of view, to quote Obi-Wan Kenobi.

Ahrens didn't seem to entirely believe me. "What do you mean by 'his case'?"

"His murder by his partner-in-crime," I explained simply.

"Hmmmm…" Ahrens said, narrowing his eyes even further. "Seems like a pretty obscure old case for a newspaper in Northern California to bother with."

I just shrugged again and smiled.

"Can you at least tell me what brought you to Universal?"

Another good question. Since my sort-of-telling-the-truth-but-not-really plan didn't seem to be very effective, I decided to go the "say nothing" route. "I'm sure you know," I said smoothly, "that a reporter has a duty to protect the privacy and confidentiality of his sources." Which technically fit, I suppose, at a stretch. Carlsen could possibly be considered a source, and to protect him I would keep silent.

"You can do better than that, Mr. Edwards," Ahrens grumbled, frustration clearing rising.

"Reporter-source privilege," I said evenly.

Ahrens stared at me, then heaved a big sigh. "I'm not gonna get shit out of you, am I?"

"Nope," I said. I'd told him as much as I was willing to give up. I also had a feeling he wasn't going to tell me what *he* knew about Carlsen, no matter how nicely I asked or how much more I divulged. No, I was done.

Ahrens stared some more at me. Then he shook his head, stood, shoved his hands in his pockets and said, "Fine. But listen to me very carefully. I would strongly suggest that you give up this investigation or story or whatever it is. Forget about Broderick Carlsen. Just walk away from this whole thing and never come back. And not a word of this in your little newspaper, or there will be serious consequences. Do you understand me?"

I stood up slowly. We were eye-to-eye across the little coffee table. "Is that a threat?"

"It's a recommendation," Ahrens replied evenly. "That's all."

"Riiiiiight."

Ahrens turned to Mr. Suit, who still hovered in the doorway. "Adam, please show this gentleman out."

"Well, thanks for the little chat," I snarked as I left the room.

Adam, the henchman formerly known as Mr. Suit, whom I'm still going to call Mr. Suit when I feel like it, led me back to the golf cart and drove me back to the Archive warehouse. I got out and started to head towards the building's entrance until I was brought up short by Adam's throat clearing.

"You're done here," the big man growled. "Time to go."

Well, it had been worth a shot. I wondered if my appointment for the next day had been canceled. Probably, since someone as high up and powerful and well-connected as Roger Ahrens wouldn't leave an "i" like that undotted. So I got in my car and drove back to the studio's main gate, where I turned in my lanyard and my vehicle pass as instructed. The entire time I was shadowed by Mr. Suit in his golf cart. Ahrens wasn't leaving anything to chance. As I left the lot and turned onto the public street, I saw the big goon in my rearview mirror, still watching me from his cart. Then I lost sight of him as I turned a corner and drove on.

Fighting my way through traffic, I began to consider what business it was of the Chief Executive Officer of Universal Studios to know about a two-bit hoodlum from eighty years ago whose only apparent connection to said studio seemed to be a plastic surgery job that made him look like that studio's famous Frankenstein's Monster. What did Roger Ahrens know that I didn't? And how could I find out what he did know? Would I be able to get back into the Archives for my appointment the following day? I sure hoped I would, but the fact that Mr. Suit had insisted on me turning in my lanyard and pass before I left gave me doubt.

If nothing else, the conversation in that little private bungalow convinced me more than ever that I really was on to something after all, that there really was a connection, a real, valid, definite connection, linking my John Doe, Broderick Carlsen, and Universal Studios. I just had to find it.

The really chilling thing was, what was it about that connection that would cause the CEO of a major motion picture studio to try to threaten me into dropping my investigation?

***

After stopping briefly for some roast beef sandwiches and an order of curly fries, I returned to my hotel. Once back in my room, I flopped down on the bed and just laid there for a while, resting. It had been a long and frustrating day, on several levels, and I just wanted to take a few minutes to do absolutely nothing.

Eventually I dragged myself back up and sat down at the little desk by the window looking out over the city. I pulled out my cellphone and was about to call my boss Lisa when I stopped and thought better of it. I didn't really have anything new to report, apart from being threatened off the story and even being threatened against reporting the threat, but I didn't care to pass that information along to Lisa at that point. So I didn't call her. And for pretty much the same reasons, I didn't call Arbor Harbor Chief of Police Raymond Parker, either.

Instead, I only made one call, to my band director to tell him I probably wouldn't make rehearsal the next night. Professor Wendahl chuckled and thanked me for the heads-up, then reminded me that there was no rehearsal that week. Oh, well, better safe than sorry.

Feeling rather stupid, I was about to put my phone away when it suddenly rang.

"Hello, Harry," said a cheerful voice on the other end.

"Hi, Dad," I said. "How are you and Mom?"

"We're both fine," said my father John Edwards.

"How's the cruise?"

"Oh, man, Alaska is just incredible!" Dad certainly sounded excited. "I'm so glad we finally decided to do it after all these years. We're having a wonderful time."

"That's great, I'm glad you could go."

"How are things with you?"

"Oh, fine," I said half-heartedly. "Working on a story. It's got me kind of frustrated, actually." I could never successfully lie to my dad, not even little white lies, so I figured I might as well just say what I felt.

"Can you talk about what it's about?" Dad asked.

I hesitated. While I would have loved to have gotten my father's take on my current conundrum, I really didn't think I should involve him in my mess. Especially not after my little encounter that afternoon. "Not really, not specifics, anyway."

"I understand."

"What's really frustrating me is that I couldn't find a certain… connection between… two things. It's like I have the beginning of something, and the very end of it, but all the important stuff in between is missing. I can't find the stuff that shows how the beginning makes it to the ending. But I know it's somewhere, it has to be."

"I see."

"So, yeah, I'm pretty frustrated, and it's starting to piss me off, and getting pissed off made me act kind of stupid this afternoon when I really should have just shut my mouth."

"What do you mean?" Dad asked, sounding a bit concerned now.

Again I paused. I did not want to over-worry him or Mom, especially not while the two of them were off on a getaway cruise, but I still wanted to be honest with him. "Well, I was sort of warned to drop the story and I didn't behave in an entirely civil manner with the guy who was warning me."

"Who told you to drop it? It wasn't your boss, was it?"

"No," I said, "it wasn't Lisa. It was someone rather high up the ladder at the place I think the connection I'm looking for is buried. But like I said, Dad, I'm sure it's there and I have to find it."

"Hmmm," I heard my dad say. "I'm guessing you're not going to drop the story."

"Of course not," I said, "you know me. Stubborn as the day is long."

"Just like your mother," Dad chuckled. "Don't tell her I said that. Although, up here the days can sometimes last a real long time…"

"Stop it," I laughed, feeling a bit better already for simply having just talked it out. "I won't tell her, Dad. But I do have to see this thing through."

"I understand. Is there anything I can do to help?"

I didn't see how a retired home builder who was currently miles and miles away on a cruise ship could realistically lend much of a hand. "No, I don't think so, not right now, anyway. But thanks for asking."

"Well, just promise me you'll be careful, okay?"

"I promise."

"I trust you to follow your instincts, Harry," Dad said. "They've always served you well. Just be careful, and don't lose your cool if things start getting too rough. Got it?"

"Yes, Dad, thank you."

"Your mother and I are always here for you no matter what, you know that, right?"

"I do, yeah, thanks. I promise I'll be careful."

There was a muffled noise on the other end of the line (can it still be called a "line" with all the cellular and satellite and computer stuff involved nowadays?), then Dad said, "Your mother's back from her walk around the deck."

"Hi, Mom," I said.

"Roger says 'Hi'," I heard my dad say to my mother.

"Hi, Harry," I heard my mother say.

"He's down in LA working on a story," Dad explained to her.

"Neat!" Mom said. "Ask him if he's found us a daughter-in-law yet."

"Geez, Mom," I grumbled in exasperation.

"Elizabeth," Dad warned with similar exasperation.

"Sorry, sorry," I heard Mom say. I didn't think she meant it, though. Mom and Dad had both been disappointed when my relationship with Sarah had ended. So much for trusting my gut on that one. I knew my parents both desperately wanted a grandchild but my mother seemed to take it hardest of all. My dad leaned somewhat more towards the "It's his life, let him lead it" side, but I knew he longed to hold a little one in his arms, too.

"Anyway," I said, "thanks for calling. I've got to get some work done before I turn in. Love you guys."

"Love you, too," Dad said.

"Love you, Harry!" I heard Mom say.

I heaved a sigh as I hung up. I hoped I'd not worried my dad too much by mentioning the threat from earlier in the day. He had his own life to manage, he didn't need to get mixed up in my crazy situation. Besides, threats came with the territory, didn't they? I just hoped my stubborn act of standing up to the CEO of Universal Studios wouldn't bring my parents any undue grief.

When I hauled out my laptop and fired it up, I'd intended to work on my story. I knew I should really start organizing my thoughts, marshal my facts and evidence and theories. But as I stared at the screen I just couldn't bring myself to get started. The day had been too long and too frustrating. So I decided to take the night off.

I flopped back onto the bed and flipped on the TV. Lo and behold, the hotel carried BBC America, and wouldn't you know it, they were running a marathon of the previous year's Series 5 of *Doctor Who* (or Season 31, if you want to include the Classic Series in your numbering) in anticipation of the forthcoming premiere of Series 6 (Season 32, naturally). I'd immediately become a huge fan of Matt Smith's goofy, dorky Eleventh Doctor. And I'd also massively fallen for Karen Gillan as the Doctor's companion, the gorgeous, sexy, leggy Scottish redhead Amy Pond.

So I stayed up late into the night watching *Doctor Who* instead of working. So sue me, I'm only human.

***

Wednesday dawned, bright and sunny, with a sky so brilliantly blue it seemed like a digital effect from a movie. Somewhat surprisingly, the temperature outside was just about perfect. Not too warm, just right, with an occasional cool breeze. A lovely day.

I threaded my way through LA and arrived once more at Universal Studios. I was still hoping Roger Ahrens hadn't thought to have my appointment at the Archives for that day canceled. So I got in line at the gate and eventually pulled up in front of the striped barrier arm. Arthur, the same kindly old guard from the previous day, ambled over to my car. I showed him my credentials again and he dutifully checked his tablet.

"I'm sorry, Mr. Edwards," Arthur said with a faltering of his usual smile, "but you're not on the list today."

Dammit, I thought. Well, maybe I could bluff my way in. "There must be some mistake," I said, matching Arthur's politeness. "I have an 8 a.m. appointment at the Archives."

Arthur checked his tablet again, tapping and scrolling. Finally, with a shake of his head, he said, "Not according to my information."

"Like I said," I smiled reasonably, continuing my bluff attempt, "it's a mistake. You know me, I was just here yesterday. I just have a little bit more to do and I'll be all done."

Arthur's eyes narrowed as he stared down at his tablet, almost like he didn't want to face me. "I'm sorry, sir, but I'm afraid I have specific instructions not to let you back on the lot. You'll have to go."

Crap. Damn that Ahrens! I smiled sadly at the nice guard, who was only doing his job, after all. "Okay, then," I said. I maneuvered my car around and left the Studios behind.

A few short blocks away I spotted an empty space along the curb and pulled in. I shut off the car and rolled down the window to let in the cool breeze while I thought things over.

What now? I didn't want to give up, at least not yet. Not until I'd seen this through to the end, if that was at all possible. I wanted at least one more shot at those Archives. I was sure that I'd find the breakthrough I needed to crack the John Doe/Broderick Carlsen case. If only I could get back in there. But how? Maybe if I had someone on the inside, someone sympathetic to my plight, someone who'd be willing to help…

Wait a minute.

Alison.

Of course! Alison! She seemed to be a friendly enough soul, someone who might lend a sympathetic ear, someone who'd be amenable to helping me out. Right? If I could just talk to her, maybe I could persuade her to help me, maybe she could find some way of getting me access to the files I wanted to look at. It was worth a shot, at least.

I pulled out my cellphone and dialed the same number I'd originally called to set up my initial appointment. But as I probably should have figured, I didn't get very far.

When the operator picked up I asked for the Archives Department. A series of short clicks followed, then a different woman's voice said brusquely, "Your number is on a restricted list. Your call cannot be connected. Goodbye." And with a final click, the call was ended.

A restricted list? Cripes, this Roger Ahrens guy didn't fool around.

I briefly considered finding a different phone to call in from, but quickly gave up on that idea. Ahrens probably had a way to thwart me even if I tried that. And he probably also had the studio's lines, or at the very least those of the Archives, tapped, and I really didn't want to get Alison in trouble by talking over a bugged phone line about getting me back inside, now that I came to think of it. Besides, asking for that kind of help felt like more of a face-to-face thing.

So how could I get face-to-face with Alison? Maybe I could camp out by the entrance gate and try to spot her in her car when she went to lunch. Except that she'd said she usually went to the studio commissary for lunch instead of going out. Well, then I'd try to catch her leaving at the end of the workday instead. I'd just have to hope I could spot her in the stream of cars that were sure to leave the lot in a huge line at the same time. Not an insurmountable obstacle, but difficult enough, to be sure.

With my sketchy plan set for later in the afternoon, I was left with several hours to kill. I thought about working on getting a rough outline of the story together, or possibly even starting a first draft, but with so much still to be learned, I felt I needed to do something else.

So I thought of something else.

CHAPTER SEVEN

Carnival of Monsters

I hadn't been there in a few years, but Universal Studios Theme Park hadn't changed much, from what I remembered. Admission prices had gone up, of course. But there were still plenty of rides and shows and shops and eateries. And today, with its sunny yet cool weather, was just about perfect for a theme park visit. Add to that the fact that, as it was a weekday, and despite it being right about spring break time, the park was not crowded at all. Wait times for rides were next to nothing. I could pretty much go where I wanted, when I wanted. I had a blast that morning, barely feeling a ripple of guilt for avoiding real work for a short time.

Just before noon, I took a little break from the rides I'd been enjoying so much. I parked myself on a bench and did a bit of crowd-watching. Suddenly I was brought up short. There, across the boulevard from me, stood three very familiar figures interacting with some park guests.

Dracula, the Wolf Man, and… the Frankenstein Monster.

Actors, of course, working as "streetmosphere" as they called it here (or was that Disney?). But with the story I was working on for several days, it sure gave me a start to see those famous monsters of filmland in the flesh. None of them bore very much resemblance to the original Bela Lugosi, Lon Chaney Jr., or Boris Karloff figures from the classic movies, but they were similar enough that the average park guest would be in no doubt as to who they were meant to be.

I waited patiently as the trio of monsters interacted with guests and posed for photos. As a smiling band of Russian tourists (or so I assumed from their accents) moved away, I saw my chance and moved over to the three characters.

"Ah!" enthused Dracula. "A new victim — I mean guest!" His fake accent was miles from Lugosi, but I could tell the man was trying his best, aided by what struck me as a natural friendly charm. Bit odd for Dracula, but… "You wish to have the… photograph… taken, yes?"

"Actually," I said, "I was wondering if I could ask you… gentleman a few questions. I'm a newspaper reporter."

"Ah," Dracula said, "I know of these. One must not believe all one reads in a newspaper."

"True, true, not everything," I said. "Actually, it's your tall friend I was most hoping to speak with." I nodded at the Frankenstein Monster.

"Ah," Dracula said yet again, "you mean Frankenstein."

Once more I bit my tongue. This wasn't the place to start splitting that particular hair, I thought with a glance at the snarling, slightly hunched-over Wolf Man. "Yes," I said, turning to the monster. "Would you mind if we discussed your makeup a bit?"

Frankenstein — dammit, now *I* was doing it! Frankenstein's *Monster* stared at me and uttered a guttural growl.

"My friend does not speak," Dracula said smoothly.

Wow, I thought, did they really hire a mute to play the Monster? If so, kudos to Universal for their progressive hiring practices. Then I realized the actor portraying the Monster was probably required to stay in character while out among the guests. Still, that could make this awkward for both of us.

"Well, then," I said agreeably, "maybe we could meet somewhere else? When do you get a break or go off shift?"

"Rrrrrrrr…" the Monster rumbled.

"Rrrrrrrr…" echoed the Wolf Man.

"Perhaps," Dracula said, looking up at the Frankenstein Monster, "we could all meet again at half past three o'clock this afternoon near the trinket merchants just inside the main entrance to the grounds."

"That sounds great," I said, "thanks, you guys."

"Would you be wanting the photograph now?" Dracula asked, still laying on the Eastern European charm.

"No, thanks," I said, shaking my head with a chuckle.

"Farewell, then, my friend," Dracula said with a bow.

So the trio of monsters trooped away, seeking more fans to please.

***

I spent the reset of my time before the agreed-upon meeting basically indulging myself. I had a big, greasy bacon cheeseburger with fries and an amazing strawberry malt for lunch. Very filling and very satisfying. I rode more rides. Jurassic Park, Back to the Future, Jaws. Though in actual fact the Jaws ride isn't all that great, I enjoyed it more for the recreation of Amity Island. I loved strolling around and soaking up the ambiance, the atmosphere of the locale of one of my all-time most favorite films ever.

As the time for my rendezvous neared, I started heading back towards the park's main entrance. On the way, I wondered exactly why I had set up the meeting with the monsters in the first place. I didn't really think the actor playing Frankenstein — dammit, I mean the Frankenstein Monster, sheesh — could contribute anything really meaningful to my investigation. Maybe I just wanted to see how the makeup artist of today would go about bringing the classic, traditional appearance of the Monster to life. Maybe I could compare and/or contrast that with what I'd seen of Broderick Carlsen's altered appearance, perhaps glean something from that. Maybe all that would do was tell me how Carlsen's look had *not* been accomplished. Hell, maybe I was just killing time before attempting to contact Alison Perry.

Whatever the actual case, I reached the entrance a bit early, so I slipped into the nearby souvenir store, soon finding myself in the small section devoted to movie props and memorabilia. Eventually I emerged from the store having spent a little bit of my splurge money on an LAPD business card of one Pep Streebek, Tom Hanks' character from the 1987 *Dragnet* movie I mentioned earlier. (By the way, just because I have now mentioned that movie twice does not imply any special fascination or obsession, it's just a silly movie I happen to have watched a lot when it was repeated ad nauseum on cable TV in the early '80s (yes, this statement is directed specifically at an ex, who will probably never read this anyway, so, whatever).)

***

Once outside in the cheery sunlight, almost immediately I spotted the trio of horror movie icons heading in my direction. Frankenstein — dammit! Okay, from hereon in I will refer to this Universal Studios Theme Park actor as *Frankenstein*, all other references will be to the Frankenstein Monster, or just the Monster, or the Creature. Or at least I'll try. Anyway, Frankenstein was clomping his way in my direction with his arms stretched forward in the traditional Frankenstein Monster (there!) manner. Though, in point of fact, this particular mannerism of the monster, walking zombie-like with arms outstretched, does not derive from the original 1931 film, or in fact any of the three Karloff *Frankenstein* films. You see, kids, at the end of the (Karloff-less) 1942 film *The Ghost of Frankenstein*, the Monster underwent a brain transplant, which caused him to become blind. In the next Frankenstein film, 1943's *Frankenstein Meets the Wolf Man*, Bela Lugosi himself finally played the Monster after having turned down the part for the original movie. So Lugosi, following on from the end of *Ghost*, played the Monster as blind as scripted, hence his arms being flung out to help navigate his way through his surroundings. However, the studio cut the scene or scenes explaining the blindness situation from *Frankenstein Meets the Wolf Man*, which then left audiences baffled or unconcerned (or more likely amused) as to why the Monster was suddenly walking around like that. Subsequent films, TV shows, toys and such followed that style from then on.

Ahem.

So, Frankenstein stomped, the Wolf Man scampered along beside him in a sort of half-crouch, and Dracula strode coolly before them both, the de facto leader, perhaps due to his ability to actually talk out loud while in public.

"Ah!" cried Dracula as he spotted me near the souvenir shop. (I don't remember "Ah!" being a particular cliche of Dracula from anything, but obviously this actor was fond of it.) "Our new friend is here! How pleasant to see you again!" He really was milking the

Lugosi/Hungarian/Transylvanian/whatever accent to the utmost.

"Hello," I said with a little wave as we all came together. "Thanks for meeting with me."

"Of course," Dracula said with a bow. He beckoned with a finger. "Come, follow."

I followed. The three monsters led me behind a food stand in amongst some tall shrubbery and eventually to a plain door built into a wall which stretched off left and right as far as I could see. Probably the perimeter cordoning off the public area from the private, behind-the-scenes area. I was proven right when Dracula produced a plastic keycard from his waistcoat, held it to a small, flat, unmarked panel by the door in the wall, then pulled the door open.

"Welcome to our home," Dracula smiled, still doing the Lugosi bit.

The three characters went in first, then I followed. The door swung quietly shut behind me. A short alley led forward then took a sharp left, ending at another door, this one leading into a building. Dracula's pass let us in, and we went down a short ramp, along a short hall, then a quick right, and finally a long walkway leading away from us for quite a good distance. The path was lined on either side by numerous separated little dressing room areas. Each little area was similar: cupboards, movable clothes racks, and styling salon chairs facing a wide mirror lined with bright light bulbs all around the outer edge of the looking glass. Various makeup tools and accessories were spread out on the counter beneath the mirror.

My trio led me down the path a short way then stepped into a dressing area off to our left. Frankenstein, the Wolf Man and Dracula each took a seat in the salon chairs, and then as if by magic, seemingly out of nowhere three people appeared, two women and one man. They immediately began working on each actor's makeup.

I was taking all of it in, dodging scurrying workers rushing through the hall, when I heard a new voice say, "So, whaddaya wanna talk about, pal?" in a thick New York accent.

I looked around for the speaker, wondering if perhaps it was the makeup man who'd just come in. It turned out to be Dracula who'd spoken and was now looking at me expectantly while his makeup woman was removing his false widow's peak. "What," Dracula continued, "you never heard a Dracula from New York before?" He pronounced it "Noo Yawk", of course. I couldn't help but smile.

"No, not really," I said. "I really just had a few questions about the Frankenstein makeup. If that's okay. No slight intended to you or your hirsute buddy."

Frankenstein looked at me uncertainly, then glanced over at Dracula on the chair between himself and the Wolf Man. "I think I might need permission from my supervisor before talking to the press…"

"I'm yer supervisor," Dracula said. "So, yeah, go ahead."

"This won't be published," I clarified. "I'm just getting some background here. Makeup styles today as opposed to, say, the 1930s, like the makeup used on the original *Frankenstein* movie."

"Oh, okay," Frankenstein said. "I'm Jack, by the way. Jack Drew. That's Don Lawe, our Dracula, and Marty Meade over there is our Wolf Man."

"Thank you," I said, "so much better than just thinking of you guys only as, well, you know."

"So it's pretty basic, nowadays," Jack said. "Sally here does the work, but basically my green skin is just colored makeup, I think pretty much like what they used back then. Except I think maybe they sometimes ended up using harsher chemicals in the early days, before they knew better. I think sometimes it took a while to get it right back in those days."

I watched as Jack's makeup person, Sally, started dabbing something via a large cotton swab along Jack's brow, down behind his ears, and across the back of his neck. Then she gently started peeling back the top of Jack's head from just above his eyebrows.

"Now Sally's taking off the main part of my makeup," Jack continued, "now that she's loosened up the glue. The headpiece is just one piece and it's mass produced, one size fits all, pretty much. I'm not the only Frankenstein the park has, so it's cheaper and faster just to make a bunch of them all at once, I guess. Especially since we can only use them once, then they're no good anymore."

Sally kept peeling the headpiece back from Jack's forehead until the full appliance had been removed. It looked very weird. She handed the floppy rubber-like piece to Jack.

"Yep," Jack said, "this is pretty much the moneymaker here." He pointed to the various parts of the headpiece as he described them. "The front, back and sides are pretty much just plain latex skin, very flexible and thankfully breathable nowadays, too. The skin and hair are painted to look as real as possible so there's hopefully no obvious join between it and my skin which Sally would have already greened up. The top of this piece, now, that's a bit different. It's a bit more tough, they stiffen it up so it keeps the famous Frankenstein flattop shape, you see. Here." Jack handed me the appliance.

I turned it over in my hands, feeling the flex of the basic latex, then inspected the more rigid top section. "I see what you mean," I said as I handed it back to him.

"Marty over there," Jack went on, nodding over at the Wolf Man, being worked on by his own assistant. "He gets a lot more of the appliance type stuff than me or Don, 'cause he has all the hair and stuff. Oh, and his big nose."

"Is this similar to what they'd use in the 1930s?" I asked.

"I think so, basically," Jack said. "What do you think, Sally?"

Sally barely looked up from her task of removing more of the green paint from Jack's skin, along with any remaining bits of glue residue from the headpiece. "From waht I've seen and read, yes," she said. "Basic head appliance, skin coloring, things like that."

I was almost afraid to ask my next question, but I knew I had to. So I did. "Do you think someone might have plastic surgery in order to play Frankenstein's Monster in a movie or TV show, or maybe even in a theme park like this one?"

Sally shook her head. "I don't think so."

Daring to continue, I asked, "Theoretically speaking, why might someone choose do that? I mean, go the plastic surgery route instead of just makeup?"

Chuckling, Sally said, "They'd be crazy if they did. Too drastic, too expensive."

"Yeah," Jack chimed in. "All they could play from then on was Frankenstein, what if they wanted to do a different thing, you know? And, like, what if they got fired, you know? Even if it was for a movie, that's like, what, a few weeks or months out of a year? Then what? It's not like they're making tons of Frankenstein movies nowadays."

"Couldn't they just get more surgery done to not be Frankenstein's Monster anymore?" I asked.

"Nah," said Sally. "The more surgery you have on the same areas, the worse it looks. They could try it, I suppose, but they'd never be themselves again, no matter how good the surgeon was."

I wasn't really getting anywhere in terms of my investigation. This was all very interesting information, but all it really told me was what I already basically knew. Broderick Carlsen's appearance as the Frankenstein Monster was not regular makeup. And there seemed to be no good reason why anyone would do that to themselves.

And then Sally said quietly as she continued working on Jack, "What if it wasn't by choice?"

Holy crap. It might have been done against his will? I had not considered that angle. So I wasn't prepared to discuss that point further just at that moment. Best to think on it myself, I thought, pursue it on my own, and leave these good people out of it, leave them to their own probably happy lives.

So I awkwardly but politely thanked them all, then had Don, who was already finished with his makeup and back in civilian clothes, show me the way out. Back in the public area, we shook hands, and Don said, "Farewell, my friend!" with one last shot of Lugosi.

As I left the park, walked back to my car, and drove back to the area of the Universal Studios entrance, I pondered Sally's question. It seemed entirely plausible, however unlikely that someone might force a person to be surgically altered to look like Boris Karloff as the Monster. But who? And why? And how? And when? And, hell, let's throw in where, for that matter.

However, it was also quite plausible that Carlsen would have the surgery done to himself, by choice, with all my attendant questions following on from that. If I could figure out if it was something that was forced on Carlsen, or something he chose himself, would knowing that somehow help me to connect the dots from a seemingly dead Broderick Carlsen in 1931 to an alive Broderick Carlsen in 2011? I had a feeling, though, that even if it did, the line between those two dots would be anything but straight.

CHAPTER EIGHT

The Waking Ally

By the time five o'clock rolled around, I had left the theme park behind and was back at the entrance to the Universal Studios lot. This time, however, I was parked about half a block away on the street running past the gate. As the shift workers started leaving, I kept a close eye out for Alison, looking carefully at each vehicle that left. I used the zoom feature on my phone's camera app to get a closer look at each driver. Well, at each driver who didn't have ridiculously tinted windows preventing a look inside. Wasn't that illegal or something? Probably not in LA, I grumbled to myself.

Anyway, a little past the top of the hour, my diligence was rewarded. I spotted Alison driving off the lot in a dark blue Honda Prius hybrid, one of many Priuses (Priusi?) I'd seen that day. I recognized her distinctive hairstyle and her dark-framed glasses as she paused to look both ways before turning out into the street, so I knew I had my gal. Alison turned left which was fortunate for me as it meant I didn't have to do a U-turn to follow her. I just pulled out swiftly into traffic and kept on her tail a few cars back.

A couple of minutes later, Alison pulled into a gas station and got out to fill up her tank. Which at the time struck me as odd, as she was driving a Prius. But hybrids still used gas, just not at the extremely gas-guzzling rate as standard cars like my rental, which quite by coincidence also needed topping off. Imagine that. So I pulled my own car up to the pump behind Alison. I got out and started filling up. Then, taking a huge breath, knowing that what I was about to do could go disastrously pear-shaped, I pretended to suddenly "notice" the driver of the car ahead of mine.

"Miss Perry?" I said with what I judged to be the perfect level of pleasant surprise.

Alison turned and looked at me. She blinked. "Mr. Edwards?" she said, clearly not having expected to see me there.

"Fancy running into you here," I went on with the appropriate amount of nonchalant charm.

Alsion smiled, tucking a stray lock of her beautiful dark hair back behind her ear. "Are you OK?"

"I'm fine," I said, "why do you ask?"

"Oh," she said, "well, you said you were going to come back today to the Archive, you said you'd booked another appointment, but when you didn't show up this morning I asked Taylor and she said your appointment had been canceled and that I really should just forget about the whole thing, and she seemed kind of nervous. I didn't know what she was talking about, I didn't know if maybe you'd gotten hurt somehow or something and she was just trying to protect my feelings or something like that."

"Protect your feelings?" I said, confused.

"Well, I'm glad you're okay," Alison continued on hurriedly. "But what happened? Why did you cancel your appointment?"

I hesitated. What could I say? I didn't want to blurt out the whole story right then and there. But I did think I needed to start. And also I *wanted* to tell her. I wanted someone on my side. Especially someone in the perfect position to help me. "I'm not the one that canceled the appointment," I said evenly.

Alison frowned. "What? I don't understand."

Hoo, boy, I thought, this is it. Brace yourself, Harry. "Miss Perry… Alison… I need your help."

Her frown seemed fixed in place as I made my simple plea. Then her eyes widened and her cheeks reddened visibly even from where I stood. "Oh," she said quietly. Then her gas pump nozzle thunked, followed a few seconds later by my own. We finished up our respective transactions, then I watched hopefully as Alison walked somewhat distractedly back over to her driver's side door. She began to open it, then stopped and looked back at me. I was almost afraid to hear what she was going to say. "Maybe we should go somewhere we can talk," she finally said. "Follow me."

Hot damn! I grinned as I got back in my car. A short time later we pulled out of the rush hour chaos into two rare adjacent parking spaces near a nice-looking little restaurant off the main drag.

Together Alison and I entered the restaurant, which was cool, quiet, hushed, dimly-yet-sufficiently lit. The maitre d' led us to a secluded corner booth, far away from the kitchen doors which for some reason I usually ended up getting stuck sitting right next to when I went out to eat. Well, except at the Earl of Essex. Apparently Alison had some good restaurant karma which outshone my bad. We placed our drinks order, then we were alone.

Neither of us seemed quite sure how to start, as we both sat there in awkward silence. I looked down at the menu.

"The Brass Lamp," I read. "I wondered what this place was called. I didn't see a sign outside."

"They used to have a sign," Alison said quietly, "but it got knocked down by a storm a while ago and they've just never bothered to replace it yet."

"And the city planning or zoning department hasn't been too bothered about it, apparently," I said, long familiar with the selective governmental sluggishness and apathy.

"I guess not," Alison agreed with a shy smile.

"Do you come here often?"

Alison looked a bit puzzled, then I realized what I'd just said. "Oh, God," I said, "I'm sorry, I didn't mean—"

"No, it's okay," Alison replied kindly, then looked down at her own menu. "Well, not a lot, but sometimes I come here. It's a nice, clean, quiet place and the food is excellent. And nicely priced, too, which is very helpful sometimes."

The waiter arrived and we placed our orders. Alone once more, I decided it was time.

"Alison," I began nervously, "I wasn't joking earlier about needing your help."

"Oh," she said, looking at me intently with those beautiful brown eyes of hers. "You weren't?"

"No," I said earnestly. "And this isn't some kind of lame attempt at a pickup line or anything like that either. Including that stupid question of mine a few minutes ago."

"Oh," Alison said, her cheeks flushing red again. Did she have some sort of medical condition, poor circulation or — No, it was none of my business.

"As I think I mentioned yesterday," I continued, "I'm down here in LA on a story. Last weekend, back home in Arbor Harbor—"

"Where is that, exactly?" Alison interrupted quietly. "I don't think I've heard of it."

I smiled. "Most people haven't. It's a quaint little town way up north, a fair distance from the border with Oregon. We're right on the Pacific coast and surrounded by some beautiful forests, a portion of which runs right up to the south edge of town. Anyway, while I was in the forest there on a story, a man came running out of the woods..."

And I told her everything, pausing only once when our food arrived. I told her about the fire. I told her about Broderick Carlsen. I told her how he looked one hundred and ten percent like Boris Karloff as the Monster from the original 1931 *Frankenstein* movie. I told her how he had been born in 1887 and reportedly died in 1931. I told her how that had led me to LA, and the records I'd been searching. I told her about Carlsen's criminal past and the circumstances of his supposed death. I told her about the funeral home that supposedly had come to retrieve Carlsen's body from the coroner not having any record of being contacted about or handling Carlsen. I told her about my frustration with the investigation. I told her everything because I figured that the truth was the only way to get her help. Also, a part of me really did not like the thought of lying to Alison. And as I narrated the story so far, I found I had become completely convinced of the whole story myself by now.

Alison took everything in, listening intently if somewhat disbelievingly. She asked a few sharp, incisive questions during my big spiel, but on the whole she really just listened.

"I know it all sounds insane," I said after I laid everything out before her. "But crazy as it sounds, I'm convinced there's truth to it. I can't just leave it alone. I need to find out exactly what the hell happened to Broderick Carlsen. Call it my journalistic duty, but I just hate leaving questions unanswered. That, plus my pretty reliable gut instincts, have served me extremely well over the years. In fact, not to blow my own horn, one of my stories even won an award."

I paused, a bit uncertain as to how to broach the subject of one her very-high-up bosses being involved somehow. I didn't know how she would take it if I started accusing the CEO of the very studio she worked at of strong-arm tactics.

"What exactly brought you to Universal?" Alison asked, rendering my hesitation somewhat moot.

"Pretty much that gut I mentioned," I said carefully. 'I was stuck without a clear lead to follow, but since Carlsen supposedly died in 1931, and *Frankenstein* came out in 1931, and since Carlsen looked like the Monster from that movie, my gut said 'Go to Universal!' So I listened and I went. Unfortunately I haven't found much of anything yet. But I am *sure* there is something in those archives that will break this story, or at the very least give me something further to follow up on."

"Then why did you cancel your appointment for today?" Alison asked with a cute puzzled frown.

I braced myself. This wasn't going to be easy for her, and it might just screw up my chances to enlist her help entirely. "I wanted to come back, believe me," I said. "But it was... recommended that I not return."

"Recommended?"

"Well, I suppose you could rework that sentence to include the word 'threatened' instead to make it slightly more accurate," I said, hoping I had played that bit casually enough.

"What?" Alison gasped. "Someone threatened you? Who? Was it that man I saw walking out with you yesterday?"

"That big bald guy? Name of Adam Suit?" Alison didn't get my little joke, obviously. "No, not him. At least, not directly. But he did take me to the man who did the actual threatening, and was also probably the person who canceled my appointment for today. Guy by the name of Roger Ahrens."

"Roger Ahrens?" Alison's eyes went wide. "The CEO? *My* CEO? Of Universal Studios?"

I nodded. "That's who he said he was. Didn't show me any ID or anything, but he seemed to have the clout. He had that kind of superior air about him."

"What did he look like?"

"About my height, a bit heavier than me, gray hair, jowly, kinda Dumbledorey."

Alison sat back, trying to take it all in. "That certainly sounds like him. What did he say to you?"

"Well, he basically told me to drop my story completely, abandon my investigation, and forget I ever heard of Broderick Carlsen."

Alison was clearly stunned. "But why would the studio CEO care about a supposedly dead person from, what, eighty years ago?"

"Another very good question. But he sure didn't want me digging up anything more about Carlsen. When I got to the lot this morning, hoping I would still be able to get in, I found out my appointment had been canceled and I'd been banned from the lot. And apparently my phone number is on some kind of restricted list, too. Which I found out this morning when I tried to call you to ask for your help. So, yeah, I don't think Roger Ahrens was kidding."

"I just… I don't get it," Alison bit her lower lip. Man, that sure looked cute.

"Me neither," I said. "But like a lot of people when they get threatened, it just encourages them all the more. And I fall into that particular category."

"So… you're not giving up?"

"Hell, no," I said. "I'm gonna figure out just what the heck is going on with Broderick Carlsen once and for all." I looked Alison steadily in the eye. "Which is where you come in. I need you."

Alison's cheeks reddened yet again.

"Are you okay?" I asked her.

"What do you mean?"

"Well, it's probably none of my business, but every now and then I've noticed your face gets very red and flushed-looking. If you have some sort of circulation or blood pressure problem, I don't know, but maybe you should get it checked."

Alison's cheeks blossomed even more red. "Oh," she said sheepishly, "I'm… I'm fine. It's just… I sometimes get… flustered when I'm with someone I kinda think I kinda like."

"Oh, okay," I said, "as long as it's nothing serious."

Just then, I could have almost sworn I actually heard a once-cent coin fall.

"Oh!" I said, my eyes widening as I felt my own cheeks flush red.

"I thought I was being obvious," Alison rushed on. "But maybe too obvious, when I get nervous sometimes I tend to babble, too. I thought maybe you might…"

And I recalled Alison's talkativeness from yesterday, her now obvious attempt to have me join her for lunch in the studio commissary, her smiles, her bright eyes… I like to think I'm pretty intelligent and insightful in general. But I will be the first to admit that when it comes to picking up signals like the ones Alison had apparently been giving me, I can be a total, blind, stupid idiot.

"Alison, I…" I began, not quite knowing what to say. I was a bit out of practice on the whole relationship front. I decided to be frank and honest. It had served me well so far today. "Look, Alison, it's… it's been a while since I've done anything like… this… so please forgive me if at any point I go all Hugh Grant on you."

Alison looked uncertain but amused. "Okay…"

"And just to clarify," I went on, "by that I mean if I start being nervous and stammer while retaining my charm, like in his movies, and not whatever the hell he was doing when he picked up that stranger on Hollywood Boulevard or wherever it was that one time."

Alison chuckled sweetly. "Got it." She grinned her beautiful, sunny smile.

"Anyway, what I mean is, I think I kinda… well, I think you're pretty nice, too. I just didn't realize it right away, I guess, because, like I said, I've been out of the game for some time."

"Me, too," Alison said sheepishly, still smiling at me. "And I will help you, in any way I can."

It took me a second to realize she was referring to my request for help in my investigation. "Are you sure?" I asked her hesitantly. "Because now I think I'm too concerned for your safety to put you in harm's way."

Alison rolled her eyes. "Oh, for God's sake, this is the twenty-first century. You don't have to be the big knight in shining armor, because I assure you I am no damsel in distress."

"Well, I'd hate for you us to get off on the wrong foot with you thinking I was un-gallant," I protested weakly.

"'Un-gallant'?" Alison said. "Is that even a word?"

"Never mind."

Alison reached across the table and took my hand in hers. "I'll be fine," she said firmly. "I'm a tough cookie."

I smiled in acknowledgment, giving her hand a gentle squeeze.

"So," my new ally said, all business-like now, "how exactly can I help?"

"I have to get back inside the Archives," I said. "My gut's still telling me the answer I'm looking for, or at least something to point me towards the answer, is in there somewhere. I think if I had at least one more day of digging through those *Frankenstein* files I'll find it."

"Well, then," Alison said, "we need to get you back inside Universal Studios."

CHAPTER NINE

Partners in Crime

Car trunks are extremely uncomfortable to ride in. I bounced and jounced with seemingly every bump in the road, banging my bent frame against the barely-padded surfaces of the interior of the trunk of Alison's car about a million times as she drove to work. Well, maybe not that many, but damn, it hurt.

Alison had picked me up from my hotel bright and early the morning after our dinner conversation. I got in front with her initially until she turned off into a quiet side street where she stopped briefly so I could hop into the trunk. This *was* Los Angeles, but even so we figured people might get concerned and call the police if they saw someone come out of a hotel and jump right into a car trunk.

So I rode uncomfortably, feeling every stop and start quite distinctly. At one point I thought I could hear the voice of Arthur, the kind elderly guard from the entrance gate to the studio lot. Then we rolled onward, and not long after that Alison parked, shut off the engine and walked away from her car. As planned, I waited about ten minutes, which we figured would be enough time for Alison to get into the Archive warehouse and make her way into position at the rear of the building.

When it was about time, I popped the trunk lid with the spare remote Alison had given me. I peered out cautiously. I saw no one about. Lifting the lid a bit further, I saw that Alison appeared to have parked in a quiet back alley of the lot. I climbed out quickly and shut the lid, then took out my cellphone and pretended to be in the middle of an important "show business" call. We'd thought that should be enough to convince any casual onlooker that I was not out of place.

I made my way over to the back corner of the warehouse, then went around to the right. Just as Alison had said, there was a steel service door a short distance from the corner. I hurried over to it, then checked my phone. Alison should be in place by now, I thought, so here goes.

I knocked three times on the door, and just as I said "Penny" the door swing outwards, barely missing me as I quickly stepped aside.

Alison had apparently heard me, as she pointed a finger in my face and hissed, "Don't even." She grabbed my arm and pulled me inside, shutting the door quietly behind me.

We were in a sort of cage tucked in the back corner of the main warehouse area, two walls of exterior wall and two walls of chain link, with a full-size chain link door set in one of the fence walls. The view to the rest of the warehouse was completely blocked by shelves on the other side of the chain link, all of them crammed with boxes, crates, bins, and whatnot. The only view out, or in for that matter, which was of much greater importance for me, was through the gate door, which showed the rest of the warehouse area to be vast, tall, and filled to the brim with row upon row of towering stacks of nearly overflowing shelving.

Taking a quick peek, I saw no one around. That was good news. Also good news was the fact that the little caged area was empty, giving no one a good reason to have to visit it at any time. Or so I hoped, anyway. But Alison had come up with the plan, and she felt comfortable using it for my workspace, so I did too.

"I don't think I've raised any suspicions so far," Alison whispered as she led me through the gate door and into the warehouse area proper. "But let's be quick about this so I can get back to my desk."

She walked briskly down a long aisle, then turned and headed down another path between towering shelves. I kept as close to her as I could, and so nearly bumped into her when she suddenly stopped in the middle of the row.

"Here they are," Alison whispered, gesturing to the shelves on our left. There I saw the familiar labeling on the three boxes I'd examined two days earlier, as well as several more just like them but with higher identification numbers. "Grab what you want."

"Can't we use a cart?" I whispered back, recalling how Alison had delivered the first three boxes to me originally.

"They're all in use already," Alison hissed back, glancing about nervously. "Come on."

I grabbed the box marked "4", then had Alison set "5" atop it, while she took "6" herself. Together we awkwardly lumbered back to the cage. We set our burdens down on the cold concrete floor, and I stood up, catching my breath and stretching my back. I needed to exercise a bit more regularly, I scolded myself silently.

Alison moved back to the gate door. "I have to go," she said. "I wish I could stay and help but I'd be missed and my boss would get suspicious and—"

"It's okay," I said with a smile, "go, I'll be fine."

Alison nodded. "I'll try to stop in around lunchtime when I can get away. Good luck." And she left, closing the gate door behind her. I listened to the click of her footsteps on the floor get fainter and fainter, heard the distant creak of the far off door opening then shutting, then silence.

I went to work.

I'd hoped for a quick breakthrough, to find whatever it was that I needed to find to put the whole Broderick Carlsen mystery together without too much time or effort. Silly me. Thursday was indeed shaping up to be a near carbon copy of Tuesday, but in less comfortable environs. I dug through reams of paperwork with no result. I waded through tons of detail and minutiae that would make a trivia geek drool with envy. Though hopefully not on the documents themselves. I browsed facts and figures I really didn't care about. I saw invoices, call sheets, accounting paperwork, pre-production stuff, production stuff, post-production stuff. I went through everything.

And found nothing.

***

By the time Alison returned several hours later, my frustration level had risen alarmingly once again. What with my fruitless searching and my fitful stop-and-start pattern brought on by the occasional sound of an archivist coming into the warehouse area yet thankfully never approaching too near my private little cage, I had not had a good morning like I'd fervently hoped.

And apparently my mood was obvious on my face as, with one look at me after sneaking through the gate door, Alison crinkled her brow in sympathy.

"Nothing yet?" she said quietly as she came over and crouched beside me, handing me a bottled water and a paper bag with a sandwich and chips from her purse.

"Thanks," I muttered as I nevertheless gratefully accepted the food. "No, nothing. Not a damn thing. I'm beginning to get rather pissed off at my gut. It's never let me down like this before. Never!" (*But what about Sarah...?* a little voice whispered inside my head. Shut up, I told it. It did. For now.) I sighed and took a bite of the sandwich. "I'm almost starting to think I should just pack it in, just give up and forget everything and move on."

Alison was silent. Then she said, "What about Broderick Carlsen?"

I looked at her. She was right, of course. I owed it to my fellow human being to figure out what had happened to him. I couldn't let go now.

"Alright," I said eventually. "I'll see what I can find this afternoon. Then maybe we can talk things over and see what we should do next. Okay?"

Alison's smile warmed me considerably. "Sounds good to me. And thank you for the 'we'. Anything you need from me before I go?"

I thought for a moment. "No," I sighed, "nothing I can think of right now." Actually there was something, but I didn't dare mention it.

"Okay," Alison said as she stood up and moved to the gate door. "Well, good luck, I'm rooting for you." With that, and another very pretty smile, she left me alone once more in the cage.

I listened to her footsteps fade before I got back to work.

***

* * *

When I checked my watch later that afternoon to find five o'clock fast approaching, I was still in a foul mood. I had dug through all the files in front of me to the point where my eyes felt strained and my temples began to throb, and yet I still had found nothing useful to further my investigation. Not one damn thing. I couldn't believe it. My gut instinct, always reliable for so long, had evidently failed me. I did not like that. And at times my mind had started to wander, to wonder what avenue I could possibly go down next, since this one had clearly led to a dead end. I couldn't come up with anything on that score, either. Which I also did not like.

Alison finally appeared at the gate door again. She easily read my mood once again, and entered quietly to help me put the boxes back in order. Then together we lugged them back to their proper place in the racks on the main warehouse floor. We returned to the cage, and Alison stopped at the doorway.

"Be careful," she said softly. "Text me when you're in place."

I nodded. Alison gave me a quick supportive smile, then turned and walked away down the long pathway back to the main door. I shut the gate door.

I peeked outside the exterior door that led from the cage, saw no one about, and hurried out. Using the same phone-to-my-ear preemptive ruse I'd used that morning, I made my way swiftly around the corner and back to Alison's car. With the remote, I popped the trunk, and with a final glance to confirm no one was watching, I hopped in and shut the lid. After catching my breath, telling myself I *really* needed to get back to the gym more regularly, I sent Alison a text telling her I was all set. She sent back a brief "K", and then I waited.

Several long, hot, stuffy minutes later, I heard and felt Alison get in the front and start up the engine. A few turns and stops and starts later, I heard the kind old guard from the main entrance gate talking with Alison, and then there was the jolt that bounced the whole car and signified we'd left the studio lot and had gotten back to the city streets.

Side note... do not hide inside a closed car trunk. Which may go without saying, probably, but, well, just speaking from experience, it sucks.

I was still in a mopey funk when Alison pulled the car over several minutes later so I could get in front with her. She gave me a sympathetic smile as she put the car back in gear and drove on.

"You okay?" she asked eventually.

"Yeah," I said, "just tired, frustrated, and pissed off."

"No luck this afternoon then, either, huh?"

"Nothing," I grumbled. "Not a god-damned thing. I almost can't believe it. So much for my ever-reliable gut. I was so *sure* I'd find something, some clue or evidence or whatever to start clearing up this whole damn Broderick Carlsen mystery. But what did I find? Nothing." I slammed my fist against the side of the passenger door. Then I remembered it wasn't my car, and I looked sheepishly over at Alison. "Sorry."

"It's okay," Alison said.

"And I'm sorry for wasting your time on this."

"No, it's fine, I get it," Alison replied comfortingly. "I haven't been involved in this nearly as long as you have and I'm feeling frustrated, too." Then I saw her smile in what seemed a shy or knowing manner, and I could have sworn I caught a slight twinkle in her eye. "But maybe your gut was right after all..."

Huh? "What do you mean?"

Alison glanced at me. "Look inside my purse."

"Uh..." I hesitated. In my experience, women's purses were inviolable no-man's-lands.

"Go ahead," Alison urged.

I took her purse from the console between our seats and gingerly prised it open. A folded sheet of paper sat atop a jumble of other items I deliberately avoided looking at. I took out the paper. "This?" I asked.

"Yep."

Unfolding the sheet, I saw what appeared to be a collection of little lists, each headed by a number, "1", "2", "3", "4", etc., underneath which were names and dates in side-by-side columns. I didn't recognize any of the names at first glance, but then I saw my own name at the very bottom of the lists headed "1","2" and "3". Next to my name on all three lists was Tuesday's date. "Is this..." I began.

"A printout of everyone who's ever checked out any of the *Frankenstein* archive boxes? Yes, it is."

I looked at the list again. Sure enough, it made sense. I'd only officially checked out the first three boxes two days before.

"That's brilliant!" I told her. "What made you think of it?"

"Well, after I saw how down you were at lunch, I went back to my office and I thought to myself, 'I wish I could help him somehow.' Then I thought, 'I wish that maybe if I can't help him maybe someone else can.' Then I thought, 'Maybe someone else already has.' I figured if someone else had been investigating the same thing you were, maybe they'd also come to Universal, maybe with some facts or knowledge you haven't come up with yourself yet and so had a better idea of what to look for in the Archives. So I printed out the check-out list of everyone who'd ever accessed any of the *Frankenstein* files. And since I didn't have to enter Broderick Carlsen's name, I knew it wouldn't pop up on Roger Ahrens' radar." She glanced at me then back at the road. "I hoped it might be a nice surprise for you," she finished with a cute little slightly embarrassed smile.

"It sure is," I said. "I'm impressed."

Alison reddened again.

"Are you sure you don't have a medical condition?" I asked teasingly. "Maybe I should drive…"

Alison stuck her tongue out at me and I chuckled.

I looked over the names on the sheet again. "I'm not recognizing any of these other names at first glance," I said.

"I didn't either," Alison said, "but I didn't have time to barney them."

"'Barney' them?" I said. "Is that a *How I Met Your Mother* reference I'm not getting?"

Alison laughed. "No," she said, "it means Google them. As in, 'Barney Google, with the goo-goo-googly eyes.' It's an old song, I think. I had a grandfather who used to sing it when I was a kid."

"Never heard of it," I said. "I thought maybe it was Cockney rhyming slang I wasn't familiar with."

"You know Cockney rhyming slang?" Alison said, glancing at me with amazement on her face.

"Yeah, but I've never met anyone else who did."

"Well," Alison said, "I must confess I'm a bit of an Anglophile."

"Me, too!" I said, grinning excitedly.

We sat in quiet happiness for a moment, Alison battling LA traffic as she drove.

Then she glanced sidelong at me and said, "You think I look like Nicola Bryant, don't you?"

Ho.

Ly.

Shit.

CHAPTER TEN

The Greatest Show in the Galaxy

"Peter Davison," Alison declared.

"Figures," I said.

"What do you mean, 'Figures'?"

"All the fangirls loooove the dishy Fifth Doctor."

"I like his character, how human he was."

"Uh-huh."

"Well, who's *your* favorite Classic Series Doctor?"

"Tom Baker, hands down."

"Like *that's* not a cliche."

"He was the best Doctor by a mile, alien, mysterious, funny, serious, everything."

"If you say so."

"Alright," I said. "Favorite New Series Doctor?"

"David Tennant."

"Wow, what a shock," I deadpanned.

"And not just because he's gorgeous."

"Riiiiiight."

"I'm serious!" Alison insisted. "He was exciting, fun, vibrant, full of energy."

"If you say so." I was teasing her, and I was pretty sure she knew and was playing along.

"Yours?" she asked.

"Matt Smith," I declared. "I know he's only had one series so far, but he's blown me away. Goofy, awkward, funny, with a sense of ancient wisdom and sadness, impressive for such a young actor. Just amazing."

"I think you just like Amy Pond."

"Well, she is nice."

"Figures," Alison teased right back.

"Favorite overall Doctor?" I asked.

"Tennant."

"Tom Baker."

"Well," said Alison, "it appears we must agree to disagree."

Finally our car reached the second drive-thru window and we took our drinks and our food. Neither of us felt like battling the crowds on St. Patrick's Day, which I'd completely forgotten about, so we had opted for the easy choice of fast food. Once we had our order, we headed for my hotel.

On the way up in the elevator, I could tell both of us were still anxious to get to work on the list of names Alison had gotten for me. For us. There were several other passengers riding up with us, so we kept quiet until we reached my floor and hurried to my room.

CHAPTER ELEVEN
City of Death

Once inside my hotel room, I set up my laptop at the desk while Alison took out our food. As I logged onto the hotel's guest wi-fi, Alison sat down on the edge of the bed so she could see the screen along with me. I typed and moused carefully so as to avoid making a mess with my food as I ate and worked.

Alison and I determined that many of the names on Alison's list were just plain unidentifiable. Oh, sure, Google came up with hits for them, but with just a name and a single date which told us nothing more than one specific day that person was alive, it wasn't really possible to narrow things down any further for them. A few names cropped up as various Universal employees from over the years, including a CEO from the mid-1950s.

Then we encountered a name that proved rather intriguing.

Joseph Holland, who we discovered was a reporter for the *Los Angeles Daily Record* newspaper, accessed the *Frankenstein* archives on January 31, 1969. Further internet digging revealed that fact that Joseph Holland was found dead three days later on February 3. I was able to find a scanned article from the *Daily Record* which reported Holland's death.

* * *

FEB 3, 1969

MISSING REPORTER FOUND DEAD

Body discovered near garbage dump

Hollywood — The body of Daily Record *reporter Joseph Holland, reported missing yesterday, was found this morning in an area of dense woods alongside the Northeast Hollywood Landfill on the edge of the Hollywood Hills, the Los Angeles Police Department announced this afternoon. A department spokesman did confirm that the discovery of the body was aided by a telephone call from a supervisor at the landfill who had reported a possible abandoned vehicle in their parking lot. Police identified the car as a 1960 Nash Rambler belonging to Mr. Holland, who had been reported as missing by his wife and co-workers the previous day. Officers were sent to the landfill to investigate the area. Mr. Holland's body was found a short time later by an officer.*

Mr. Holland was a well-respected journalist for this newspaper for many years, and he will be sorely missed. The thoughts and prayers of everyone on the staff go out to his family and loved ones. A tribute to Mr. Holland is in preparation and will appear in the near future in this newspaper.

I looked at Alison as she stared at the screen. "I think we might be on to something here," I said quietly, hoping I hadn't just jinxed us. Alison nodded.

We found another article, this one from the following day.

FEB 4, 1969

CORONER: REPORTER MURDERED

Missing reporter was strangled

Hollywood — At a press conference held today at City Hall, the Los Angeles Police Department announced the results of the autopsy performed on the recently discovered body of Daily Record *reporter Joseph Holland. The coroner's office determined that Mr. Holland's cause of death was asphyxiation due to strangulation, which likely also accounts for Mr. Holland's broken neck. The coroner's office also estimated that Mr. Holland most likely died a few hours after he was last seen by employees of the Northeast Hollywood Landfill, probably the afternoon or evening of January 31. The LAPD is now treating Mr. Holland's death as a homicide.*

Authorities also provided further information as to Mr. Holland's activities during his final hours, based upon interviews with several Northeast Hollywood

Landfill employees. At approximately 1:00 p.m. on January 31, Mr. Holland arrived at the landfill in his vehicle and requested permission to search the property, both within the fenced dump site and outside in the surrounding area. After spending close to two hours inside the fence at several locations, including a long period spent at the far north end of the dump, Mr. Holland exited the enclosed area and moved his car to the adjoining parking lot outside the fence. Mr. Holland then proceeded on foot, exploring the surroundings of the dump and eventually disappearing within the densely-wooded area among the hills just north of the dump site itself. Mr. Holland was not seen alive by any eyewitnesses after this point.

On February 3, landfill employees called in a possible abandoned vehicle in their parking lot which had been undisturbed for several days. The vehicle was identified via Department of Motor Vehicles records as belonging to Joseph Holland. Mr. Holland's wife had, in fact, officially reported her husband missing just that morning. Officers were dispatched to the landfill, and shortly thereafter Mr. Holland's body was found in the wooded hills to the north of the dump.

The Police Department declined to take questions at the press conference.

Mr. Holland's final work for the Daily Record, *a telephone interview with film legend Boris Karloff, who himself passed on Sunday, will be published in this newspaper at a future date.*

Both of our jaws dropped as we read the final sentence. We looked at each other in stunned disbelief.

"Holy crap," I breathed.

"Oh my God," Alison said shakily.

"I definitely think we're on to something," I said.

"Yeah."

We reread the article. I couldn't believe it. Boris Karloff? It couldn't be a coincidence.

"So your gut was right after all, I'd say," Alison said.

"Yours was, too," I said. "Brilliant idea to print out that list."

"But what does it all mean?" Alison said as she stood up from her hunched-over position to look at the laptop screen from the edge of the bed. "Boris Karloff ties in with the *Frankenstein* thing, but what's the connection with Carlsen?"

"I don't know," I admitted. "What date did Holland access the *Frankenstein* records?" I pulled out my pocket notebook and a pen as

Alison brought her printout over to me.

"January 31st," Alison said.

I started scribbling a rough timeline. "Okay," I said, "and that same day he visits the landfill. Then his body is found…"

Alison read from the laptop, "February 3rd."

"The article doesn't say when Holland interviewed Karloff, does it?"

"No," said Alison.

"Hmmm," I mused. "I'm guessing it wasn't too long before Holland's visit to Universal. But what sent Holland to Universal in the first place? And what sent him next to the landfill?"

"I don't know," Alison said quietly.

I felt myself getting a bit frustrated once more, having found something relevant and then running into the same problem yet again — not having answers and not knowing where to find them. "Alright," I said, "who else have we got on your list? We'll come back to this. Let's check the rest of the names on that list before we go any further." Maybe something will occur to me in the meantime, I hoped silently.

We Googled the rest of the names. Only one seemed connected to our investigation. ("Our"? Was I automatically thinking in those terms already? When did *that* happen? I wondered.) Victor Locke, apparently an LAPD detective in the 1960s and '70s, accessed the *Frankenstein* files on February 6, 1969, just three days after Holland's body was found.

"Probably following up on the Holland murder, I'd guess," I said.

"Can we find him, maybe talk to him?" Alison asked.

I Googled some more. "Doesn't look like it," I said eventually. "He died in 1986."

"Oh," Alison said, disappointed.

"Let's dig a little more into the murder," I suggested. I set to work again as Alison sat on the bed behind me once more. It took some doing, as not every issue of the *LA Daily Record* was available online. However, what little we did find told us that Joseph Holland's murder was never solved. No one was ever arrested or charged, no one ever confessed, nothing. The case was presumably still technically open, now a long-forgotten cold case.

"Crap," I muttered in frustration.

"Now what?" Alison asked. "Would it be worth looking at the LAPD's files on the case, maybe?"

I thought about that. It was probably a good idea, but at the moment I didn't feel it was the right move. "I'm not sure I want to go that route just yet," I told Alison.

"Why not?"

"Well, if the police couldn't solve it, I'm thinking we won't find much in their files that would help us in our own investigation."

"You never know."

"True," I admitted. "I'm just not sure it's our best move right now."

Alison was quiet for a moment. Then she smiled at me shyly. "Your gut?"

I chuckled lightly, still feeling the sadness of Joseph Holland's fate. "Yeah, I guess so."

"I know!" Alison chirped suddenly, her pretty brown eyes brightening. "Let's find that interview that Holland did with Boris Karloff. If he interviewed Karloff and then started investigating whatever it was that sent him to Universal and then to the landfill, maybe it was something Karloff said in the interview that got him going?"

'That's good," I said, smiling at Alison. I stood and gestured to the chair I'd been sitting in. "Go ahead."

Alison sat before the laptop while I took her spot on the edge of the bed. A few moments later she found a transcript of the interview, the last one either man was a part of. "It's on a Boris Karloff fan site," she said. "It's all I can find. I would've liked to have found the actual newspaper scan, though."

"It's fine," I said encouragingly, "this is great. Good job."

Alison smiled shyly again, reddening only slightly this time.

We read the interview together. It was a fine piece of work, a fitting tribute to both men. Joseph Holland was an excellent interviewer, smart, methodical, insightful, able to easily pick up on comments from his subject and following up logically on them, always avoiding obvious or cliched questions. Boris Karloff was just as much a wonderful interviewee, smart, charming, witty, openly honest and truthful and seemingly willing to talk about just about any aspect of his life and career. The interview ranged from Karloff's youth and early days in the theatre to the start of his film career as an extra in the 1916 film *The Dumb Girl of Portici,* running all the way up to his later work, such as the host of the television horror anthology series *Thriller* and his role in an early Roger Bogdanovich movie called *Targets,* one of his final film roles. There was happiness, there was sadness, there was failure, there was triumph. It was a thoroughly engrossing interview.

However…

"Hmmm…" I heard Alison say as we reached the end of the transcription.

I looked over at Alison. "Did you just not read the same thing that I think I just did not read?"

"You mean the fact that there was absolutely no mention of *Frankenstein* at all?"

"Not one mention," I said, "not even in passing."

"That is too weird."

"Yeah, what the hell?" I said. "Why? Why would they so completely avoid talking about Karloff's most famous role by far?"

"I don't know."

"I suppose it's possible they agreed not to talk about it ahead of time," I pondered, working it over in my head as I talked it out. "Either because Karloff didn't feel like going over yet again what he had to have talked about ad nauseum for decades. Or maybe Holland was trying to be tactful and not bring it up himself and thereby avoiding rehashing what Karloff interviewers over the years had already gone over so many times."

"I have no idea," Alison said. "But it's still weird that they don't talk about it at all."

"Especially since Karloff seemed open to just about anything else," I said.

"And another weird thing," Alison went on. "The interview ends so abruptly."

"You noticed that too, huh?"

"It just… ends. There's no nice wrap-up, no thank you, no summation, nothing. It just… stops."

"It does feel unnatural, that's for sure," I concurred. "Maybe the person who typed it up for the website was working from an incomplete copy of the printed interview? Maybe there was more in the published version."

"Is there a way to find out?" Alison asked.

"The newspaper might still have Holland's notes, maybe, or if he recorded it they might have the original audiotape. At the very least, they should have a copy of the original printed article. And that's why I think tomorrow I want to start at the *Daily Record*."

"That makes sense," Alison said. She stood up and moved over to the window and looked down at the lights of Los Angeles twinkling in the dark. I hadn't quite realised how late it had gotten. "What time do we want to head over there?" Alison asked.

"'We'?" I said with a slight smile as I rubbed my tired eyes.

Alison turned to look back at me. "Yes, 'we'," she said with determination. "I'm involved in this thing now, you know."

"Yes, but—"

"'But' nothing," Alison butted in (see what I did there?). "I've already told you I'm no frightened damsel in distress. I want to help."

"I understand," I said, holding up my hands defensively. "I'm not saying that at all." (Though admittedly my chivalrous male nature was a factor, I will admit, but a small one.) "But so far no one else knows you're involved. And I think we should keep it that way for as long as possible." I could see her start to bristle so I hurried on. "At least until it's no longer an issue. I think you need to go back to work tomorrow as if nothing is going on. If anyone gets suspicious, by, for example, noticing that the archivist who'd been assigned to the guy who'd later been banned from the lot, if they noticed she called in sick right after that… Well, our whole investigation could be shot." I'd thrown in the "our" for Alison's benefit. Mostly.

It seemed like she got it, though she did continue to glare at me, albeit with more resignation than defiance.

"I really think that's how tomorrow should go," I said. "Then afterwards we can figure out what we'll be doing on Saturday."

Finally Alison's face softened. "Promise?" she asked.

"Promise," I told her with a smile. "And I promise to keep you updated tomorrow with anything I find."

Alison smiled back, still not one hundred percent on board, but willing to follow the plan. "Alright," she said. She moved away from the window and picked up her purse from off the bed. "As long as you promise," she mock-growled.

"I already did," I said as I stood and walked to the door of the room with her.

"I'll talk to you tomorrow," she said.

"Sounds great." I was glad she understood my reasoning behind wanting her to go back to work the next day. If Roger Ahrens found out I was still sniffing around the Carlsen case I'd be in a world of trouble, I was sure. And if he discovered Alison was helping me… I didn't want to think about that, actually. Reaching for the door, I hesitated, then thought, "What the hell," and gave Alison a hug. A nice, firm, but gentle "we're good friends" hug. "Thank you for everything you've done for me," I said as I felt her arms embrace me back. We ended the hug and I opened the door for her.

"You're welcome," Alison said quietly. She stepped out into the hallway and gave me another pretty smile, her cheeks reddening again, of course, then turned to go.

Then suddenly she turned back, took my face in her soft, gentle hands, and kissed me.

Oh, that kiss.

It was sweet, it was gentle, it was oh, so nice.

It felt amazing, it felt like… Imagine you've been living out in the wilderness for a long time, sleeping on nothing but hard, bare, uncomfortable ground. Then finally you're back home, and you fall into your own bed, your beloved, comfortable bed, with your favorite plush pillows, your coziest blanket, and you just collapse into the softness, and it feels so incredible, so comfortable, so *right*. *That* is what Alison's kiss felt like.

Then suddenly it was over, and by the time I recovered and opened my eyes, Alison was already at the elevator bay down the hall. As one of the cars arrived and an elderly couple exited, Alison looked back at me and gave me a cute little wave. Then she got on the elevator and was gone. I was still standing in my doorway, recovering, as the elderly couple frowned at me then moved off in the opposite direction.

I lifted my jaw up from off the floor (how did it get down there?) and shut the door, wandering back to the bed in a daze.

Where did *that* come from? I wondered in giddy amazement. Then I remembered Alison saying she liked me. In my obsession to solve the Carlsen mystery I'd completely set that statement aside in my brain, as if it was something to be addressed later when I had the time to more properly examine and process it. Of course, I also knew my tendency to retreat from emotional commitment like that was rearing its ugly head again, a result of my breakup with Sarah intensifying my natural nervousness in affairs of the heart. I'd been burned badly the last time I'd put my heart out there so far. I knew I was afraid of getting hurt like that again.

But Alison had said the words and she'd initiated the first kiss. Surely this wasn't Sarah all over again, this was different. It had to be. I wanted it to be.

Well, now what? Should I call her? No, that was way too desperate. She'd just left! I figured I should probably just do what we'd planned for tomorrow. I'd visit the *Daily Record* and see what I could find. I'd update Alison like I'd promised. And then I would take her out for a real dinner date tomorrow night, not like the last two meals we'd had, an "ambush" plea for help and a fast food meal in a hotel room. Then we'd see where that took us.

It was time to break out of my shell. And who better to break out of it for than a beautiful, lively, smart, fun, sweet woman who was already into me?

I was too distracted to work anymore the rest of the night, so I shut down my laptop, straightened up the room, changed, and got into bed. I fell asleep to some *Big Bang Theory* reruns. Which would explain my dream that night where I was Leonard pining for Penny from across the hall. Except that Penny wasn't a blonde in my dream, but was instead a dark-haired beauty who bore a more-than-passing resemblance to Nicola Bryant from *Doctor Who*.

CHAPTER TWELVE

The Caretaker

The bright but hazy sunlight the next morning did no favors for the ugly, drab, functional 60s-style structure that housed the *Los Angeles Daily Record*. The interior, however, was thankfully quite a different story, cool, smooth marble floor, sleek steel-and-glass furniture pieces, tastefully placed flora. Much more inviting. Clearly the newspaper industry wasn't on its last legs here if all the recent-looking renovations were anything to go by.

I bypassed the already busy touchscreen information kiosk and approached the main reception counter, where several staff members were helping other customers. I stepped towards the one worker seemingly not busy with anyone else, a cute young woman wearing a small bluetooth bud in her ear. She reminded me somewhat of Shevonne from the *TMZ* TV show, the curly-headed cutie with the beautiful eyes and the most wonderful dimples when she smiled. The woman I approached was wearing a fake, non-dimpled smile on her face. As I stood in front of her, her gaze shifted slightly in my direction, though it felt like she wasn't quite looking at me, exactly.

"This is the *LA Daily Record*," the woman said brightly, "how can I help you?"

"Yes," I said, "I'm looking for your archives or records section, please."

"Certainly, sir," the woman said as she continued to fake-smile sort of at me but almost not quite.

After a moment of silence from the woman, I went on. "So if you could please show me where it is…"

"Of course, sir," she said. And still the same smile and somewhat off gaze.

"Um, hello?" I said when the woman again just stood there.

"Excuse me a moment," the woman finally said politely. Then slightly shifting her gaze so it felt a tiny bit more at me, ish, she said, "This is the *LA Daily Record*, how may I help you?"

Ah, I thought, she'd been on the phone, with her bluetooth thing. That explained it. "Yes, I'm looking for your archives or records section, please," I said with a smile.

"Yes, sir," the woman said brightly. And once more the silent grinning stare.

"Uh…" I began, not quite sure what to do.

Then another staff member behind the counter how had just finished with his customer quickly stepped over towards me. "I'm so sorry," the man said, "Britta's on phone duty today." The man gently but firmly shifted Britta so she faced the wall behind the counter. It didn't seem to phase her at all, from what I could see. The man turned back to me. "I've told her time and again not to just stand there like that, but, well, you know how it is."

I didn't, exactly, but didn't want to open another can of worms. "That's okay," I said. "I'm just looking for your archives or records department, please."

"Of course, sir," the man said. He pointed to a hallway over to my right. "Just follow that hall all the way to the end, then left, then go down that hallway until it ends, then take a right. At the end of that hall is the door to the archives."

"Sounds simple enough," I said.

"Anything else, sir?" the man asked.

"I think that's it for now," I said. "Good luck with…" I nodded towards Britta, who was still facing the wall, still talking and still probably fake-smiling.

The man chuckled. "Thanks," he said with a rueful smile. "I'm just glad she's not like this at home."

Not wishing to pursue that thought any further, I smiled politely and headed for the hallway the man had indicated. Soon I was at the end of the final corridor, darker, narrower, and less busy than the rest of the building I'd seen so far. I was facing an old-fashioned door with a frosted glass window with the word "Archives" seemingly hand-lettered on the glass. In the corner of the window on the corridor side was a little card that read, "Come on in." So I went on in.

The large, spacious, airy room I found myself in made me think I had seemingly stepped back in time, into a classic newsroom of the early 1960s. Several rows of big, clunky desks, metal filing cabinets, water cooler in one corner, and an old telex machine in another, a big chalkboard on one wall, several old clocks showing multiple time zones on another wall. Typewriters and big, chunky ashtrays on the desks. All that was missing to really nail the period was the haze of cigarette smoke and the background clacking of typewriters. The only real anachronisms were the computer monitors and keyboards on the desks.

A few people sat at the computers, a few paged through articles in oversize binders. Across the room, behind a low half-wall with a swinging door set roughly in the middle of its span, was a kindly-looking white-haired older woman. Behind her were more of the seemingly ubiquitous racks of storage shelves I was beginning to think I'd never escape. The woman looked up at me as I approached and gave me a smile. "Be right with you," she said cheerily as she stood and made her way over to me. We met in the middle of one of the rows between desks.

"Hi, I'm Harrison Edwards, I'm with the *Arbor Harbor Coast Post*," I said, showing my press badge. "I'm doing a piece on an old unsolved case and I was hoping to look at some contemporary accounts about it."

"Of course," the woman said, nodding. "Here, have a seat at one of these desks and we'll get you started. Oh, and I'm Betty, by the way."

"Nice to meet you, Betty," I said as I sat in a hard yet not uncomfortable old wooden desk chair. "I have to say this room is very impressive."

"Oh, thank you," Betty said. "It was quite a battle to keep it like this, I don't mind telling you. When the newsroom moved upstairs some years back they wanted this whole space converted to storage, but I wanted a workspace for anyone who needed to do research, and I insisted on keeping this place as-is as much as possible."

"Well done."

"Thank you. I must say, I like to think of this place as sort of an attempt to archive the newsroom itself, along with all the articles and such back there." Betty waved a hand in the direction of the storage racks behind the half-wall.

"It definitely works," I said, "I like it a lot."

"I hoped it would work," Betty said, "and it seems to, from the feedback we get. Now, what can I help you with?"

"I'm hoping to look at whatever you have on the death of Joseph Holland from 1969," I said.

"Oh, dear," Betty breathed, her face turning pale, her smile falling. She looked about to collapse, so I hurriedly stood and guided her gently down into my chair. "It's alright," she said with a weak smile at the other patrons in the room who'd started to gather around. "I'm fine," she insisted gently. "I'm just old, don't worry. Now shoo, I'm not useless yet." The other customers accepted her word and went back about their business.

"I'm sorry," I said quietly as I rolled another desk chair over and sat next to Betty. "I didn't mean to upset you."

"It's alright," Betty said, also keeping her voice low so as not to worry the others. "You weren't to know."

"Know what?" I said, though I had an inkling.

"I knew Mr. Holland," Betty said. "We worked together here for a time. Until..." She trailed off.

I slipped into caring interviewer mode almost without thinking. "Can you tell me about it?" I urged quietly, gently.

Betty took a deep breath. "I first met Joseph Holland when I was a little girl," she began. "My father was an editor here at the time, and he would sometimes bring me and my older sister Nellie to work with him. Mr. Holland was always very nice, very kind to us. He was one of the top reporters then, though of course I didn't know or understand any of that, being so young." She chuckled wistfully. "I remember one time, I lost a button on my sweater. I was very upset about it, it was my favorite sweater. Well, Mr. Holland said he could fix it for me. Sure enough, he brought out a little portable sewing kit from his desk and went to work. I remember his kit had little spools of thread, and mini-compartments for buttons, pins, needles, and suchlike. A few minutes later, my sweater was as good as new. Better, actually, Mr. Holland said, because now one of his buttons had found a new home. He was like that, you see, always thinking, always finding a way to make things better.

"Anyway, a few years later I became an intern here. Mr. Holland was still on staff, but the new management that had been brought in when the newspaper was bought kicked him from the main newsbeat, which was really Mr. Holland's passion. They kept him because they knew how popular he was with the staff and the readers, but they put him on the Arts and Leisure beat. Mr. Holland was hurt, but professionally he didn't show it. He did the same amazing job in his new position. But I could see he missed his old job. A bit of his spark was gone. It was sad, but what could you do?

"That last week, he…" Betty broke off, dabbing quickly at the corner of her eye. "Mr. Holland was assigned to interview Boris Karloff, the movie star, over the phone. I think Mr. Holland was a fan of Mr. Karloff, as he seemed excited to get to interview the man. He seemed to brighten a bit. Well, the day of the interview, he came in and went into his office, shutting the door for privacy and telephoned Mr. Karloff. He left shortly afterwards.

"Mr. Holland came in the next morning, but he was very quiet. He really didn't talk to anyone like he usually did, friendly and chatty. He came in, went straight to his office, shut the door, spent about an hour in there all by himself, then he came back out. And then he left. We never saw him again."

Betty heaved a sigh, then looked at me sheepishly. "I'm sorry, Mr. Edwards, this must seem silly to get so worked up over something that happened over forty years ago."

"No, it doesn't," I said, hopefully reassuringly. "It's perfectly understandable."

Betty took my hand and patted it. "Thank you, young man," she said. "You asked me to talk and I will keep going."

"Take your time."

"Well," Betty continued, "the next day Mr. Holland didn't come in to work. At first we really didn't think anything of it. He did that, sometimes, you see. Especially if he was working on a story, so it didn't strike us as anything out of the ordinary. The following morning Mr. Holland still hadn't come in to work, and then we got a phone call from Mrs. Holland. Her husband hadn't come home the night before, and she wondered if we'd seen him or knew where he was or what he was doing. We told her we didn't know. He hadn't told any of us. The next day... they found his body."

Betty stopped to collect herself.

Betty made an effort to smile. "Let me go get the clippings file for you," she said. "I'll be right back." She stood and walked back to her area behind the half-wall, disappearing around the corner for a moment. I took the opportunity to get out my iPad and my Star Trek communicator-like pocket notebook.

Betty returned, setting a slim folder before me on the desktop. Sitting again, she said, "That's what we have on Mr. Holland's... passing."

"Thank you so much," I said, carefully opening the folder. Betty moved off to give me some space, and also to check on the other customers she had in the room.

The folder appeared to be your basic clippings file, something many newspapers used to do, clipping articles out of a printed copy of an issue and grouping them into files by subject, topic, story, or what have you. My own *Post* did something similar. The *Daily Record* went an extra step further, putting each clipped article into a clear plastic sheet protector. Each sheet protector bore a label noting the date of the article, as well as the section and page number. There was also a numeric code on the label which I assumed to be the identifier for the folder. I didn't know if this extra treatment was something the *Daily Record* did as a matter of course, or had done specially in this particular case.

The first article in the file folder was the first article Alison and I had found online the previous night, the one that broke the news of the discovery of Joseph Holland's body. The second article in the file was the follow-up we'd also found that night, giving the cause of death along with more details on the discovery of the body. My mind started to wander a bit, I must admit, as I recalled reading those articles the previous night with that beautiful woman, and that incredible kiss. With difficulty, I dragged my mind back to the task at hand and the folder before me.

The third clipping in the file was new to me. It was dated February 7, 1969. I took an image of the clipping with my iPad, then read the brief article.

FEB 7, 1969

NEW LEAD IN REPORTER'S DEATH?

Police to investigate possible Universal Studios connection

Hollywood — The Los Angeles Police Department issued a statement today giving new details on the investigation into the murder of long-time Daily Record *reporter Joseph Holland. On February 4th, one day after Mr. Holland's body was discovered, an employee at Universal Studios contacted police saying he recognized Mr. Holland's face from the news reports. The employee stated he believed Mr. Holland had visited the Universal Studios Archive several days earlier. A detective was sent to follow up on the tip.*

Police confirmed Mr. Holland had indeed visited the Universal Studios Archive on the morning of January 31st, the day he was last seen alive. Police are now looking into what might have brought Mr. Holland to the Archives, what he may have accessed there, and what may have led him to then visit the Northwest Hollywood Landfill. Mr Holland's body was later found strangled in the hills adjacent to the landfill.

When the Daily Record *contacted the LAPD to ask if there was a connection between Mr. Holland's visit to the Universal Studios Archive and his last assignment to interview film star Boris Karloff, star of numerous Universal Studios films, including the famous original Frankenstein and two of its sequels, in England over the telephone, a police department spokesman declined to comment.*

To me there seemed an obvious connection, but I was in possession of more facts than the *Daily Record* was at the time. At least, I thought and hoped I was.

The next clipping was a follow-up to the one I'd just read, one week later.

FEB 13, 1969

POLICE NO CLOSER TO SOLVING REPORTER'S MURDER

Universal Studios investigation a dead end

Hollywood — The Los Angeles Police Department released a statement today declaring the investigation into a possible connection to Universal Studios in the murder of Daily Record *reporter Joseph Holland, has proved to be a dead end. No evidence was found to directly link Universal Studios with Mr. Holland's death, and police were unable to find a specific reason for Mr. Holland's visit to the Universal Archives the very morning of his death, apart from Mr. Holland's telephone interview the previous day with Boris Karloff, star of Universal's* Frankenstein *films in the 1930s. Similarly, police were unable to find a specific reason for Mr. Holland's subsequent visit to the Northwest Hollywood Landfill, where he was last seen alive. Police did acknowledge that the landfill did hold the contract to receive all garbage and waste from Universal Studios from 1928 until 1951, and revealed they also found an invoice from the landfill in the records from the original 1931* Frankenstein *film. Police noted that the only files accessed by Mr. Holland were those of the 1931* Frankenstein. *The invoice in question was simply noted as "for services rendered." Further inquiries by the LAPD apparently turned up no further evidence or leads. Police are now widening their net in their attempts to find the murderer of Mr. Holland.*

Hmmmm, I thought. There's something there. Not a fire, perhaps, but some smoke, definitely some smoke.

Next in the clippings folder was the somewhat out-of-sequence obituary of Joseph Holland. Above the text was a studio photograph of a man who I assumed must have been Holland himself. He looked a handsome, older man, roughly in his mid-fifties, perhaps. Remember I have always been horrible at guessing ages. But that was what Holland's approximate age appeared to be, in my lowly opinion.

I read the obituary in silence. It was extremely respectful, almost reverent, detailing Holland's long career at the *Daily Record*. Some of his story I'd heard from Betty, but there was a good deal I hadn't learned at that point. All in all, Joseph Holland sounded like a very professional reporter, dedicated to his career and the ethics of his profession, and through all the ups and downs a smart, thoughtful man. He seemed like a man I would really have looked up to if we'd been on staff together. I thought I could understand why his death in such a terrible manner had affected Betty so much, even after all these years. Unfortunately, there was very little, if anything, in the obituary that was of relevance to my investigation.

The next item I came to was the interview Holland did with Boris Karloff, the final interview for both of the men. It filled an entire newspaper page. The headline, "BORIS KARLOFF: THE FINAL JOSEPH HOLLAND INTERVIEW" was bracketed by two photos, one being the same portrait of Holland used for his obituary, the other a headshot of Karloff from about the time he hosted the *Thriller* TV series. The famous face and the not-so-famous face were a well-matched pair, both had strong, magnetic eyes gazing out piercingly at the reader, drawing them in.

The interview seemed identical to what Alison and I had read on the Karloff fan site the night before. I used my iPad to double-check, but apart from a few very minor and inconsequential typos on the fan site transcription, the two were identical in content. And identical in their omissions, such as the fact that *Frankenstein* was never mentioned, and the awkward lack of a proper wrap-up or conclusion to the dialogue between the two men.

"Betty," I said, catching her attention as she was filling up a cup from the water cooler.

"Yes, sir?" Betty said, smiling as she came over. A smile, but a very slightly wary one, probably due to what I was looking into.

I held up the protector sheet with the Karloff interview. "Did Mr. Holland usually end his interviews like this, without any thank-yous or a wrap-up of any kind?"

Betty leaned closed to peer at the article. "It does seem rather abrupt, doesn't it?" she said. "No, I think he usually put a proper ending on all his interviews. He usually did his own transcription of his tapes and then typed the full articles up himself. Maybe because he was, well, gone, maybe the editors just published a straight transcription right from the audiotape. Usually Mr. Holland would write up his interviews into prose form, not like a plain script like this one. I think Mr. Holland usually did end his interviews with a little something, now I think of it."

"Would it be possible to look at a few other, earlier interviews of his?"

"Sure," Betty said. "Do you want to see the printed originals or the scanned versions?"

"Scanned is fine," I said. Betty instructed me as I typed and moused on the computer at the desk. It was a pretty simple system, and I quickly found an earlier Joseph Holland interview.

It was from 1958, and Holland had interviewed a Los Angeles City

Council member who was running for re-election. Like Betty said, the interview had been elaborated into a prose dialogue article, quite unlike the script-like form of the posthumously-published Karloff interview. The article concluded with Holland saying to the interiewee, "Mr. Collings, thank you very much for giving your time to the *Daily Record*." Now, *that* sounded more like a finish.

The second interview was from 1967, and was with an up-and-coming sculptor gaining some popularity in the LA arts scene. Once again, Holland concluded the interview by saying, "Mr. Depkins, thank you very much for giving your time to the *Daily Record*."

I checked a few more Holland interviews. They all concluded the same way, apart from the interviewee's name changing, with the exact same sentence. A sentence entirely missing from the Karloff interview.

I pondered that for a moment. The absence of Holland's trademark sign-off could have just been an editorial decision maybe by the paper's staff after Holland's death. Or…

Or maybe there was more to the interview?

"Betty," I said, "was there a 'Part Two' to the Karloff interview, perhaps?"

Betty shook her head. "No, that's all there was. And if there had been a second part, it would be in the file here."

The possibility that struck me at that point was something I would definitely have to run down. The Karloff interview had continued beyond the point where the published interview stopped, and the editors had, for one reason or another, not published the rest of it. But would it be possible, after all these years, to uncover the truth? The possibility needed to be checked. "Would you still have the original tape of the interview, by chance?" I asked Betty as casually as I could.

"I should think so," Betty said after a quick think. "The police ran off a copy but they returned the original to us. I have to get it from the climate-controlled storage room we have, it'll just take a few minutes."

"No rush," I said. "Thank you."

"Just doing my job, sir," Betty said with her kind smile. She went back behind the half-wall and disappeared around the corner once more.

I took the opportunity to finish the rest of the folder, which didn't take long. There were only two articles left, one from July 31, 1969, marking six months since Holland's death, and bemoaning the lack of progress in the case by police. The other item was from Jaunary 31, 1970, exactly one year since Holland's death, an editorial harshly criticizing the LAPD and their inability to solve the Holland murder. Neither piece was useful to my own investigation, apart from highlighting the depth of pain felt by Holland's co-workers after his death. I still imaged them with my iPad, along with all of the other items in the clippings folder.

Then I pulled out my phone to text Alison as I'd promised.

"Lots of background but no smoking gun yet," I sent.

"K," was the reply from Alison.

"Archivist here knew Holland," I added.

"Wow, OK," I got back.

"Will keep you posted," I finished.

"K," Alison sent back.

***

Betty soon returned, carrying a small, flat square box. She led me over to a corner of the retro newsroom area where there was an old-fashioned reel-to-reel tape machine on top of a small metal cabinet with wheels.

"Right where it was supposed to be," Betty said proudly as she opened the box and gently withdrew a smallish reel of audiotape. "Always nice to see my system working properly," she said as she placed the reel on the empty spindle of the machine. She then threaded the leader through the machine's heads, and finally wound the leader onto the empty collector reel which was already in place. "Almost forgot," Betty added as she grabbed a bulky pair of padded headphones from the cabinet underneath. She plugged the large jack into the proper receptacle on the machine and donned the headphones. "Just want to make sure it's working properly," she said, hitting the "play" button.

As I watched, Betty's face transformed, slipping from all-business to a wistful sadness. With slightly glistening eyes, Betty stopped the tape, rewound it, and handed the headphones to me. "All set," she said rather huskily.

"Are you sure you're alright?" I said gently.

"Yes," Betty said, putting on a brave smile. "I just… I knew what I was going to hear, but I just… I hadn't heard Mr. Holland's voice in, oh, so long."

"I'm sorry," I said, "I didn't—"

"No, no," Betty said hurriedly, "don't be silly, it's fine, it's fine. I'm alright. It was just a bit of a jolt, is all. Well, go on, whenever you're ready. I'll be nearby if you need anything." With another of her kind smiles, Betty moved off to check on her other customers again.

I settled the quite comfortable Koss headphones on my ears, then reached out and pressed "play". I had pulled up the interview transcript on my iPad and read along as I listened.

It was interesting to hear the two men's voices. The first to speak was Joseph Holland. His strong, somewhat deep voice, a bit gravelly from age (or perhaps smoking?) was neatly counterpointed by the cultured, refined, slightly lisped British-accented voice of the interviewee, Boris Karloff. His voice was instantly recognizable, although weaker than what moviegoers would have been used to, but undeniably still Karloff himself. You could tell this was a recording of a long-distance phone call, crackly and buzzy at times. The actor had been very ill and weak at the time, in fact only a few days from death, and the wheeze and hacking in his voice definitely betrayed his poor condition. But he soldiered valiantly on, answering Holland's questions earnestly and with considerable good humor.

By the time the tape ran out, the loose end of the tape thwacking in the machine until I pressed the "stop" button, it was quite evident that the transcription as published had omitted nothing from the recording. Once again, though, distinctly noticeable by their absences were any mention of *Frankenstein*, Karloff's breakout film, and Joseph Holland's signature sign-off. Something was scratching at the back of my mind, but I couldn't pin it down.

I waved again for Betty's attention and she soon came over.

"Are you sure there wouldn't be a second tape from this interview?" I asked her, still hoping against hope.

Betty shook her head. "This is all there ever was," she said. "I helped go through everything after…" She trailed off quietly.

Very gently, I asked her, "Is there anything you remember that you can tell me about the case that wasn't in the newspapers at the time?"

Betty raised her head, thinking. "I don't think so," she said eventually. "There really wasn't much information at all anyway. The police were stymied. We'd told them about Mr. Holland's last assignment being the interview with Mr. Karloff, but by that time Mr. Karloff himself had passed away. They talked to Mr. Karloff's friends and family, but nothing of note came from that, I guess. They found the audiotape of the interview but didn't feel there was anything in it that had anything to do with Mr. Holland's death. Nothing that explained why he went to that landfill.

"When the police were done with the audiotape and made their own copies of it, they returned it to us, along with a few other personal things from Mr. Holland's office they had taken. Since none of it was apparently relevant, they didn't need it. We boxed up all of Mr. Holland's personal items and passed them on to his family. His work material we kept here as property of the newspaper, of course. I'm sorry I'm not much help."

"Betty, you're doing just great," I reassured her gently.

Something struck me just then. A suspicion, or more strictly speaking a noticing of something I'd witnessed but not quite seen, if you take my meaning. I leaned forward and took the collector reel, which now held the interview audiotape, and looked closely at the end of the physical tape itself. The end was sharply squared off, as was typical of audiotapes of the time. But there was one significant difference.

"There's no leader," I said, showing the end of the tape to Betty.

You see, children, back in my day, when audiotape wasn't typically found in self-contained plastic cassettes for playing, but instead were reel-to-reel, as this one was, audiotapes would have what we called "leaders", basically a short length of material not used (or even able to be used) for recording. (There are leaders on cassette tapes, too, but I digress…) It was usually some kind of plastic, white or some other color, or sometimes clear. This non-recordable material was used to thread the tapes through the heads of tape machines and wind them onto collector rolls, just as Betty had done. That way the valuable recording material wouldn't be wasted. I'd seen the leader on the front of the Holland-Karloff tape as Betty had worked it into the machine.

But this tape had no end leader.

"Would someone have edited this?" I asked Betty, pointing at the neatly sliced and leaderless end of the tape.

"I really don't think so," Betty said. "I don't believe the police would have, and I'm certain nobody here would have done that."

Just to be sure of things, I asked Betty if she could find a couple of other tapes of the same brand and size from that era that had been used for various articles. She did, and we discovered that they all had both front and end leaders. We also noticed that the diameter of recording material on the Holland-Karloff reel was noticeably smaller than that of the other sample reels.

Betty and I looked at each other, both of us understanding what the most obvious explanation was. Joseph Holland had cut the last part of the interview tape, the part that most likely contained whatever it was that had sent him to Universal Studios and the landfill and ultimately his death.

I didn't voice my suspicions, however, as I was reluctant to get Betty mixed up in this mess any further than I already had. It was bad enough Alison was so deeply involved. I was hugely grateful for Alison's help, of course, but I was uncomfortable at the thought of any possible negative consequences that might affect her.

But there was perhaps one more innocuous way Betty might assist me just a little bit more.

"What happened to Mr. Holland's personal effects afterwards?" I asked.

"We boxed everything up," Betty said, "and Mrs. Holland came in and picked it up herself in person."

"I don't suppose Mrs. Holland is…"

"Mrs. Holland passed on a few years after her husband," Betty said with a small shake of her head. "As for their son, Josiah… Last I heard he was still up in the Bay Area where he'd gone to college, I think for engineering." I noticed Betty's face brighten a bit as she spoke of Holland's son.

I jotted a few additional quick notes in my flip-up notebook. "Josiah Holland," I said as I scribbled. "No address or phone number that you know of?"

"No, sorry," Betty said. "All I can really tell you is, he was born I think in '46? I think. He went to school in the San Francisco area, and I believe is still there. I'm sorry, I wish I had more to tell you, but… When his father was working here, Josiah would occasionally stop by, but after his father was gone he only ever came back to LA for his father's funeral, and then his mother's a few years later. He was pretty upset about his father's murder, as you can imagine. He blamed the media, particularly newspapers, and most specifically the *Daily Record*. He thought his father would never have been killed if he'd been allowed to stay on the main news desk, instead of getting bumped down to Arts and Leisure. But who knows? I don't."

"And he's not been back here since, huh?"

"Not as far as I know," Betty said. "He never stopped by to see us, at any rate, if he did."

I didn't want to push Betty too hard on an obviously sensitive subject that was, in all probability, probably rather tangential to my investigation. I started packing up my things. "Well, Betty," I said, "I cannot thank you enough for everything you've done for me."

"I assume you're going to try to talk to Josiah Holland," Betty said softly as I hefted my shoulder bag.

"Yes," I said.

"If you do find him, tell him…" Betty paused, took a breath. "Tell him there are still a few of us old-timers her that still remember him and think of him."

"I will," I said quietly. Then, with a grateful smile, I turned to go.

"Will you find out who killed Mr. Holland?" Betty said even more quietly.

I stopped, turned, and looked back at the kindly old woman who clearly carried around these painful memories from long ago. I wanted to tell her everything I knew at that point, all about Broderick Carlsen, his *Frankenstein* appearance, hell, that he was still alive, for Christ's sake. But I just didn't think she was ready or capable of hearing it right now, of taking it all in. Hell, I wasn't all that sure I believed it all myself. But my instinct was to reassure her, in some way.

I said, "I'll do everything I can."

"Thank you."

I nodded, then quietly left her to her memories.

* * *

***

I got in my car and headed towards City Hall, keeping an eye out for a decent-looking place to grab lunch. I was soon pulling over to find a parking spot outside GrumB's, a little but busy restaurant with an old-fashioned ship's wheel with "GrumB's Fresh Seafood" as a sign out front. The name of the place rang a bell, for some reason, but I could not put my finger on it. I was pretty sure I'd never been to GrumB's before, so that wasn't it. Oh, well, it would come to me or not. Before going in, I called Alison, as she should have been on her lunch break by then.

"So, what's up?" Alison asked right away.

"Just stopping for a quick lunch," I said, "What about you?"

"I'm eating my lunch out in my car," she said. She added hurriedly, "Don't worry, it's not suspicious, I sometimes eat out here when I want to just get away from everything and everybody."

"And no one's said anything to you today?" I asked. "No big, mean-looking goons asking about me or anything like that?"

"No, nothing, everything's been business as usual."

"Good, good," I said, my mind put to ease on that score, at least.

"So, what have you found out?"

"Well," I said, "Betty, the very nice lady at the archives, was very helpful."

"Betty, huh?" Alison said with what I took to be a playful tone of jealously in her voice.

"Relax," I said smiling, "she's nothing like Betty Roberts from *Remember WENN*."

"Betty who from 'Remember' what?"

"In a nutshell, Betty Roberts was the very pretty main character on a TV comedy show called *Remember WENN*, spelled W-E-N-N, which were the call letters of the late-'30s/early-'40s Pittsburgh radio station the show was set in."

"Never heard of it," Alison said.

"Not many people have, sadly," I said. "It was a wonderful, sweet, charming , funny little show which AMC axed rather abruptly and rudely after five seasons. And now the network seems to be denying it ever existed, even claiming *Mad Men* was their first original series, even though that over-hyped critics' darling came years later. They never even released *Remember WENN* on VHS or DVD."

"But at least you're not bitter about it," Alison said. I could almost hear the twinkle in her eyes.

"Anyway, getting back to what I was saying, Betty actually worked with Joseph Holland at the *Daily Record* for a while, way back when. She gave me a good idea of who Holland was, and it sounds like he was a good man and a good reporter. I looked through their clippings file they kept on his murder, but there wasn't much there. Most of the useful info we already found online last night."

"OK," Alison said.

"I also saw the printed version of the Holland-Karloff interview, and not only that, I got to listen to the actual audio of the interview."

"Wow! So was there anything more there that wasn't in the article?"

"Sadly, no," I said, "they both match the version we read on the fan site. However…" I trailed off, just to mess with Alison.

"What?" she said anxiously.

"The tape appears to have been cut."

"What?"

"Edited, sliced, the last part of the interview, it's missing."

"Really?"

"Yeah," I said. "So that would explain why there was no *Frankenstein* talk in the published article, and why it ended so abruptly."

"Did they have the second part there at the paper?"

"No, Betty had no idea it had been edited. I have to think Holland himself cut the critical, important part out and, I don't know, hid it somewhere maybe, before he went off on his investigation."

"Because he wanted to confirm whatever was discussed in that second part before it was published?" Alison suggested. "Because whatever it was was so, I don't know, so unbelievable, he wanted proof before publishing?"

"Makes sense to me," I said.

"Do you think the last part of the tape still exists?"

"I can only hope."

"But where could it possibly be?"

"If it's anywhere," I said, "I'd guess that the family still has it, whether they know it or not."

"Do you know how to get in touch with the family?"

"Not exactly," I admitted. "Betty thought Holland's son Josiah might be in the San Fran area, so I guess I'll start there. But first I want to see what the LAPD has in its files on Holland's murder."

"All right," Alison said. "Well, be careful. And good luck!"

"Thanks," I said, "I'll keep you posted."

We hung up, and I went inside the restaurant and had the best basket of fish and chips I'd had in a very long time.

***

After a delicious lunch, I struggled my way through non-rush-hour-but-still-crazy-busy traffic to City Hall. Inside the iconic landmark, I soon found myself back in the LAPD Records department, also finding the same woman who'd helped me earlier in the week, back at her station.

"Welcome back, Mr...." Holly began, trailing off as she tried to recall my last name.

"Edwards," I supplied, "Harrison Edwards."

"Yes, of course, Mr. Edwards, I'm so sorry."

"No worries," I said amiably. "I have one of those forgettable faces." Ah, self-deprecation, hello, my old friend.

"Nonsense," said Holly, "you have a very fine face. I'm just very forgetful when it comes to names and putting them to faces."

"You're too kind," I said, feeling a bit embarrassed.

"What can I do for you today?"

"I'm hoping I can look at your files on the murder of Joseph Holland, back in early 1969. I'm sorry I don't have a case number or anything."

"1969," Holly said. "We should have that scanned in, I think, so you can use one of the computers over there." She slid a brochure across to me. "That'll tell you how to get started, then you can start searching for whatever you need. Providing it's been entered, of course. And as you can see there are printers at each station, if you need it."

"Sounds good, thank you." I took the brochure with me over to one of the available computer workstations and sat down. The login instructions were very straightforward, and soon I was looking at an index screen detailing the various documents in the Holland murder file.

There was a lot to go through, but it was fairly quick work. A lot of it I'd already learned from the contemporary news reports. Much of it was written in "official-report-speak", where a simple statement which could have been summed up in one sentence was needlessly expanded into a too huge paragraph. Having read plenty of those over the years, even back home, I knew how to get right to the heart of the matter. But still, that government-speak still annoyed the crap out of me.

I dug through the incident reports, the eyewitness interviews, the report from Detective Locke's visit to the Universal Archives, I examined the crime scene photos, the autopsy report, everything in the file, from the first phone call to report Holland missing right through to the point where it seemed the police just gave up on the investigation as they saw they were getting nowhere. (OK, so maybe sometimes I'm just as guilty at over-writing…) And unfortunately there was very little new information in the entire file that was relevant to my own investigation. A few items did crop up, though, which made me feel a tiny bit better that my return visit to City Hall hadn't been a complete waste of time.

The first new item I came across had somehow not been reported in the papers. At the crime scene, police had discovered a small cave opening several yards from where Holland's body had been found up in the wooded hills behind the garbage dump. There were a few photos of the cave entrance, as well as a description in the report. The narrow opening led into a very cramped, low-ceilinged, well, cave, obviously, which ran back a fair distance into the hillside. Inside the cave the police found several small piles of animal remains. Later testing confirmed there was no human matter in the piles, just animal debris, bones, fur, feathers, and the like, including the partial remains of a deer. The police concluded that the killer had been living in the came for some unknown length of time prior to Holland's murder, after which the killer fled the scene. They were unable to find any trail to follow.

Among the numerous crime scene photos in the report, there were several which I printed out, including a couple from inside the dump, at the north end, where several eyewitnesses had placed Holland for a considerable length of time.

A brief notation in the file reported the items found on Holland at the time of his body's discovery. He'd had nothing unusual on him, just the expected, such as his wallet, his keys, a pen, and a pencil. What this meant for my purposes was that no work-related documentation or notes were found with him, meaning no potential clues to follow up on. Not that I was really expecting anything, but it definitely would have been nice.

And that was about it for "new" stuff. With so little to go on, I could almost see why the police never got anywhere in their search for the killer. But still, isn't it their job to keep digging, keep going, never rest until the perpetrator or perpetrators were found and brought to justice? Then again, what the hell did I know?

Printing out a few possibly useful documents for future reference, I then logged off, waved a thank-you to Holly, and headed back to the outside world.

I stopped on the steps in front of City Hall to text Alison.

"Not much in LAPD files," I sent.

"That sucks," I got back. I chuckled.

"Gonna try to find out where Holland's son is now, will let you know."

"K."

***

On the way back to my car, I spotted a little coffee shop, its inviting aroma drifting out to the sidewalk. It seemed like a nice place to park myself while I searched for Josiah Holland, especially with its free wi-fi. I glanced at the sign above the door. "Mister Beans", the place was called, with no apostrophe after the "n". I assumed that was the way the place avoided possible litigation from whatever company owned the rights to Rowan Atkinson's Mr. Bean character. I also had to assume the cartoon figure on the sign was apparently just dissimilar enough to also avoid any lawsuits. I chuckled, partly in fond remembrance of Mr. Atkinson's hilarious character, but also for a recollection of something I'd read about some years back. A bar somewhere in the Midwest, Wisconsin maybe, called itself "Grumpy's" and had painted an image of the dwarf Grumpy from Disney's *Snow White and the Seven Dwarfs* on its door. Well, the Disney folks didn't think too highly of that and so the bar's owner was "persuaded" to modify the picture. I could understand the corporate viewpoint, not wanting people making money off of unauthorized Mickey Mouse products and so on. And the bar owners had to have known they might get in trouble. I wondered if the not-quite-Rowan-Atkinson cartoon was pre- or post-litigation in this case.

Shrugging to myself, I went inside, where it was very modern and stylish, all sleek lines and fashionable colors. I ordered my usual iced mocha frappuccino and carried it over to one of the empty plush chairs in a quiet corner. I took a sip from my frapp, pulled out my laptop, and set to work.

Using all of the regular search engines and people-finder websites I usually used to hunt people down, I eventually came up with a long list of potential candidates in the San Francisco area Several "Josiah Holland"s, a bunch of "Joe Holland"s, and a slew of "J. Holland"s comprised the initial long list I put together. Breaking the huge task into smaller, more manageable chunks, I started with the names listed as being in San Francisco proper, leaving Oakland, Alameda, and so on for later.

Finally, after numerous wrong numbers, and with a growing sense of frustration building in me, I dialed up another "J. Holland".

"Hello?" the voice on the other end of the line said.

"Hello, sir," I said, using the same polite voice I'd used on all the other calls I'd made that afternoon. "My name is Harrison Edwards, I'm a reporter with the Arbor Harbor newspaper. I'm looking for a Mr. Josiah Holland, please."

There was a slight pause, then the man on the phone answered, "Yes."

"Are you Josiah Holland?" I asked straight out.

"I just said I was," the voice replied.

Easy, Harry, I told myself. If this *is* your guy, you don't want to lose him. "I'm sorry, yes, thank you, sir," I said, hoping he could hear my apologetic smile over the phone. "Specifically I am looking for the son of Mr. Joseph Holland, who was a reporter with the *Los Angeles Daily Record*."

There was another, longer pause.

"Mr. Holland?" I prompted gently. Maybe I'd simply confused the man, and he had nothing to do with Joseph Holland, just like everyone else I'd called that day.

"Why?" the voice eventually said.

"I'm sorry?"

"Why are you looking for him?"

It *was* him. I was sure of it now. "Mr. Holland," I explained, "I'm doing a story for my paper on Joseph Holland's murder, and I was hoping to talk to his son about it, to get his take on it."

Another pause.

"Hello?" I ventured.

"I'm here," the voice grumped at me.

"Thank you, sir," I said. "So… are you the son of Joseph Holland of the *LA Daily Record*?"

"Yes, I am," the voice replied quietly.

I knew it! I knew it was him! Now I had to keep him talking, not spook him, and arrange an interview with him. "Mr. Holland," I said, "I wanted to tell you first off how truly sorry I am for your loss."

"Thank you," Josiah said.

"Would you be agreeable to an interview to discuss things?"

"What newspaper did you say you were with?"

"The Arbor Harbor newspaper," I said carefully. Please don't make me say it…

"But what's it called?" Josiah persisted.

"The *Arbor Harbor Coast Post*," I muttered reluctantly.

"That's a dumb name," Josiah said.

"I couldn't agree with you more, sir," I said. "But let me assure you, we are a legitimate, respectable, professional, accredited newspaper, not a tabloid or gossip rag or —"

"Yeah, I can see that," Josiah said. Evidently he'd decided to check out the *Post* online as we'd been talking.

"So, would you be willing to consent to an interview, sir?" I asked.

"I'm kind of busy tonight," Josiah said.

"That's all right," I said. "We could do it tomorrow sometime, if that's possible."

"How 'bout bright and early, say seven a.m."

"That would be fine," I said, jotting some notes. "Would this be the best number to reach you at, then?"

"Huh?" Josiah said.

"For the interview."

"I'm not doing this over the phone," Josiah said emphatically.

"You are not?"

"I just said I wasn't."

"Well," I explained. "Right now we're in LA so it'd take us a while to get there. Perhaps late tomorrow afternoon? Wherever you'd like to meet, it's up to you, your place, a restaurant, a park, wherever you'd feel most comfortable."

The pause returned. "I thought you said you were from Arbor Harbor," Josiah said.

"Well, yes, but right now I'm in Los Angeles working on the story."

"Oh," Josiah said. "I guess that makes sense. Yeah, sure, tomorrow afternoon. We can meet at my place." He gave me the address, and we set a time.

"Thank you, sir," I said.

"Who's 'we'?" Josiah said.

"I'm sorry?"

"You said 'we're in LA' earlier," Josiah said. "Who's 'we'?"

"Oh," I said. "Myself and my assistant Alison." That technically described Alison's unofficial role, didn't it? Not that Alison would be entirely happy to be called an "assistant", mind you.

"I see," Josiah said. "All right, I'll see you tomorrow afternoon then." And he hung up.

Well, that had been… interesting. Not exactly super-friendly, but at least he was willing to be interviewed. But tomorrow… that could be rather tricky.

I dumped my empty cup in the trash on my way out. It was just after five, so I felt safe calling Alison. The suddenly gusty wind outside felt refreshing after the climate-controlled interior.

"Hello?" Alison said when she finally answered.

"Hey," I said, squinting in the sunshine as I trooped back to my car. "I found him. I found Josiah Holland."

"You did?" said Alison. "That's great! How did it go?"

"We set up a time and place to meet tomorrow for the interview."

"Oh," Alison said, "you didn't interview him right then and there?"

"I was getting a bit of orneriness from him, and I didn't want to push things. I had hoped to just do it over the phone sometime tomorrow, but he wanted it to be in person."

"I see. So when and where are we going to meet him?"

"Tomorrow afternoon, at his place in San Francisco."

"I can't wait!" Alison said happily. "Maybe we can finally get some answers."

"I sure as hell hope so," I said tiredly. "You wanna meet someplace and go over everything I found out today?"

"I really don't feel like going out tonight," Alison said. Uh-oh, I thought. What did I say or do wrong? I thought she liked me. Before my panicky thoughts got too panicky, Alison eased my fears. "Would you like to have dinner with me at my apartment?"

I was a bit taken aback, especially since I had begun rejection-panicking. But I was pleasantly surprised by the invitation. "Uh, sure," I said as casually as I could muster. "That sounds fine."

Alison gave me her address. "About 7:30?"

"Sounds good," I said.

"Well, then, I will see you then."

After we hung up, I couldn't have wiped the smile from my face if I'd tried.

CHAPTER THIRTEEN

Deep Breath

Back at my hotel, I showered, shaved, put on a nice set of clothes, then, checking the time, realized I still had time to kill before I had to leave for Alison's. I didn't feel like doing any work just at that moment, so I switched on the TV, reclined on the comfy bed, and just vegged out for a while.

I stumbled upon one of my guilty pleasure TV shows, *TMZ*, the daily gossip/celebrity/paparazzi show. I actually didn't care for most of the "celebrities" they discussed, but they still presented even those stories in a funny and entertaining way. And then, of course, there were the *TMZ* Hotties, as I called them. The *TMZ* staff had a number of extremely attractive women reporters/correspondents who appeared on the show. There was the slim, black haired pretty one. There was the grumpy blonde one who often displayed a sizable amount of her ample cleavage. And then there was my absolute favorite, the beautiful blondish-brownish curly-haired woman with the gorgeous eyes and the cutest dimpled smile I had ever seen. I was entranced by her from the first time I saw her. And she wasn't just a pretty face, either, he had some book learnin', too. I remember grinning hugely one time when she railed at another staffer who was British and wasn't fully up on his British history, and she lectured him a bit sassily on Henry VIII's dissolution of the monasteries in the sixteenth century. I was impressed.

Lounging back and enjoying the show, I suddenly thought to myself, what the heck was I doing? I shouldn't be objectifying pretty women on TV, women I would likely never meet, much less ever get to go out with. I had an amazing, sweet, intelligent, beautiful woman — *in real life!* — who had actually professed to like me. I didn't need any fantasy TV woman, I had a real opportunity with a real woman.

So I flipped the channel and found something else.

Then another thought struck me. I had a date that night. A date! It had been a long time since I'd been on one of those. Or had I? I wondered if the last two evenings together with Alison counted as dates. I didn't really think so. Tonight felt more "official", in a way.

And yet another thought hit me. I should probably bring something tonight, right? Isn't that something you do on a date? Crap, I didn't have anything. I'd have to stop somewhere on the way to Alison's. I checked my watch again. It was time to get going.

I hurried down to collect my car, then started following the GPS instructions to Alison's place, keeping an eye out for a store along the way. I soon spotted a small grocery store. It would have to do. I pulled over and dashed inside.

Figuring wine would be a safe, decent thing to bring, I headed for the liquor section. Once there, I stood dumbly before the vast selection on hand. Should I get red or white? What were we having for dinner? Should I call and check? No, that would make her think the wine was a last-minute afterthought. Not entirely incorrect, but I didn't want her to think that, did I? No, I'll just get one red and one white, that should work.

I scanned the racks, not sure which label to buy. Then a familiar label grabbed my eye, and my choice was made. I made my purchase, put the little box with the bottles in the trunk, and resumed my drive to Alison's.

Her apartment building was fairly easy to find, a modest high-rise in what looked like a busy mixed-use area. I parked a short distance away, the closest spot I could find, and walked back to the building's main entrance, carrying the box with the wine bottles. Taking a deep, fortifying breath, I pressed the intercom button next to a neatly typed label reading "A. Perry".

Alison's voice crackled over the grille. "Yes?"

"It's Harry," I said, noticing the security camera tucked discreetly in a corner near the door.

"Come on up," Alison said.

The door buzzed, I pulled it open, and walked into the comfortable foyer which was very neat and clean, but rather spartan. I rode the elevator up to the fourth floor and emerged into a similarly clean and spartan corridor. I located apartment 407 quickly. Taking another huge breath, I knocked. And, with difficulty, restrained myself from repeating the "Penny" episode from the day before. The tiny pinprick of light in the peephole darkened, then brightened again. I heard the sound of several locks being worked, then the door opened, and there was Alison.

As lovely as ever, she looked comfortable and relaxed. At least, more relaxed than I was at that moment. She wore a pale yellow blouse and a very nicely snug pair of black slacks. I couldn't help but notice she was barefoot.

"Hi, hi," Alison said chirpily with a grin, "come in, come in." I did, and she shut and locked the door once more.

Alison's apartment wasn't as austere or spartan as what I'd seen so far of the building, but it was just as clean and neat. As she led me through the short entry hallway, past a modest-sized living room off to the right, I noted with appreciation the tasteful decoration, the little touches of art on the walls, the healthy green potted plants here and there, the comfortable-looking furniture. The place felt nice, neat, homey.

Reaching the kitchen, from which delicious aromas had permeated the apartment and told me Alison had been busy fixing dinner for some time, I handed Alison my box with the wine bottles. "Here," I said, "I brought a little something."

"You know you didn't have to do that," Alison mock teased. She set down the box and opened it.

"Well, I wanted to," I said with a smile.

"Thank you," she said. "I don't think I've had Vaughn Steele wine before."

"My favorite winery," I said. "I hope you like it. I wasn't sure what we were having, so I got a red and a white."

"Well, we're having ribeye steaks."

"I do like steak," I said happily. I sure did.

"You did strike me as a meat-and-potatoes kinda guy," Alison said lightly.

"Yep," I said. "And the Satin Red here pairs beautifully with steak."

"Oh, good. Shall we have a seat? It'll be just a bit before the main course is ready."

We sat at the small dining table which already had two places set, as well as a large bowl of fresh-looking greens.

"A little garden salad to begin with?" Alison offered, handing me the tongs. I thanked her and placed a modest portion on my plate.

Alison did likewise, then asked, "Dressing?"

"No, thanks," I said.

"Excuse me?"

"I just never liked how the taste of the ingredients gets overwhelmed by the dressing, so I just skip the dressing now."

"Oh, okay," Alison said. "Interesting. Is it all right if I have some?"

I chuckled. "Of course." We enjoyed our salad for a bit. Then I said, "Well, I sure had a long day today."

"I'm sorry," Alison broke in, "could we wait to talk shop until after we're done eating, please? I'd just like to enjoy the meal with you."

"Oh," I said, taken somewhat aback but not displeased. "Yeah, that's fine, fine."

"Thanks," Alison said shyly, her cheeks reddening slightly.

Our salads finished, Alison brought out the just-finished ribeyes, accompanied by fresh baked potatoes and crisp, fresh green beans. And it all tasted amazing.

"So," Alison said before taking another petite bite of her steak, "tell me about yourself."

I gulped a chunk of ribeye, somehow managing not to choke on it and embarrass the hell out of myself. "Uh, what would you like to know?" I asked.

"Anything you care to tell," Alison smiled at me. Lord, she had a beautiful smile.

"Hmm," I said. "All right. But I warn you, I'm pretty boring."

"Oh, I doubt that," Alison said cheekily through her lessened-but-still-there blush.

"All right," I said. "Let's see. I was born and raised in Arbor Harbor, went to UC-Sacramento for journalism because I realized I wasn't a good enough trumpet player to make a career out of it, got a job with the Arbor Harbor newspaper right out of college, and that's what I've been doing ever since."

"How did you settle on journalism?" Alison asked. "And by the way, this wine is amazing."

"I'm not going to say 'I told you so,' but you were informed of that fact earlier." Alison playfully stuck her tongue out at me. "But it ain't nothin' compared to your steak, my dear."

"Thanks," Alison said, blushing again. Was it my compliment or the "my dear"? Why did I say that? Man, I'm awkward.

"Well, I'd always enjoyed writing, in fact I was editor of my high school newspaper my junior and senior years. If you'd ask me if there was one clear thing that got me interested, I don't think I could pinpoint anything specific. I think basically I've always wanted answers. I've never liked leaving things unsolved or unanswered. In fact, I actually have difficulty listening to Charles Ives' *The Unanswered Question*."

"Whose what?"

"Oh, sorry, a classical piece featuring a haunting solo trumpet. Beautiful, but I don't know, maybe just the title sets me on edge."

"I see."

"Anyway, I guess maybe it was my nitpickiness, too, that got me into journalism. But, yeah, I always wanted to dig deeper, figure things out. Even with *Doctor Who*, I'd watch and enjoy the episodes, but I also loved all the behind-the-scenes stuff too, the production side of the show, how it got made, who made it, all of that. So that curiosity or nosiness or whatever you want to call it, well, it went hand-in-hand with my love of writing and so, voila, journalism."

"Makes sense," Alison said, nodding. "Any good at it?" she asked teasingly.

"I have won an award for my work, actually."

"Oh, so it's bragging time now, is it?" Alison grinned.

"Maybe?"

"By the way, who the hell ever thought that was a good name for a newspaper, the *Arbor Harbor Coast Post*?"

I laughed. "I know, right? I sure as hell never did."

"Seriously, though, who came up with that stupid name?"

"Well," I said, "it was originally called the *Arbor Harbor Post*. That's not quite as bed."

"True," Alison said. "The Arbor Harbor part is still kinda silly."

"The town itself was named after its locale. It's right on the Pacific, in a natural bay, and surrounded by forest. So I guess it sorta makes sense, in a way."

"Still sounds silly."

"Can't argue with you there," I said. "The founder of the newspaper, Michael Kirke, named it the *Post* originally. Then a few years later some little towns that had popped up along the Pacific just north of Arbor Harbor formally requested to be covered by the *Post*. They didn't have to do that, actually, they would've been covered anyway. But it did flatter the founder, who was also the editor-in-chief, chairman of the board, and everything else, basically, so he changed the name, and lo and behold, it became the *Arbor Harbor Coast Post*."

"Can't they change the name now after all this time?" Alison asked.

"Me, personally? I wish. No, it'd have to be the board of directors. And they're all a bunch of old, stick-in-the-mud, fixed-in-their-ways old-timers who are terrified of change of any kind. There have been a couple of attempts over the years to propose a name change, but every time the old fogeys on the board start grumbling and protesting and crying out 'Tradition!' as if they were auditioning for *Fiddler on the Roof*. The motions fail every time. The last try was about five years ago. No luck."

"Wow, that sucks."

"You're tellin' me," I said, shaking my head. "And speaking of you tellin' me, it's your turn. What's your life story?" I took a bite of my steak and lifted my eyebrows expectantly as I watched Alison flush red again.

Alison took another swig of wine, then started, "All right. Well, I guess I kind of followed the same rough pattern as you. I was born and raised here in Los Angeles. I went to San Diego State for my degree in library science, then got a job with the LA Public Library System after I graduated. I worked there for a while until I got let go because of some massive budget cuts. My dad pulled a few strings and got me the job at the Universal Archives, and I've been there ever since."

"Your dad pulled strings? Does he work at Universal?"

"Yeah," Alison said brightly, "you've met him, actually. His name's Roger Ahrens."

My jaw dropped. I didn't know what to say. "I, uh…" I tried.

"I'm kidding!" Alison said hurriedly to put me out of my obvious misery.

"Oh, thank God," I breathed.

"No, Dad doesn't work at Universal," Alison went on, still smiling at my panic-stricken response. "Not directly, anyway. He's a camera operator and gets hired per project, some union thing, I never really understood that stuff all that well."

"Has he worked on anything I might have seen?"

"Well, he prefers the smaller, lower-budget character-driven movies," Alison said. "But he did do a bit of work on *Jurassic Park III* as a favor for a friend. Hated it. Hated the 'glorification of spectacle over substance', as he put it."

"Yeah, the third one wasn't that great."

"No."

"So what made you take up library science as a career?"

Alison's smile shifted from silly to wistful. "I've always loved books, loved reading. I think my dad started reading to me the day I was born, it feels so ingrained in me. Plus I really dig the organization side of things, too, making lists, cataloging, working with databases. I guess I'm kinda OCD in that way. I like things neat and organized and arranged just so. There's way more to library science than just the Dewey Decimal System. But, yeah, that's where that came from."

"Do you miss being in an actual library, working with actual books, instead of in the archives of a movie studio?"

"A bit, sometimes, yeah. But what I do now is very similar, so it's not like I'm doing something completely opposite or anything."

"That's good," I said.

We finished our main courses, then Alison said, "I hope you have room for dessert."

"Absolutely," I said. "Especially if it's as good as everything else has been."

"Well, it's nothing fancy," Alison said as she got up and puttered about the kitchen briefly. "It's just your basic homemade cherry pie. I figured I couldn't screw that up too much." She brought over a warm pie tin heaped with a full-to-bursting crust with cherries peeking out. She served us each a slice. I took one bite and, oh, my Lord, it was incredible.

"Wow," I said. "This must be where pies go when they die."

"Thank you, Agent Cooper," Alison said with a chuckle.

"And she knows *Twin Peaks*, too," I said in wonderment from not just the pie but also the latest geek culture revelation from Alison. "How is it that no one has snapped you up yet?"

Alison's smile faltered, and her face fell. Oh, God, I thought, I screwed up, she is seeing someone and I just put my foot in it. But wait, what about that kiss? Her blushes? What she said before about liking me? She *had* to be single… didn't she? And wow, what a cliched old-person thing to say, too.

Looking down at her plate and toying absently with her pie, Alison said quietly, "There was someone, but… he's gone now."

Oh, Lord, I'd really done it now. I didn't know what to say. I never knew what to say in emotional situations like this one. Clearly I'd hit a sore nerve, albeit unwittingly and unintentionally. Summoning up some rare courage, I went with my gut and decided to try to carefully coax her into talking it out.

"I'm sorry," I said softly. "I didn't mean to—"

"No, it's OK," Alison said, still not looking up. "It's… I was engaged. To a wonderful, sweet man. He was in the Army. On his first tour in Afghanistan, he… They said it was an 'IED', an 'improvised explosive device'. Which is a bullshit military way of saying a stupid bomb killed him. A stupid bomb." She ate a bit of pie, then went on. "It… it hurt, you know? It was a shot to the gut like I'd never felt before in my safe little world. And it still hurts. But… I've gotten better."

"I didn't know," I said quietly.

"And now I sometimes overcompensate," Alison said, finally looking up and once more drawing me into her beautiful eyes. "I still get nervous around guys I… like." Another blush. "My therapist had a hell of a time getting me to the point where I stopped feeling like I was betraying Matthew whenever I realized I was becoming... liking another man." She stopped and cocked her head. "Why am I telling you all this? God, I'm such a mess." She gave a tiny little laugh.

"Maybe," I ventured, "you feel comfortable enough with me to talk about it? Maybe it's my natural talent as a journalist that brought it out of you."

"Bullshit," Alison chuckled, tossing her napkin at me, taking that last comment as the mood-lightening "joke" it was meant as. I was rewarded with another of Alison's dazzling smiles. "So what about you?" she said. "How come you're not attached to anyone special? Ha, your turn now!" I swore I could see the ghost of Taylor Swift song lyric in her eyes. *Please don't be in love with someone else..."*

Even though I'd known it was coming, I still felt the uncomfortableness wash over me as it always did when my love life came up. It was something I'd gotten used to thinking about as the past, as dead, never to return. But now... "Well," I began slowly, "there *was* someone once. Not anymore. We weren't engaged, but we came close. We broke up the night I had planned to propose to her."

"Oh," Alison said softly, reaching for my hand to give it a little squeeze. God bless her. "What happened?"

I sighed. "We got into an argument. Again. We'd been doing that a lot by that point. And mostly they were about stupid, little, inconsequential things. I had the dumb idea that maybe if we got engaged and got married, maybe things would change and it would be better. So I set everything up, made reservations at her favorite restaurant, prepared my little speech, had the ring all ready. Then even before we ordered anything we started going at each other angrily again. And I'd finally had enough. I walked out. And we've not seen or spoken to each other since."

"Not once?"

"Nope. Her brother came to my place the next day and collected her things. That was rather uncomfortable, too. And that was it."

"Wow," Alison said.

"Well, to tell the absolute truth, it was for the best. It was a toxic relationship. I don't want to get into details, but... dammit, this is hard to admit."

"Whenever you're ready," Alison said with another hand squeeze.

"No one ever really gives much thought to those situations where the female partner is abusive to the male. But it happens. Much more than people think. And, well… that's what I was stuck in. And didn't realize it. Not until later, after I was well out of it for a good long while."

I took a deep breath. "But it still hurts. I'd thought we'd had something special, but… apparently not. Even though I know it was the best thing for me to get out of that abusive relationship, there are still times when I… kinda… well, no, not really, I suppose. I was going to say 'miss her', but that would be a lie. I miss being with *someone*. Doing stuff with someone, going places with someone. Having *fun* with someone. But not her, hell, no."

Alison just held my hand.

"So," I said, putting on a brave smile, "long story short, I'm a free and single man."

"OK," Alison smiled shyly back at me, giving my hand one last comforting, supportive squeeze. Then she stood and said, "Well, if you want to head into the living room, I'll just clean up here and—"

"Nonsense," I said as I stood as well. "I'll give you a hand."

"You're my guest, you don't have to—"

"I know," I said smoothly. "But I want to help. You did all the hard work to cook the meal, it's the least I can do."

Alison shrugged, admitting defeat. "All right."

As we worked at washing the dishes, Alison asked, "So where did you end up having lunch today?"

"A little seafood place," I said, "called GrumB's. That name has been ringing a bell in my head for some reason all day, even though I'm positive I've never eaten there before."

"It's a shortened version of the owner's name," Alison said. "Grumberger. Apparently they thought it was too long and awkward of a name, so they shortened it. Then someone told them it was also the last name of the Skipper from *Gilligan's Island* and—"

"Of course!" I cried. "Jonas Grumby! *That's* why it sounded familiar!" I washed another plate, then said casually, "I once met Roy Hinckley, you know."

Alison looked at me blankly.

"Roy Hinckley," I repeated. "Oh, come on, someone with your

amount of pop culture knowledge should know Roy Hinckley was the real name of the Professor from *Gilligan's Island*, as played by Russell Johnson."

Alison smiled and shook her head. "Nope," she said, "that I did not know."

"Ah," I said, "well, now I have to dock you a couple of 'cool-geek' points."

Alison mock-pouted. Even *that* looked damn cute.

We laughed, then Alison said, "So where did you meet the Professor?"

"In Minneapolis, about, oh, fifteen years ago or so," I said. "He was one of the celebrity Guests of Honor at the *Mystery Science Theater 3000* ConventioCon Expo Fest-a-Rama 2: Electric Bugaloo."

"At the what the fuck?" Alison said as she fought back laughter.

"An official convention for fans of the TV show *Mystery Science Theater 3000*," I said.

"That's the show where the guy and his robots watch really crappy movies and make jokes during the movie, right?"

"That's the one," I said.

"I kinda liked that show. Wow, so they had whole conventions dedicated to just that one show?"

"Two of them, as a matter of fact. Russell Johnson was there because he was in a movie called *This Island Earth*, which they riffed in the *MST3K* movie."

"A movie, wow," Alison said. "I guess that show was more successful than I thought."

"It did all right, ten seasons and a movie."

"Nice. Anyone else there I might know?"

"Oh," I said, thinking back, "there was also Kim Cattrall, and—"

"Hold on," Alison said. "Do you mean to tell me that you actually met Kim Cattrall? Samantha from *Sex and the City*?"

"Well, I don't know about that," I said, shrugging, though I was generally aware of Ms. Cattrall's career. "But if you asked me if I met the mannequin from the movie *Mannequin*, yep, I sure did."

"Wow," Alison breathed. "You just went up a notch in my estimation."

I lifted an eyebrow. "I wasn't aware it was possible to go any higher."

"Oh, please," Alison said, rolling her eyes teasingly. At least, I hoped it was teasingly. "You have no idea how my estimation scale works."

"True enough."

We finished the dishes, and Alison took a deep breath, letting it out slowly. "Thank you for helping, you really didn't have to do that."

"I wanted to help."

"Shall we go into the living room and get to work?" Alison asked cheerfully.

I was a bit reluctant to move on from the mostly relaxed, casual, personal talk we'd been having thus far, but I knew it was time to get down to business, so I said, "Sounds good to me."

We went into the living room and sat down next to each other on the plush sofa. I pulled my laptop out of my shoulder bag and handed it to Alison, who fired it up and logged into her wi-fi. I did the same with my iPad, once she'd given me the password.

"So," Alison said, "how was your day?"

I laughed. "Oh, it was all right," I said.

I proceeded to tell her all I'd learned that day, starting with my visit to the *Los Angeles Daily Record*. I told her about Betty and her stories of Joseph Holland, the clippings file they had on Holland's murder, and the discovery of the audiotape from Holland's interview with Boris Karloff, and how it appeared that a fair chunk of the last part of the interview was missing from the tape.

"So whatever they talked about at the end of the interview," Alison said, *"that* had to be what led Holland to Universal, and then to the landfill, right?"

"I think so," I said. "I have a feeling that whatever they discussed, it was so shocking, or so "out there", that Holland wanted more proof of whatever it was before he published it. That's probably why he removed the last part of the interview tape."

"Makes sense."

"Then," I went on theorizing, "whatever he was following up on led him to Universal and the *Frankenstein* files, and from there to the dump, where someone killed him." I felt it was time to voice a suspicion of mine that had been growing all day. "And I think we both know who killed him."

Alison looked up sharply from her typing. After a moment, she nodded. "I think so. Broderick Carlsen."

"I don't know how, I don't know why," I said. "But I feel it. It was him. He killed Holland. Then he ran. And showed up last weekend in Arbor Harbor."

Alison mused quietly. "Well, without any proof or evidence, it'll be dang near impossible to actually link Carlsen to the murder, at least beyond a reasonable doubt."

"I know," I sighed, running a hand through my hair. "We're still missing a chunk of the story. How are Holland and Carlsen linked, beyond the murder? There has to be a connection of *some* kind."

"Was there anything helpful in the police records about Holland's murder?" Alison asked.

"Hard to say, exactly," I said, "but possibly so." I went on to tell Alison and show her the information I'd gotten and printed out from the LAPD records, I told her of the police reports I'd read, the crime scene photos, the eyewitness interviews. I told her about the cave the police had found near Holland's body.

"That's where you think Carlsen might have been hiding out before he killed Holland?"

I nodded. "I think so. The police estimated that someone, possibly the killer, had been hiding in the cave for several years, at least, based on the forensic evidence and analysis of the animal remains and such found inside."

"Yuck," Alison said, wrinkling her face. Even so, she still looked so amazingly cute.

"Yeah," I said.

"Why do you think Holland might have spent so much time at that one end of the dump when he was there?" Alison asked. "Could he see the cave from there, maybe? Or maybe he spotted Carlsen and was watching him for a while, or maybe even talking to him?"

"I don't know," I admitted. "But I don't think he was talking to anyone. None of the eyewitnesses who reported seeing him there ever mentioned seeing him with another person. When he was inside the landfill, he was either looking north, towards the outer fence or the hills beyond, or one saw him walking towards the actual mounds of garbage."

"Ewww," Alison said with another cute frown, her nose crinkling adorably. Jesus, I sure had it bad for this gal, didn't I? Sheesh!

"We're still missing something big, something very important. Something that explains all this, that ties everything together."

"I bet it's on that missing last portion of the audiotape," Alison said.

"I think so, too."

"Does Holland's son have it?"

"I didn't ask about it specifically," I said. "He was a bit… prickly on the phone. I just wanted to set up a meeting and go from there."

"I sure hope he has it."

"He might not even know he does, if his dad hid it well."

Alison sighed.

"By the way," I went on, a bit hesitantly. "When I was on the phone with Josiah, I happened to mention that I'd have my assistant along with me."

"And?" Alison prompted when I paused.

"Well, I wasn't sure how you'd take it, being called my 'assistant'."

"Oh, that's fine," Alison said happily. "I kind of feel like I *am* your assistant. Even if it's unofficial."

"OK, good," I said. "I thought maybe you'd think it was sexist of me or something."

"Oh, stop playing Mr. Chivalry," Alison said. "I appreciate the thought, but I am my own woman. I'm all growed up and everything."

I chuckled. "Point taken."

"How much does it pay, by the way?"

"Nothing."

"Guess I'll have to live with it," Alison said with an exaggerated sigh.

"Yep."

"Now," Alison went on, cracking her knuckles and setting to work at the laptop, "let me try a little something, since I am your assistant, after all." She tapped and swiped the tracking pad as she went on, ignoring my raspberry in response to her teasing. "I want to put together a timeline with everything we know so far. It'll help us narrow down exactly what we're missing, what we still need to find out, what questions we still need answering, things like that. Sound good?"

"But I already started one," I said, pulling out my little pocket notebook.

"Oh, this'll be much more useful," Alison said as she continued typing and swiping.

"All right," I said, putting my notebook away and feeling slightly hurt. But it didn't last long. One look at Alison, and I could see how invested and enthused she was in the investigation. It felt like she was really committed to seeing it through to its conclusion. And since that meant she'd be continuing to work with me, how could I not be thrilled? But I still had to tease her a bit. I looked at the laptop screen as she worked. "A spreadsheet?" I said, quirking an eyebrow.

"It's a very helpful and versatile tool," Alison said. "I use them all the time at work and at home. I even track my bills and my bank account with spreadsheets."

"Nerd," I said.

"Says the guy with a picture of the TARDIS on his desktop," she replied smoothly, referring to the Doctor's time and space machine in the shape of an old London police box.

"Says the spreadsheet nerd who knows what a TARDIS is," I shot back just as smoothly.

"Touche," Alison grumbled with a good-natured sigh.

"Seriously, though," I went on, "a spreadsheet is great."

"I know it is," Alison replied. "So let's get to it."

While we worked, Alison did the actual entering of data and information on the spreadsheet, while I called up information in the documents and notes on my iPad, as well as the chicken scratchings in my notebook.

"So," Alison said, "Broderick Carlsen. The man of the hour. Let's see, the failed burglary attempt where his partner killed him was..."

"August 24th, 1931," I supplied. Suddenly I felt something scratch at the back of my mind. "Hang on a sec," I said, searching my notes. Then I found it. "I thought that date sounded familiar."

"Why?"

"It's the same date that principal photography began on

Frankenstein," I said.

"That's going into the timeline, too," Alison said. Then she paused. "A connection?"

"Maybe," I said, "but if so, I don't know what yet. It sure feels like way too much of a coincidence."

"That's for sure."

"Moving on for now, next we have, also on August 24th, Carlsen's official autopsy."

"Got it," Alison said as she typed.

"Next day, August 25th, 1931, Carlsen's body is picked up by someone claiming to be from Heavenly Rest Funeral Parlor."

"Do you have a copy of that paperwork?" Alison asked. "I'd like to see that signature."

"Yeah, but it's not very legible," I said. I brought up the document image and showed it to Alison.

Alison peered closely at the signature. "You're right," she said, "that's pretty crappy. I was hoping maybe we could get the initials at least, use that as a clue."

"Assuming the 'bodysnatcher' signed his real name," I said.

"Good point. All right, let's move on, what's next?"

"A whole lot of nothin'," I said, "until 1969 and Joseph Holland enters the story."

"OK, let's keep at it."

"Right," I said. "Let's see… OK, January 30th, 1969, Joseph Holland interviews Boris Karloff. And we have our suspicions about part of that interview, don't we?"

"We sure do," Alison agreed, not looking up from her typing but giving me a smile nonetheless.

"January 31st, 1969, Holland stops by the *Daily Record,* then visits the Universal Archives, looks at the *Frankenstein* files, then goes to the Hollywood City Dump. And is murdered."

"By Broderick Carlsen," Alison said, looking up at me then. "According to your gut, anyway."

I nodded. "That's all I have at the moment, but that's what it's telling me, so I'm listening."

"Me, too," Alison said. "So it goes into our timeline. Next?"

"All right," I said, feeling grateful for Alison's continued support and faith in me (and my gut), even though we'd only known each other for a few days. "February 2nd, 1969, Holland's wife reports him missing. Oh, and Boris Karloff dies."

"Same day?"

"Same day," I said, "February 2nd."

"OK."

"February 3rd, Holland's body is found just north of the dump where he was last seen. After that, well… the LAPD investigates but gets nowhere. And that's about it, until Broderick Carlsen shows up in Arbor Harbor last weekend, March 12th, 2011. And by that point, he's been altered somehow to look like the Frankenstein Monster."

"Got it." Alison finished typing, then scanned her work. She tweaked it a bit, then turned to me. "OK, I think we've got a good framework to work with now."

I looked at the screen and was impressed. The spreadsheet was very neatly arranged and organized, columns logically set up, data entered fully yet succinctly, and good use of conditional formatting. "Very nice," I said, meaning it. "Better than I could have done."

"Of course," Alison said with a twinkle in her eye. "But thank you."

"We've got some pretty big gaps in there," I said. "Between 1931 and 1969, then between 1969 and 2011."

"We'll fill 'em all in," Alison said. "It'll just take a bit more digging."

"As for our unanswered questions…" I began.

"I can log these in here, too," Alison said, keyboarding again. "And let's start with the big one. How the hell is Broderick Carlsen still alive in 2011 when the records show he died way back in 1931?"

"I think if we had the answer to that," I said, "things would really start to fall into place."

"What else don't we know yet?" Alison asked, fingers poised.

"Why does Carlsen look like the Frankenstein Monster?"

"Boy, you are definitely a stickler about that, calling him the Monster," Alison said, typing. "Wouldn't it just be easier to say 'Frankenstein'? I mean, I'd still know what you were talking about."

"Yeah, but it wouldn't be accurate," I said. "Sorry."

"Hey, no problem, it just feels a bit clunky."

"Anyway," I said to move things along, "Who altered Carlsen to look like the Monster? Was it his choice? Or someone else's? When was he altered? What happened with Carlsen's supposedly dead body after the coroner's office released it to whoever was posing as a funeral parlor worker? If that even *was* Carlsen's body. Why was Carlsen in that cave by the dump? How long had he been there? What led Holland to the dump? What made him go up the hill to the cave? Why did Carlsen kill Holland? What did Carlsen do after he killed Holland, where did he go? How long did it take him to get up to the forest near Arbor Harbor? Had he been hiding out somewhere up there? If so, where, and for how long? And what the hell do we do with him now? Dammit!"

I realized my gradually crescendoing rant had stilled Alison's hands. She looked at me with concern and asked, "You OK?"

I sighed. "Yeah, sorry," I said. "But Jesus Christ, that's a lot of questions. I hate unanswered questions."

Alison nodded. "I know. Me, too." She smiled at me encouragingly and grasped my hand, giving it a tiny squeeze. "We'll get there." And I did feel better having her support.

"Thanks," I said. "Sorry for swearing."

Laughing lightly, Alison said, "Hey, no problem, I do it all the time."

"All the time?"

"Well," Alison said, returning to the laptop, "not literally all the time. But we're all human, and we're gonna swear sometimes. Just one thing, though."

"Yeah?"

"Could you repeat those questions for me, please? You were going so fast that I couldn't keep up."

I went back over my recitation of unanswered questions, this time more calmly. Alison typed them all into her spreadsheet.

When the questions were all logged, Alison sat back and looked at the screen before her. "That is a lot of stuff we don't know yet," she said. "But we're gonna get it all figured out, just you wait and see."

Yet again, Alison's use of "we" gave me a little thrill. It may seem silly, that such small, simple words such as "we" and "us" could make me happy, but they did. So deal with it. I just hoped Alison felt the same when I made similar reference to our partnership. Such little things gave me hope that this relationship might go on, might blossom into something more one day in the not too distant future. Out loud, I said, "If only it were as easy as just waiting and seeing."

"I know that, you silly, literal man," Alison teased with a huge grin on her beautiful face. "Anyway, I think maybe we should call it a day where work is concerned."

"Probably a good idea," I said, still feeling a bit embarrassed by my little rant from earlier. "How do you want to coordinate things tomorrow morning for our trip to San Francisco?"

"I had a thought about that," Alison said as I packed up my shoulder bag. "I can drive."

"I know," I said patronizingly. "Congratulations, by the way. How long have you had your driver's license?"

"Shut up," Alison growled at me. "I mean, I am volunteering the use of my car for the trip. You can ditch that gas-guzzling rental of yours."

"Hey, I like my Corvette," I protested, but not very vehemently. I liked where this was going. "What are we doing after seeing Josiah Holland?"

"Well, I thought I could just run you back home to Arbor Harbor," Alison said. "Save you the plane ticket money."

"I'd be on the paper's corporate account," I said.

"Whatever," Alison said. "I like my plan. Unless you needed to come back here to LA for some reason…?"

I couldn't think of anything off the top of my head. But I sure wanted to. Any excuse to spend more time with Alison… But I felt like I'd checked out everything I could have based on the information as I had it then. Unless something came up during our talk with Josiah Holland, I figured my legwork in LA was done. "All right," I said, "if you're sure."

"I'm sure," Alison said.

"I don't really like the thought of you driving all the way back to LA all by yourself, though."

"I'll be fine," Alison said with a knowing smile. Knowing what, exactly, I wasn't sure. But I knew I liked the smile.

"All right," I said.

"Good. It's set. You drop your car rental off at LAX, I'll pick you up there, and off we'll go."

"All right," I said again. She sure could get an idea fixed in her head, I thought to myself.

Flipping on her TV casually to some *How I Met Your Mother* reruns, Alison said, "A little TV break before you head out?"

"All right," I said yet again as I settled back on the comfy sofa. Alison snuggled up close to me, which felt really good. Tentatively, I put my arm around her shoulders. She snuggled even closer, which felt even better. And so we watched TV together for a short while.

Eventually, just as the *HIMYM* gang was discovering the cheesy greatness of the Robin Sparkles music video for "Let's Go to the Mall", I suddenly felt Alison's hand on my thigh. I froze, tensing. Oh, God, I thought, I'm not ready for this. It'd been so long since I'd been with a woman, not since Sarah, and I just didn't feel ready. Don't get me wrong, I was completely smitten with Alison, but I didn't think the time was right. I glanced cautiously at her. Her eyes were shut, her mouth hung slightly open. She was asleep. Oh, thank God, I thought. I had no idea what Alison's thoughts were on the situation, but I knew that I didn't want to lose her.

I glanced at my watch and saw it was getting late, especially if we were going to be up extra early the next morning. "Alison," I whispered, nudging her gently. "Alison."

"Mmm-hmm," Alison muttered groggily, shifting and stretching.

"It's late, I'm gonna head out," I said as I gathered up my things.

"Mmm-kay," Alison said as she blinked her weary eyes open.

I stood and helped her stand, holding her hand as I led her over to the door. "Thank you for a delicious meal," I said as she looked at me blurrily. "And thank you for your help. Everything tonight was wonderful."

"Yes, you were," Alison murmured sleepily.

I chuckled quietly and hugged her. Then, hoping to give Alison at least a fraction of the amazing, dreamy sensation I'd experienced from her surprise kiss the previous night, I gently cupped the back of her head in one hand, circled the other around her back, pressed her close to me, leaned down slightly, and gave her what in my humble self-critical opinion was one of the best kisses I'd ever given a woman.

When it was over, I stepped back, and it took Alison a few seconds to open her eyes again. I believe that did it, I thought happily, judging by the sweet smile that slowly but surely spread across her sleepy face.

"Good night, Alison," I said softly as I opened the door. "I'll see you bright and early tomorrow morning."

"Mmm-kay," Alison said, still not quite all there.

I left her apartment with what I'm sure was a goofy grin on my face. A glance in my car's rearview mirror on the drive back to my hotel confirmed it. But I didn't care how ridiculous I looked.

CHAPTER FOURTEEN

The Expedition

Saturday morning came way too early for my liking, the alarm shaking me to wakefulness. I checked out, then collected my car and headed to Los Angeles International Airport, the sun not officially up just yet, though its glow was brightening the eastern horizon.

The process of returning my rental car (goodbye, sweet Corvette) took longer than I'd hoped, so by the time I lugged my luggage out to the curb outside the terminal, Alison was already waiting. We kissed (amazing how natural that greeting felt now), I loaded my luggage into Alison's trunk, and we were off.

As Alison threaded us through traffic, I entered Josiah Holland's address into my phone's map app. I turned to Alison and said, "Are you still sure you want to do this?"

"What, go to San Fran and talk to Josiah Holland with you?" she asked. "Hellz, yeah."

"No, I mean drive me the whole way back home to Arbor Harbor after we're done in San Francisco, then drive all the way back to LA all by yourself. It's a hell of a long drive, especially for one person on their own."

"Oh, that's all right," Alison said. "I've got plenty of vacation days saved up if I don't make it back in time for Monday morning. I'll be fine."

"If you're sure," I said. I did feel somewhat bad about the long solo drive Alison had ahead of her. But I also felt rather selfishly excited that Alison would be coming to see my hometown, to glimpse my life, I guess you could say. So I didn't press the point too hard.

"I'm sure," Alison said with a smile. And as I looked at her, her face lit by the freshly-risen sunlight with the Pacific Ocean just visible past her underneath a bright cloudless sky, I didn't know which sight before me was more beautiful. Actually, that's not true. I did know. It was Alison.

As my "assistant" drove us out of the Los Angeles metropolis, I decided to make a few perhaps overdue phone calls.

"What've you got?" Lisa Takagi barked over the phone.

"Still working on the John Doe story," I said.

"I know you are. Where are you on it?"

"On my way to San Francisco to meet with someone that will hopefully be able to get me some good solid information that I need."

"Have you got proof that your John Doe is the guy who supposedly died eighty years ago?"

"Well, no," I admitted. "Not definitively."

"But that's what I need, Harry," Lisa said firmly. "I need definitive, incontrovertible proof of this crazy story before I'll publish it. I won't be the laughing stock of the news industry. Get me hard, concrete proof, or I'll have to pull the plug on the story." She paused, then continued in a somewhat softened tone. "You know that, Roger. Do what you can, but if you get nowhere, I need you back here at your desk. All right?"

"All right," I said. "I'm doing everything I can."

"I'm sure you are," Lisa said. "Good luck." She hung up.

Alison glanced at me. "Your boss give you a hard time?" she asked.

"No more than I deserve," I said. "She's a tough boss but she's fair. Which is why it sometimes feels like I'm letting her down, too, not just myself, if I can't crack this story."

"We will," Alison said, throwing me another encouraging smile.

The next call was likely to be even more awkward. The comm tech at the Arbor Harbor Police Department told me Chief Packer was on duty but out of the office. Fortunately, intrepid reporter that I am, I had his cell number, which I then dialed.

"Harry," Chief Ray Packer said with evident surprise. "How's it going?"

"Fine, fine," I said. "Listen, has there been anything further happening with that John Doe in the hospital?"

"The guy in the coma? No, no change, not that I've heard. Why?"

"Have you done any more checking into his identity?" I asked.

There was a pause, then the chief said, "I thought we'd settled that."

"I know you're reluctant to believe—"

"'Reluctant'?" Ray snapped. "Look, here's how it is. The fingerprint match was an error somewhere in the database. He's not Broderick Coleman or whoever you think he is. He's not a hundred-and-whatever years old. We tried IDing him but we've come up empty. It happens. And that's that. End of story."

"But—"

"End. Of. Story." The chief sighed. "You should have listened to me and not gone on this wild goose chase of yours. Unless you've actually found something?" His sarcastic tone told me he wasn't going to be receptive to anything I might have to say.

"Well…" I began carefully.

"I didn't think so," Packer went on. "Because there's nothing to find. Drop it, Harry, just drop the damn story. Before you make a complete fool of yourself. Got it?"

I frowned. Closed-minded idiot, I thought angrily. "I hear you," I said, echoing James T. Kirk's words from *Star Trek III* when a superior officer tried to warn Kirk off from a crazy scheme that Kirk went ahead with anyway.

"I'm just trying to help you, Harry," Packer said, easing up a bit.

"I know."

"I'll see you around," Chief Packer said before hanging up.

"Another fan, huh?" Alison said sympathetically.

I shrugged. "Not everyone is as open-minded as you." I dialed another number.

"Not another one?" Alison said worriedly.

"Don't worry," I said, "this one'll be a happier call."

"Mr. Edwards," said the calm voice at the other end.

"Mr. Goldschmidt," I said just as evenly to my house- and cat-

and dog-sitter. "How are you, Johnny?"

"Oh, things are fine, Harry," Johnny replied smoothly. "How's your story coming along?"

"Getting there," I said, not really wanting to get into the details, but I knew Johnny wouldn't press the issue. "I just wanted to give you a heads-up that I'll probably be home in a day or two."

"All right," Johnny said.

"I don't know for sure yet but I'll try to keep you posted. How are my boys?"

I caught the surprised, wide-eyed look Alison shot at me.

"They're both fine," Johnny reported. "Sam is behaving in typical cat-like fashion, acting like he owns the place and everyone in it. Sonny, well, he's still missing you a lot. He keeps going to the back door and waiting for you to walk in."

"Awww," I said, smiling. "Give them both hugs for me, and tell them Daddy loves them and misses them and will see them soon."

Alison glanced at me again, this time narrow-eyed.

"I will," Johnny said.

"And thank you, guys, for helping me out like this. I had no idea I'd be gone this long."

"Not to worry, Rachel and I are happy to help. Now go finish that story like the rockstar reporter you are."

"Thanks," I chuckled. "I'll do my best."

"You always do."

I quietly put away my phone. I knew Alison had been thrown by a couple of things I'd said to Johnny, and I decided to have a bit of fun. After a few silent moments of gripping the steering wheel tightly, Alison finally spoke up. "Do you, um..." she began. "Is there, um, something I should know? Like maybe something you forgot to tell me?"

I tilted my head, pondering. "Not that I can think of. What do you mean?"

"Not that I have a problem with it or anything," Alison went on. "But, um... who exactly were you referring to when you asked about your 'boys', 'Daddy'?"

"Oh, that," I said off-handedly. "Sam and Sonny. My boys."

Alison nodded slowly. "And they are..."

"Let's see," I said, "Sam is almost seven years old, and Sonny is almost six."

"Oh," Alison said quietly.

"Or I guess you could say Sonny's almost thirty-six."

Alison frowned, clearly confused. "What?"

"In dog years. Sonny's my dog, and Sam's my cat."

Alison shot a glance at me. "You jerk," she growled. "You deliberately had me thinking…"

"Thinking what?" I asked, all innocence.

"You know what," she grumbled sulkily.

"Hey, I'm sorry," I said, easing up on my obvious enjoyment of her discomfort. "I was just having a little fun with you."

"Uh-huh," Alison said evenly.

I looked out the window at the passing California scenery. "I really do think of them as 'my boys'," I said reflectively. "They've always been there for me, through thick and thin. They helped me get through my rough patch after my break-up, among other things."

"Your pets did?" Alison said softly, her irritation of a moment before having disappeared and been replaced with sympathetic interest.

"Well, not just them, of course," I said. "My family and friends helped me a lot, too. But those times when it was just me, all alone at home, they were there, Sam and Sonny, 'my boys'. Sam is usually your typical aloof cat, but when I was really down and really struggling, he was always right there. When I'd be sitting on my couch he'd curl up in my lap. Well, at least until Sonny noticed and got jealous and jumped up and nudged Sam out of the way so *he* could be in my lap. But Sam would just hop up behind me on the back of the couch and lay down against my neck and shoulders. Sometimes he'd even reach out and rest a little paw on my shoulder and fall asleep like that."

"Awww."

"Yeah, even little things like that helped make me feel better. And Sonny, well, he's always been my best buddy, but when things were bad he definitely proved that and then some. Sometimes I'd trip over him, he'd be keeping that close to me. And like when he'd push Sam out of the way to be on my lap, it was like, 'Hey, *I'm* his best pal, not you.' And whenever I found myself crying, yes, I can admit it, I have feelings. Anyway, when I cried he'd always kiss my face with his big tongue to wash away all my tears. And that sweet gesture, whether he knew what was going on or what he was doing for me, it always made me laugh and cheered me up."

"That's so sweet," Alison said.

"Yeah," I said, smiling as I remembered all the times my best buddy had lifted my spirits.

"I can see why they're 'your boys'."

"Absolutely. I'm glad I've got good people to look after them when I'm away from home."

We drove on a bit, then, in a very quiet voice, Alison said, "I sure could have used a kitty or a puppy."

My stomach lurched. I felt horrible. There I was, moaning about my poor self after a simple (albeit difficult) break-up with my girlfriend, when this woman's fiance had *died*, for God's sake. What the hell was *I* whining about? "Oh, God, I'm sorry, I—" I began.

"No," Alison said very firmly, tightening her grip on the wheel again. "I didn't say that to get your pity. I just meant it as an observation about myself, a statement about something I didn't think of back then. That's all. OK?" She glanced over at me, her expression stern, but with more than a touch of softness there as well.

"OK," I said. And my estimation of her, of her strength, notched upwards yet again.

Some minutes later, Alison said, "Let's get some music going." She switched on and tuned in her satellite radio's 80's channel, and, lo and behold, "Our House" by Madness was playing.

"Love this song," I said.

"By the only band ever to appear in more than one episode of *The Young Ones* during its too-short twelve-episode run," said my fellow Anglophile.

"And the name of the other song they did on the show?" I asked, figuring she probably knew.

"'House of Fun'."

"Correct," I said with a smile for my fellow nerd, who smiled warmly back.

* * *

***

The rest of the morning was mostly uneventful, yet pleasant and fun. I enjoyed having a partner on my investigation, and I especially enjoyed the fact that my partner was Alison. We picked up a quick drive-thru breakfast at McDonald's, then later, in the interest of fairness to both sides of the Burger Wars, we grabbed lunch at Burger King. I tried out my "I'm not Herb" line there, but no one recognized my reference to one of many failed Burger King promotions from the 1980s. Oh well, maybe one day.

Back on the road, we kept driving. I spelled Alison at the wheel for a time, which she appreciated. More choice 80s hits blasted from the car radio, and we had an enjoyable, comfortable early afternoon with each other as we continued north.

Eventually we left one interstate for another which angled towards San Francisco. As we neared a particular green road sign, I pointed and said to Alison, who was driving again, "Alameda, where the nuclear wessels are."

"Aye, Keptin," Alison replied with a quick mock-salute. The nitpicking side of me wanted to point out that she had responded as Chekov to my Chekov, and that at that point in the *Star Trek* chronology, Kirk was still technically an admiral. The non-nitpicking side of me told me that her "Keptin" could just as easily have been referring to Captain Montgomery Scott or some other captain, and that I should shut the hell up and not say anything. I settled on an appreciative smile and chuckle.

Alison drove on, and eventually we arrived at the city of San Francisco.

Ah, San Francisco. I've always loved the place, ever since my first visit with my family when I was about eight or nine years old. My dad was attending a homebuilders' convention, and while he was at his various seminars, Mother and I went out, seeing the sights and doing some shopping. Well, Mother did the shopping, I just went along. Since then I've been back many times, both for work and for pleasure.

Over the years, I've tried to express just what it is about San Francisco that captivates me so much. Yes, I'm a 49ers fan, but not a Giants fan (go, Dodgers!). I think perhaps it's the innate feeling of aliveness the city has, its vitality, its great variety of people, cultures, beauty. A sense of bright, sunny optimism always seems to come over me when I visit. I love the broad multicultural range of the city's residents, the beauty of its architecture, the landscape with the hills and the shorelines, the great bay, and the magnificent ocean. Even the cheesy tourist sights, like the impressive Golden Gate Bridge, the grand Palace of Fine Arts, pleasant Golden Gate Park, Coit Tower with its how-the-hell-can-this-be-legal super tiny elevator that takes you up to a breathtaking view of the city, the crazy-fun zig-zag of Lombard Street, the gritty history of Alcatraz, even clilched Fisherman's Wharf. It all blends into a wonderful brew of beauty, happiness and hope. I absolutely love it.

But not as much as Arbor Harbor, of course.

"This place is almost like a little home away from home for me," I said wistfully as we rolled through the streets of San Francisco.

"I've only been here a few times," Alison said as she kept an eye on the GPS directions. "But I do really like it, too."

CHAPTER FIFTEEN

The Empty Child

Finally we arrived at our destination. Josiah Holland's home was in a quiet residential area just north of Golden Gate Park. There were few cars parked in the area and even fewer people walking the sidewalks. But the neighborhood looked clean, neat and well-maintained. Josiah lived in a small cluster of townhouse condominiums, each unit painted a different light pastel shade. We parked and walked up to the small, waist-high iron gate set into the fence surrounding Josiah's unit. We double-checked the number on the plate affixed to the bars of the gate against the address Josiah had given me over the phone. This was the place, all right. We stepped through the unlocked gate and walked the short flagstone walk up to the front door. I pressed the doorbell button on the wall by the door.

After waiting a minute or so with no response, I pressed the button again. Again there was no response. I cast a worried glance at Alison, who shrugged. Once again I pressed the button.

"Hello?" a voice crackled from the speaker beside the doorbell.

"Mr. Holland?" I said.

"Who's asking?" came the response.

"It's Harrison Edwards, Mr. Holland, we spoke on the phone yesterday."

"Who?"

Uh-oh, I thought. "Harrison Edwards," I said patiently. "From the Arbor Harbor… newspaper."

"From the what?"

I sighed. "From the *Arbor Harbor Post*."

Another pause. "I don't remember talking to anyone from anything called that."

I gritted my teeth. He was doing this deliberately, I just knew. "From the *Arbor Harbor Coast Post*," I said.

"Well, why didn't you say so? I'll be right there."

A moment later, the front door finally swinging open, Josiah Holland turned out to be a rather short, stocky, gray-haired man. He looked to be about in his mid-sixties, his thin hair wispy on a wrinkled head, his eyes somewhat sunken over his jowly, stubbly cheeks, his frame slightly hunched over. His broad grin, unexpected as it was, showed what was almost certainly a relatively new set of dentures. "I'm sorry," Josiah said, "I was just having a bit of fun. But that really is a dumb-ass name for a newspaper."

"Believe me, I agree with you one hundred percent in that," I said.

Josiah shook my hand enthusiastically, and I fought desperately not to show any pain from his amazingly powerful grip. I did feel somewhat relieved at our welcome. Was today's talk going to be more good-natured that yesterday's phone call had led me to believe? I sure hoped so.

Josiah glanced over at Alison. "And you are…?"

"Alison Perry," she said with a confident, friendly smile. "Mr. Edwards' assistant." I had the impression that the handshake between Alison and Josiah was decidedly less forceful.

"Do you work for the same paper as he does?" Josiah said with a nod in my direction.

Alison chuckled lightly. "No, I'm freelance."

"Probably wise," Josiah said with a shake of his head. "Well, come in, you two. I've got some tea ready if you're interested."

Josiah led us inside, down a short hallway and into his living room. It was large, but still felt cramped and cluttered in a way often typical of homes of older persons who'd lived full lives and struggled to find a way to accommodate all of their accumulated souvenirs and remembrances of their lives. Several tall, crammed bookcases, an old entertainment center with a record player above a shelf full of vinyl record albums, an old tube-style television, a fireplace with a mantle covered in chintzy but probably treasured knickknacks, a big, tired-looking sofa, and two easy chairs, one decidedly much more worn that the other. Throw in a big oak coffee table and matching end tables, plus a few lamps, and that was Josiah Holland's place in a nutshell.

The old man motioned us to the sofa while he plopped himself wearily in the well-used easy chair. "Help yourself to tea," he said, indicating the tea service on the big coffee table before us. "I've already got mine," he added, nodding at the cup on the end table by his chair. "It's just simple green tea, I hope that's all right."

"Thank you, sir," I said as I took the delicate looking pot from the tray and poured a cup for Alison and then one for me. Alison took hers with two sugars, while I added just a small amount of milk to mine. I sipped, and was pleasantly surprised at the rich, warm flavor. So apparently not just "simple" green tea, but wonderful nonetheless. "This is excellent, thank you," I said.

"Mmm, yes, it's superb," Alison added enthusiastically after she'd sampled her tea as well. "Thank you."

Josiah waved a hand dismissively. "You don't need to flatter me," he said. "I know you're here on business."

I glanced at Alison, then back to Josiah. Careful now, Roger. "Yes, sir," I said politely. "But it really is delicious. I mean that. However, if you like, we can get right down to—"

Josiah held up a hand to cut me off. "I'm not ready to talk yet," he said gruffly.

I fought the urge to glance over at Alison again. I was getting a sinking feeling about the meeting, after such a promising start. Had we really just driven all that way only to be denied the interview after all? Why the hell had Josiah agreed to meet with us in the first place? Was this some cruel trick, a petty little way for him to get even, to pull a fast one on a member of the media which he apparently still held at least partly responsible for his father's death? I bit back my first response, knowing it would absolutely nix any chance I might have of salvaging the situation. Instead, I merely said, quietly and evenly, "I'm sorry?"

Josiah pulled himself out of his chair and shuffled over to the old entertainment center. There he spent a few silent moments rifling through his record collection. Finally he pulled out an album, took the paper inner sleeve out of the album, and removed the actual vinyl disc, slipping it carefully out of the sleeve. He placed the record on the spindle of the record player, where it hung suspended about two inches above the surface of the turntable itself. Josiah slid a control on the player, then stood back as the record flopped onto the turntable which had begun rotating. The long player arm moved over from its resting cradle, then quietly lowered itself to the outer edge of the vinyl record. After a few pops and crackles, a gloriously bright, brassy big band sound blasted from the speakers. After a few seconds of intro, we then heard the unmistakable smooth croon of Mr. Frank Sinatra.

As the legendary singer hit the second verse, Josiah turned the volume down to a much more reasonable background level. Then, with a satisfied smile, he shuffled back to his chair.

"Ah, the Chairman of the Board," I said with a smile. I did like Sinatra, but wasn't a huge fan, but I thought maybe playing into this could bring Josiah out of his shell if I played my cards right.

"The best there ever was or will ever be," Josiah said happily as he sat back.

"And he always had the best backing bands, too," I said, nodding. "Same with the arrangements of his songs, they're always such fun to play." There, I thought, that should hook him.

Josiah's eyebrows lifted. "You play?"

"I sure do," I said, noticing the look of wonderment I was getting from Alison. I guess I hadn't mentioned to her that I still played, had I? "I play trumpet in a local big band back home, as well as a more traditional concert band, but the big band is much more fun."

"Please tell me your band doesn't have a stupid name like your newspaper," Josiah said.

I laughed. "No, the founder of the music program was a lot more sensible than the idiots who named the paper way back when. We're called the Oceanside Big Band, and the Oceanside Concert Band."

"Much better," Josiah said approvingly. He turned to Alison. "Do you play, too?"

"No," Alison said, "I took piano lessons when I was a kid but never kept it up."

Josiah nodded. "You ever heard him play?"

Alison lookied over at me with an amused smile playing about her pretty lips. "No," she said, her eyes twinkling, "not yet, anyway."

I felt my cheeks burn and earned a teasing "Turnabout is fair play" grin from Alison. "Are you OK?" she asked. "Is your circulation —"

"I'm fine," I said swiftly.

Josiah chuckled. "Well, I think I'm ready now," he said.

It took me a second to catch his meaning. Then I carefully said, "Are you sure…?"

With a nod, Josiah replied, "Yeah, I just need some Frank. He helps me relax and focus my mind better. I assume you're going to want me to use my mind?"

OK, so he still wasn't going to be a pushover, even with Sinatra in the background. Fair enough. Time to get to work. Alison slid my iPad out of my shoulder bag and tapped it on.

"Mr. Holland—" I began, then was cut off by Josiah.

"Just Josiah, please," the old man said with a touch of irritation.

"All right," I said. "Josiah, perhaps we could begin with telling us a little bit about your father, you know, what kind of person he was, what kind of a father he was, that sort of thing. Whatever you feel comfortable sharing with us."

"I thought you were here to talk about his murder," Josiah said with narrowed eyes.

"We'll get to that," I said. "This is for background, a bit of context for the article."

Josiah's expression softened, and he settled back in his chair. "All right," he said. "I'm just not sure what exactly you want to know. He was a pretty good dad, I think. He just wasn't around as much as I maybe would've liked while I was growing up. And probably not as much as he would've liked, too. But he was always so busy with work that he was out of the house a lot. When he was home, though, he sure did spend as much time with me as he could, and with Mom. We read books together, listened to radio programs together, went to the park, lots of things like that. I remember him as a good, kind father."

"What can you tell us about his work?" I asked.

A frown crossed Josiah's face. "That's the *one* thing I resented," he rumbled. "His job. That's why he was gone so much, working on his stories. I know he loved what he did, he sometimes told me he felt he was doing one of the most important things a person could do, working to help other people, in his case by bringing them the news. I kind of got his point, but not totally. And I was a selfish kid who wanted to see his dad more often, you know?" Josiah sighed, releasing some of his frustration. "But yeah, he did love his job. When he'd take me to the office, I could see how happy he got just being there, doing his job and working with his colleagues. And from what I could tell, he seemed to be damned good at it, too."

I nodded. "I agree," I said, "I've read some of his work. He had a great gift of insight, finding the truth of a situation. And he had a wonderful personal touch with people."

"Exactly, exactly," Josiah said. "And, boy, did he resent it when they kicked him off the main news desk down to Arts and Crafts."

"Arts and Leisure," I found myself automatically correcting.

"Whatever," Josiah said. "He did not like it one little bit, no sir."

"What can you tell me about that?"

"Well, he was getting older, but he was still as sharp as ever. Yeah, maybe he got a bit of a limp in his right leg, but that didn't mean he couldn't go out and do the big stories. It wasn't like he was chasing down bad guys like a cop or something. No, it was pretty much a case of new blood running the paper wanting new blood doing the big stuff, or some shit like that." He broke off and glanced at Alison. "Pardon my language, ma'am," He murmured embarrassedly.

Alison smiled back. "It's all right," she said. "I've heard and said worse."

Josiah gave her a thankful nod. "Well, thank you. So, anyway, yeah, Dad hated getting booted to Arts and Crap..." (I bit my tongue) "...but he made damn sure he did just as good at his job on those 'puff pieces' as he sometimes called them as when he was doing the big stories on the main desk."

"How old were you when he got, erm, reassigned?" I asked.

"I think about, oh, nineteen maybe? Dad was only fifty-five when they booted him down. Fifty-five! It's not like he was decrepit and senile for Christ's sake!"

I steeled myself for where I had to go next. This could go OK, I thought to myself, or this could go royally pear-shaped, as they say. But it was why we'd come to see the man, after all, so I had to move forward. "Josiah," I said gently, "how did you learn about your father's death?"

I could see Josiah's jaw tighten somewhat as he paused a moment before answering. When he eventually replied, he was quiet, gazing into that middle distance where somehow we're able to see things that aren't really there, or are long gone. "Mom called me and told me the police had found his body. She'd called me the day, no, two days before that, asking if I'd seen him or heard from him. I told her I last talked to him about a week before, just talking on the phone, catching up. I was at Cal Tech at the time and we talked on the phone now and then, just checking in, you know.

"Anyway, sometimes Dad would work late and stay at the office and forget to call Mom to say he wouldn't be home, but he hadn't really done that since he was put on the Arts and Leisure beat. I had told Mom that's probably what had happened and she shouldn't worry, he'd show up. But when Mom called two days later, I knew what she was going to say before she said it, somehow. She was so calm on the phone when she told me he was dead. Then she asked me to come home, and of course I did.

"When I got there, Mom came outside before I even got out of my car. She hugged me and cried and just collapsed in my arms. After we took her inside and put her to bed to rest, Uncle Bob told me how brave and strong she'd been the whole time, right up until I got home."

Josiah took a deep breath and collected himself. "At the reception after the funeral, a lot of Dad's co-workers came up to me and told me how sorry they were. I think that was when I realized that Dad's job had killed him. And could they figure out who his killer was? Could they figure out who had killed one of their own? No, they were useless, just like the pathetic police department. Nobody could solve my Dad's murder. Even now, over forty years later, those idiots still haven't figured it out. They can solve all kinds of other cases, other murders, but the one I needed them to solve, they couldn't do shit." Josiah shook his head. "If they hadn't booted him to Arts and Shit, he would never have gone to that damn garbage dump and never been killed."

Over forty years later, Josiah had said. And he was still so bitter. I have to say, part of me could hardly blame him. If my dad had been murdered and no one could solve the case, I'd probably be pretty bitter the rest of my life, too. Another, perhaps biased side of me felt his grudge against the newspaper was somewhat unfair. Granted, it did appear that a story he was working on had led him to the landfill, probably something from the Karloff interview. But the fact that a newspaper with a limited budget and limited resources couldn't solve a murder that had stymied the LAPD was no reason to throw so much responsibility for the murder on the newspaper's back.

"Can you think of anything from that time," I said quietly, "that might not have been in the news or not generally known to the public? Anything that might be relevant to your father's murder?"

Josiah was quiet for some time, looking distant. I was about to check that he hadn't fallen asleep when he finally said softly, "No."

Damn, I thought. I looked over at Alison, who looked back at me with a sympathetic "Now what?" look on her face that succinctly reflected exactly what I felt in that moment. Had we come all that way for nothing? I had been sure, my gut had been telling me we needed to talk with this man. We were supposed to be getting closer to the answer, not just spinning our wheels in the mud, going absolutely nowhere.

"What about you?" Josiah said, his voice barely above a whisper.

I turned back to him. "Pardon?"

"Do *you* know of anything new about my Dad's murder?" Josiah said evenly, his eyes locked on mine. "You do, don't you? Otherwise, why would you be here?"

And that was a very good question. I could have tried to dissemble, just put him off with the standard "Just looking into an old case" excuse. But his eyes wouldn't let me do that. I saw his pain and frustration. It felt wrong to lie to Josiah, especially about this. Another quick glance at Alison decided me. Her eyes and her face told me she had come to the same conclusion I had. But I also knew I had to go about it very carefully. I turned back to that angry, pained gaze. "Are you familiar with the name Broderick Carlsen?" I asked.

Josiah's brow wrinkled as he pursed his lips, thinking. "No, I don't think so," he said.

Damn. Guess that would've been too easy. "Are you sure?" I asked.

Josiah shook his head. "Doesn't sound familiar at all."

"Maybe from your father's notes or something?" I paused. Here goes, I thought. "What about in the personal effects the paper returned to your family?"

Josiah gave a small, silent guffaw. "No," he said. "I never even looked inside that damn box."

"Never?" I asked, trying not to get too hopeful.

"Nope. I don't think Mom ever did, either."

With another quick glance at Alison, I ventured, "You wouldn't still happen to have the box, would you?" I could feel Alison tense up slightly.

Shrugging, Josiah said, "I think so." He stood up from his chair, stretched his back with an audible crack, then led us down a short hallway from the living room. We followed him closely, Alison giving my hand a quick, excited squeeze which I returned. Josiah led us into a den/office/library (delete as applicable) that was just as crammed as the living room. More stuffed bookcases, piles of cardboard boxes scattered haphazardly here and there, and opposite the door was a large wooden desk and an old wooden desk chair. Both sat oddly un-piled-upon next to a window with a view of the lowering sun. On one of the bookcases in the room I noticed a small framed photo of Josiah looking about ten years younger with a lovely woman of roughly the same age. It struck me then that Josiah was probably a widower, as I had seen no evidence of a woman's current presence or a woman's touch about the place. Nor had Josiah ever mentioned anyone. Figuring that it might be one of the causes for his general grumpy disposition, I decided not to bring up the subject with him just then.

Josiah paused in the middle of the cluttered toom, then turned and headed to the far right corner. There he began to shift and dig through the pile of boxes. After a moment he shuffled over to a different stack of boxes and began hunting through them. Then, with a small grunt of triumph, Josiah lifted out a box and, wheezing slightly, brought it over to set it on the clear surface of the desk. "That's it," he breathed as he plopped himself into the old desk chair and wheeled it away so we could approach the box.

"Are you all right?" Alison asked as she moved over to Josiah's side.

"Yeah, I'll be fine," Josiah said, waving her off. "Too many years of cigarettes, that's all."

"Are you sure?" I asked. It wouldn't do to have another Holland die in the middle of this sad, crazy story.

"Yeah, yeah," Josiah grumped with just a hint of gratefulness lacing his tone. "Go check out your box."

I looked at Alison, who nodded. She'd keep an eye on Josiah for me. So I turned to the desk and examined the box. It was a 24" x 24" x 24" cube, very plain, very old-looking, very standard. No distinguishing marks, apart from the name "HOLLAND" written neatly in black marker on all four sides and the top, which was sealed with box tape.

I pulled out my swiss army knife intending to slice open the top, but when I touched the tape, the tape just came away as if it had barely been hanging on by the skin of its teeth. Probably due to how long it had been sitting, I figured. I put my knife away and peeled the now useless tape from the box. The cardboard itself had also aged, and felt somewhat weak and not very sturdy or rigid. But it had held together for so many years, and for that I was grateful. Who knows, if it had fallen apart Josiah might have just chucked everything in the trash and been done with it.

Opening the lid, I found loosely crumpled wads of old, crumbly newspapers filling the empty space at the top. Well, I say "empty space" but obviously since there were newspapers there it wasn't "empty" per se, but I was referring to the portion of the box not taken up by any of the personal effects of the late Joseph Holland. I started tossing the crinkly crumpled papers away, but Alison started picking it all up, opening the pages and smoothing them out, arranging them neatly.

I paused and looked at Alison, quirking an eyebrow.

"What?" Alison said. "I'm just seeing if I can reconstruct a whole newspaper with these.

Josiah and I looked at each other.

"So I'm a bit OCD," Alison grumped defensively, "so sue me."

I chuckled. Josiah shrugged.

Turning back to the box, I finally cleared out all the filler paper and reached the actual items. Some were wrapped in additional newspaper sheets, which I dutifully passed to Alilson. Most of Joseph Holland's personal items turned out to be standard office supply items, albeit in somewhat larger, chunkier 50s or 60s style. Pens and pencils, a heavy stapler (not a red Swingline), an even heavier Scotch tape dispenser still holding some tape, a box of staples, a pencil case, a real live plastic pocket protector (nerd!), scissors, paper clilps, a slide rule, and so on. There was also a compact weekly desk calendar, which I handed to Alison. "See if there's anything in there," I told her. I didn't really think there'd be anything useful in Holland's calendar, since he'd died only a few weeks into the new year, plus the fact that the police had had it before turning it back over to the newspaper. I continued with the box, finding a small, expensive-looking wooden humidor, which Josiah asked for as soon as he saw me lift it from the box.

"I remember this on his desk at work," Josiah said quietly as he gently opened the lid. There appeared to be only cigars inside, no clues or leads. But to Josiah it was apparently very significant, judging by how his eyes misted over as he stared into the box.

At the bottom of the collection of personal effects in the box I found a portable tape recorder. Now, when I say "portable" in this instance, I mean portable in terms of late 1960s technology. It was actually fairly large, much larger than today's mini-tape recorders, with big almost piano-key-like buttons on one end, and empty spindles for tape reals above the complex of tape heads and mechanisms. Attached to the unit was a long, sturdy-looking leather shoulder strap.

"Dad's tape recorder," Josiah breathed as I examined the device. "I remember that, too."

Also in the box were a couple of empty plastic tape reels and an old-fashioned microphone which looked very much like the one that Johnny Carson used to have on his desk on *The Tonight Show*, back when *The Tonight Show* used to actually be good. The microphone cord ended in a large jack that looked exactly the right size to plug into the receptacle on the side of Holland's recorder. There did not appear to be any reels with audiotape in the box.

Only one item remained at the very bottom of the box. It was a small plastic container with an opaque frosted lid. Opening the container, I found inside a collection of neatly arranged spools of various colored threads on little spindles on one half, and some small covered compartments on the other half, containing needles, pins, buttons, and small swatches of fabric.

"Dad's old emergency sewing kit," Josiah said, a little smile lightening his features a bit.

"Oh, yeah," I said, remembering, "Betty mentioned him sewing something for her."

"Betty?" Josiah said. "Betty Reynolds? She's still at the *Daily*

Record?"

"In charge of the Archives there, in fact," I said. "She said to tell you she and some others still at the paper still think of you."

Josiah sat back in his chair, his hands wrapped around the humimdor. "She... she remembers me?"

I nodded. "She sure does," I said. "And very fondly, too, I think."

Josiah shook his head. "I can't believe it. Sweet little Betty Reynolds, after all these years."

"I can give you the phone number for the newspaper if you want," I said with a quick wink at Alison.

Then Josiah's face, which had briefly brightened at the mention of Betty, clouded over once more. "No, thank you," Josiah murmured, shifting in his chair and shooting a glance over at the framed photo I'd noticed earlier. Almost a guilty look, I thought.

Presumably to nudge us from the current side track we'd gotten onto, and the somewhat awkward situation, Alison set the calendar she'd been going through down on the desk among the other items from the box. "Well," she said, "there's nothing in this that's of any relevance, as far as I can tell."

"I figured it was probably a long shot," I said. I hoped we could discuss Betty, and Josiah's obvious interest in a long-lost friend in a bit. For now, though, we were back at the frustrating task in hand. I looked one last time at the sewing kit in my hands before closing its lid.

Then I opened it again, as something had struck me as... off. Something wasn't quite right. A quick scan of the kit's contents and I had it. One of the spools of thread was significantly more full than any of the others. I plucked the odd spool off of its spindle and held it up before me. The thread was wound around the core right up to the outer edge of the metallic little round TIE-Fighter-like holder. The other spools were only about half as full, some even much less than that.

"What is it?" Alison asked, moving closer to my side to look at the spool with me.

"I think..." I hesitated to actually say it out loud, but, "I think we might have something here."

"What?" Josiah said from his chair.

"There is just too much thread on this spool as compared to all the others," I explained, "especially considering this is black thread and I'd almost bet it would be used much more often than any other color in this kit."

"Could be a new spool," Alison suggested.

"I don't think so," I said, shaking my head.

Alison peered at the other spools in the kit, seeing the same thing I had noticed. None of the spools had anywhere near as much thread as the black.

Taking a deep breath, knowing that somehow this could be the clue that gave us the break in the case we so desperately needed, and also perhaps subconsciously knowing what I was about to find, I tugged the end of the black thread from the tiny notch in the rim of the spool holder and began pulling. In a short time, all of the black thread was gone, revealilng—

"It's audiotape!" Alison said in an awed voice.

It was indeed, a length of clear leader and beyond that black-brownish audiotape was wound around the inner core of the spool. It appeared to be in good shape, from what I could see, which could be possible, considering it had been protected from the elements by layers of black thread, the sewing case itself, and having been sealed up (well, mostly) in a box for over forty years.

Josiah wheeled his chair over to take a look for himself. "Why is there audiotape on a spool of thread?"

I hesitated. But again, I felt Josiah deserved the truth. "We think this might be the missing segment of audio from your father's interview with Boris Karloff."

Josiah frowned. "What? I don't understand."

Briefly I told Josiah about the abrupt end of the published version of the interview, and how the original audiotape was cut short, in this case quite literally.

As I spoke, I began to wind the tape, starting with the still present leader from the end of the tape, onto one of the empty reels that had been in Holland's box.

"And we think there is probably something on this tape that will explain your father's actions during his final days," I said as I finished winding the tape onto the reel.

"That means..." Josiah began. He swallowed, then continued, "...

Maybe we'll know who killed Dad and why."

"We can't be sure of that, but I sure hope so," I said as I picked up the portable tape recorder.

Josiah looked from the tape to me. "Do you think it's that Broderick whatever you mentioned before?"

"It's possible he comes into play here somehow," I said evenly. I didn't want to give away too much just yet, nor did I want Josiah jumping to conclusions or getting his hopes up. I noticed Alison giving me a "May I?" eyebrow lift. I nodded, trusting her to be careful with her explanations.

"Josiah," Alison said, and the old man swiveled in his chair to face her, still keeping an eye on what I was doing as I continued to get the audiotape segment ready to play. "Broderick Carlsen was a bad man, a criminal from… back in the day. The police caught him after a burglary went bad and he… escaped. We think he hid out in the hills behind the Hollywood City Dump for a while, and we think he may have been the man who… who killed your father." She looked at me with a "How'd I do?" look, which of course was very distinct from her "May I?" look from earlier. I smiled and nodded. She'd done an admirable job of telling Josiah the essentials of Carlsen's story without going into the more, shall we say, unusual aspects of the tale.

"But why?" Josiah said. "He was just a newspaper reporter."

"We're not sure yet," Alison said. "We're hoping this tape may explain things. It might just boil down to a case of being in the wrong place at the wrong time."

"How did you connect this Carlsen guy to my dad's murder?"

Again Alison looked at me, this time giving me a "Your turn" look.

"Well," I began as I had Alison get the iPad's audio recording app ready, "it's sort of complicated. Like Alison said, we're hoping this tape will clear it up." By that point, I had the audio all set to go in the portable tape deck. I'd had a bit of a problem making a makeshift length of leader to attach to the neatly sliced end of the recording material so we wouldn't miss any of the contents of the tape, but eventually everything was good to go. I looked at Alison. (I looked at her a lot, if you can't tell. She was nice to look at.) Alison pursed her lips and nodded. Then I looked at Josiah. "Josiah, hearing this may be difficult for you. If you'd rather —"

"Oh, just shut up and play the damn thing already," Josiah

growled.

I nodded at Alison, she tapped the "record" button on my iPad, then I reached out and pressed "play" on the old tape deck.

CHAPTER SIXTEEN

Revelation

JOSEPH HOLLAND: -haps we could turn to your time working on the *Frankenstein* films.

BORIS KARLOFF: Of course.

HOLLAND: What was your first impression of the makeup you were to wear as the Monster?

KARLOFF: I was quite impressed just from the initial sketches by Jack Piece, makeup artiste extraordinaire. Even the unfinished makeup we used for the screen tests was very striking. Unfortunately when they put on the full, final makeup on the first day of filming, I had a severe allergic reaction!

HOLLAND: Really?

KARLOFF: Oh, my, yes! I forget what exactly it was in the mixture for the makeup that I reacted to, but it was strong enough that I was rushed to hospital.

HOLLAND: How long did that delay filming?

KARLOFF: Two days, I think, I'm not entirely sure.

HOLLAND: Well, fortunately you recovered, and quickly, too, it seems.

KARLOFF: Oh, no, I was in hospital about two weeks.

HOLLAND: So they just shot around you while you were gone?

KARLOFF: No, they used —

[Brief silence]

HOLLAND: What did they use?

[Another silence]

HOLLAND: Mr. Karloff?

KARLOFF: [sighs] Well, shit. I guess everyone's dead and buried now, what does it matter anymore?

HOLLAND: What do you mean?

KARLOFF: They used a double on the first picture. I never shot a frame on the original picture myself.

HOLLAND: But… it's you. I've seen the film, we've all seen the film. It's you, it looks exactly like you, in Frankenstein makeup.

KARLOFF: The director, James Whale, had another person brought in and altered to look like me as the Monster.

HOLLAND: And this other person didn't have the same allergic reaction to the makeup as you did?

KARLOFF: Oh, they didn't use makeup on him.

HOLLAND: What?

KARLOFF: They had a surgeon physically alter his head and his face to look like me in the full Monster makeup.

HOLLAND: You mean they actually found someone to voluntarily agree to such drastic surgery? For a movie?

KARLOFF: Well, it's my understanding that the person in question didn't actually have a say in the matter.

HOLLAND: They *forced* him to have the surgery?

KARLOFF: Not exactly. When I said he had no say in the matter, I mean he literally had no say. He couldn't speak. He was dead.

[Silence]

HOLLAND: I don't… OK, maybe we should back up a bit here. So. First day of filming on *Frankenstein* you have an allergic reaction to the makeup.

KARLOFF: Yes.

HOLLAND: And it was such a severe reaction that you had to go to the hospital. For two weeks.

KARLOFF: Correct.

HOLLAND: And then…

KARLOFF: Then the director and one of the heads of the studio,

Carl Laemmle, Jr., came to see me. They kicked all the doctors and nurses out of my room and told me their plan. They'd spent too much money on the film by that point to lose me, like when they'd previously had to let Bela Lugosi go when they hired Mr. Whale as the new director. And they'd promoted Lugosi heavily as the Monster and then replaced him. They felt that it that happened again the public would think the picture was cursed and it would be a box office disaster. You see? They had too much money wrapped up in it already. And the filming dates were locked in, the release date of the picture was locked in. So they came up with an idea. They would find a body, make it look like me as the Monster, and pass it off as Karloff playing the Monster. They even had a rather naughty wink-to-the-audience in the opening credits of the picture, where they listed the person playing the Monster as just a question mark. Of course, their new plan meant that they would have to bring that replacement body back to life. But they had a plan for that, too.

HOLLAND: What? I don't — How on earth did they think they could accomplish *that*?

KARLOFF: Mr. Whale and Mr. Laemmle knew so many people. They found an electrical engineer who agreed to get Mr. Strickfaden's fantastic electrical props hooked up with some additional components in such a way that, once the setup received an electrical burst from a bolt of lightning, it would do just what they wanted: bring a dead man back to life. A lightning rod on top of the soundstage where the laboratory set was built was the last bit they installed. This was all done very quickly. All they needed once it was ready was a thunderstorm. Which they got I think only two days later after I went in hospital. Mr. Whale brought on a doctor he knew from somewhere or other to alter the body to look like I did in the photos taken during the screen tests and makeup tests. Then they were ready to bring him back to life.

HOLLAND: Wait a minute, you had makeup tests before filming started?

KARLOFF: Of course. But the makeup used in the tests wasn't the final formula they used for the actual filming makeup.

HOLLAND: Couldn't they just use *that* makeup, the test makeup, instead of going to all this trouble?

KARLOFF: You would think so, wouldn't you? Well, I was in no condition to come back to film in the timeframe of their locked shooting schedule. And to use that makeup on anyone else, it just wouldn't look right, would it? It would look nothing like me.

HOLLAND: I guess, but... I don't... How on earth did they think they could accomplish bringing someone back to life?

KARLOFF: Everything and everyone were kept separate, and only a very, very few knew the whole plan and its ultimate purpose. And, of course, most men are corruptible if you just find the right amount of hush money.

HOLLAND: Who else knew the whole plan?

KARLOFF: Apart from myself, Mr. Whale, and Mr. Laemmle, I believe it was just Colin Clive, Dwight Frye, and Edward Van Sloan. They needed to be told because they were the ones who were to be directly involved in the actual process during the filming of the resurrection scene. They had to be aware of what was really going on.

HOLLAND: And... and it actually worked?

KARLOFF: You saw the picture, you saw it happen. Everyone did. But no one really knew the truth except us few. The resurrection of, I think his name was Broderick Coleman? No, Carlsen, I think that was it, Broderick Carlsen, I believe that was the poor man's name. His rebirth was filmed and shown to the unwitting general public. Those first twitches and movements you see, that is Mr. Coleman's actual resurrection, his first initial stirrings upon being brought back to life. And do you remember that line Henry Frankenstein says when he sees his creation come to life? "Now I know what it feels like to *be* God!" That was not in the script. That was poor Colin Clive letting things get to his head. It wasn't just for religious considerations that that specific line ended up being cut from the picture.

HOLLAND: This is... It's all just... so unbelievable.

KARLOFF: Unbelievable and yet quite true, all too true, I assure you. And with everything being so tightly scheduled, so many contracts and bookings and rentals had been signed, they couldn't push the filming back. It would have been disastrous to them. Disastrous. When I did get better, I was smuggled onto the set in disguise to see how things were going. I had to admit, Mr. Carlsen was quite good. Obviously he didn't really understand all that was happening to him. What you see on the screen is very much him dealing with what he was going through after being brought back to life. Confusion, anger at times, quite pliant at other times. Mr. Whale explained it all away to the rest of the cast and crew as being a result of my staying in character the entire time. Apparently they believed him. Now, I'm not sure if that's a compliment or not, but I like to think it was, in a way. Anyway, it basically worked like this: Mr. Whale told Mr. Coleman, I mean Carlsen, what to do before they filmed a scene, and Mr. Carlsen did as he was told. Usually. He did get carried away once in a while, like in the scene with the little girl. When they ran out of flowers to throw in the water, Mr. Carlsen tossed the girl in the water. That was not quite how it was supposed to go. They cut that from the picture, too, didn't they? I can't quite remember now.

HOLLAND: The girl was OK, though, wasn't she?

KARLOFF: Oh, yes, fine, just shaken up. Scared, of course, but physically unharmed. It did upset Mr. Whale quite a bit. He started losing faith in Mr. Carlsen, and kept on even tighter hold on him after that. And he started trying to figure out how to get rid of Mr. Carlsen once they no longer needed him for filming.

HOLLAND: Get rid of him?

KARLOFF: Yes. Apparently Mr. Whale didn't have the stomach to try to return Mr. Carlsen to his former undead state outright. Funny, that. He had no qualms about bringing life back to him but he couldn't bring himself to take that life away again. At least not directly. So when the Monster's scenes were all finished, Mr. Whale cleared the set. He put Mr. Carlsen in the collapsing windmill set and had the whole thing brought crashing down around Mr. Carlsen. When that didn't kill the poor man, he had Mr. Carlsen packed up and sealed in a giant steel box and had him hauled away to the rubbish dump along with the rest of the debris from the windmill set.

HOLLAND: Good God.

KARLOFF: And everyone that knew the truth about Mr. Carlsen agreed to pretend that none of it ever happened, and that I was present for every day of filming.

HOLLAND: How? Why? I almost can't believe no one ever talked.

KARLOFF: Well, only a few of us actually knew the full story. And I think, once the filming had been completed, I think we all deeply regretted our parts in the whole sorry situation. I know I certainly did. And I still do. Mr. Whale and Mr. Laemmle kept silent to protect their careers. As did the other actors who knew, though as I said the guilt of their complicity ate at them. They would visit me or phone me occasionally, commiserating with me. They were never the same after that picture, and in fact they each passed away not long after the first *Frankenstein* film was released. Poor Dwight Frye had a particularly hard time before he was gone, much too early, the poor fellow. Such a shame. He was such an excellent actor, and a very kind person. I know that Mr. Whale, for the rest of his life, truly and deeply regretted his part in meddling with life or death. He felt it was an additional sin for which he was paying penance. Mr. Laemmle, well, I never spoke much to him afterwards, so I don't know what his true feelings were. But he certainly never shared the secret with anyone, so far as I am aware. The engineer who wired everything together to make it work, I believe he was paid off, never spoke of it again, just as we'd all agreed. He'd also assisted in the dismantling and destruction of the laboratory set once all of its scenes had been completed, to prevent anything like what we had done to happen again.

HOLLAND: And what about you? Why did you keep silent for so long?

KARLOFF: [Deep sigh, followed by a brief coughing spell] I do apologize for that. Thank you, I'm all right. As for me... I would like to think I was merely frightened into remaining silent... Frightened of what had happened, frightened of what might happen if the truth came out. But I think I must admit to being somewhat motivated by vanity.

HOLLAND: Vanity?

KARLOFF: Yes. My career really took off after *Frankenstein*, of course. I basked in the glowing reviews I received. Or, rather, that Broderick Carlsen received. I parlayed that into a successful career, including the two *Frankenstein* sequels in which I did actually play the Monster, further other Universal films, and a whole host of other pictures, some good, some bad, some successful, some not. I had convinced myself I'd earned it. But I hadn't. Not really. A part of me knew that, but sinful nature afflicts me as it does everyone else, so I ignored my conscience. Well, at least as much as I could. And, like everyone else who knew what we'd done, I was ashamed. Greatly ashamed.

HOLLAND: My God.

KARLOFF: And so, here I am, confessing my sins. I've kept quiet long enough, damn it. I know I won't be around much longer, so I might as well speak while I have the chance and go to my rest with at least a little bit of, well, let's call it peace.

HOLLAND: I can't… I mean, this is just so… so unbelievable.

KARLOFF: But it's all true, every word of it. I don't have any proof, I admit, and like I said everyone else who knew is gone now. But it all happened just as I described it to you.

HOLLAND: There is no way I can publish this without *something* to corroborate it.

KARLOFF: That is up to you. I wish I had something to offer you on that score, but alas I do not. All I can suggest is, dig. Look. Search. Find out what you can, if you can.

HOLLAND: Where? Where do I look? And what do I look for?

KARLOFF: Anywhere, anything. I don't know what's out there. I don't know what might still be around. I'm sure someone with your journalistic prowess can manage to uncover something.

HOLLAND: Well, thank you, but…

KARLOFF: I am sorry I have passed the burden of this dreadful story on to you. I know it won't be easy carrying the truth around with you. Believe me, I know. But if you can find proof, you can tell the world what truly happened in 1931. And then, maybe, the world will learn it truly should not meddle in the realm of God. Or nature. Or whatever one chooses to believe in. If you print this story without proof, the public might just pass the story off as the ravings of a senile old man on his deathbed. That's probably what I would think. Except for the fact that I was there. I was part of it. And I wish to God that I hadn't been. Or don't print anything about it at all. Keep the story buried, like it has been all these years. It's all quite up to you. Perhaps I truly am mad, and these are just the insane ramblings of a tired, old man who knows his time on this world is nearly up. Perhaps convincing yourself of that can ease your conscience, at least somewhat.

HOLLAND: I think… I think I believe you. Dear Lord, but I believe you. Am I sane?

KARLOFF: I believe so.

HOLLAND: I'll do whatever I can to find… something. Anything.

KARLOFF: Then I wish you all the luck in the world. I am sorry. I am so sorry you had to be the one to learn the story. But I do wish you luck, in whatever you choose to do with this.

[Brief silence]

HOLLAND: [Shakily] Mr. Karloff, thank you very much for... giving your time to the *Daily Record*.

KARLOFF: Thank you, sir. God go with you.

CHAPTER SEVENTEEN

Human Nature

The tape ran on silently for another minute. When it finally ran out, it stopped the machine, and Alison tapped "stop" on the iPad.

All three of us were quiet for some time, stunned expressions on our faces, none of us daring to move, none of us quite willing to break our shocked silence. Finally I looked down at Josiah. He was staring at nothing in particular. "Are you all right?" I asked him.

Josiah didn't move, didn't respond.

Alison put away my iPad and crouched down beside Josiah. "Are you OK, Josiah?" she asked gently as she touched his arm.

Josiah stirred at the contact. "What?" he said, blinking. "Oh. Oh, yes, I'm fine." He smiled wearily. "Just a bit shocked, you know. Hearing my dad's voice like that after so many years. I'd forgotten what his voice sounded like, can you imagine that? Forgetting the sound of your own father's voice."

Yeah, *that* was the shocking part of what we'd just heard, I thought wryly to myself. Then I scolded myself for such an insensitive thought. But at that point I just wanted to get out of there and deal with what we'd just learned. I looked over at Alison, who looked back at me as she stood up. I nodded my head toward the doorway and gave her a "We should get going" look.

"Josiah," Alison said, "we're going to get to work on this now. We can call you when we've developed anything further. Would that be OK?"

Josiah smiled at us both, pushing himself up out of the chair. "Oh, yes, I imagine you have a lot of work, you two. Don't worry about me."

"Are you absolutely sure?" Alison asked.

"Absolutely," Josiah said, guiding us back to the front door of his home. "I know the work of a newspaperman — or woman — is very difficult. But please do keep in touch."

I smiled appreciatively. "Thank you so much, Josiah. I can't begin to tell you how helpful you've been."

As Alison and I walked back to the car in the fallen dark of the evening, I kept looking back to see Josiah still standing in his doorway, watching us silently.

"Maybe we shouldn't have left so quickly like that," Alison said as we got in the car. "He seems a bit… out of sorts."

"Wouldn't you be," I said, "if you'd just heard your father's voice forty years after he'd died?"

"I suppose so," Alison said a bit uncertainly as she started the car. "But it was almost like he didn't even hear all the things Karloff said."

"Well, that's probably part of it, too."

"Yeah," Alison said. "So maybe we should have stayed to make sure he's actually OK."

I shook my head. "I'm sure he'll be fine. He just needs to take some time to process it all."

"That makes two of us," Alison muttered uneasily.

"Make that three," I said, waving to Josiah as we drove off.

***

We drove back towards downtown and checked into the hotel we'd booked earlier in the day on our drive north. After dropping our luggage off in our room (upper floor, non-smoking, two queen beds, very nice and clean) we went around the block to a small Italian restaurant. I went for the traditional spaghetti (or as the lovely chef Giada De Laurentiis says, "spah-gee-tee") and meatballs, while Alison was more adventurous and ordered something I couldn't even pronounce correctly, but which smelled delicious.

Neither of us spoke much during the meal. I know I was feeling overwhelmed by the revelations we'd heard a short time earlier, and I was struggling to comprehend and accept it all. I figured Alison was having similar difficulties in processing the craziness we'd been confronted with.

Neither of us had the courage to broach the awkward subject until we'd gotten back to our hotel room and were sitting across a small glass end table from each other in matching easy chairs.

Finally, after quite a while of silence in the room, I said, "Holy shit."

"I know, right?" Alison said, suddenly galvanized into action by my plain statement.

"Can you believe it?" I went on. "They used Broderick Carlsen for their own selfish purposes. For a movie. A *movie*!"

"Mind-blowing," Alison said.

"And then they literally just threw him away with the rest of the garbage when they were done with him. I mean, how can you treat a human being like that?"

"Horrible."

"And covered the whole damn thing up for years."

Alison was quiet, then said, "And…?" in a very leading way.

I looked at her. "And what?"

Alison threw her arms up and said, "Really? Are you maybe overlooking something? Like one very large thing?"

I shook my head. "I don't think so, but maybe I am?"

Alison stared at me, then reached across to give me a whap on the back of my head like she was Gibbs and I was DiNozzo and we were in an episode of *NCIS*. Then she said, very deliberately. "They brought a dead man. Back. To. Life."

"Oh, that," I said quickly, "well, that's obvious, isn't it? I mean, it goes without saying." Gee, nice cover, Roger. But Alison had not been far from the truth. I had sort of let that huge fact slip to the back of my mind, probably because I was afraid to think about it too much, afraid to consider the ramifications. And maybe also because it still seemed too fantastic to be true.

"Riiiiiight," Alison said, clearly not entirely believing me.

"So, now what?" I said, only partly hoping to shift the conversation.

"You're the reporter, Woodward or Bernstein," Alison said with a smirk, "you tell me."

"Nice timely reference," I teased, relieved we were starting to feel a bit more relaxed again, a bit more like ourselves, enough to banter a bit again. "You couldn't decide on which name to use?"

"Well, I never remember who was who," Alison confessed sheepishly.

"I always considered myself more of a Robert Redford type than a Dustin Hoffman type, so I'd say Woodward."

Alison looked me up and down. "Yeah, I think I could see that," she said with a twinkle in her eye.

"But getting back to business," I said seriously.

"Where do we go from here?" Alison said. "Am I still driving you back home tomorrow?"

"I think we need to go back to LA," I said.

"Really?"

"Yeah. I want to take another look at those files at Universal, now that I know more of the story, I'm sure I can find some relevant evidence now."

"Are you sure?" Alison said. "I mean, you were pretty adamant about not making my boss suspicious of me. Won't this be extremely risky, sneaking you in *again*?"

"Maybe," I said. "But if we're going to get this story figured out and get it published, we're gonna need solid proof. Because no one is going to believe this crazy story just based on Boris Karloff's say-so. He knew that, too. People will think he was just an old, senile lunatic like he said."

"I see your point," Alison said. "But we'll have to wait until Monday, I can't get us back in the Archives on the weekend without really raising suspicions."

"That's fine," I said. "I have a feeling it'll be a long drive tomorrow anyway."

Alison sighed. "I was really looking forward to seeing your home, though," she said quietly.

"We'll get there," I said, not really sure how or when that might happen. In the meantime, little inklings of doubt started running through my brain. If I did end up publishing this story, I wondered, even with corroboration and proof, would anyone seriously believe it? And then I wondered, should I even publish it at all, even if I did get my proof? Did the world really need to know what had happened? Was it my responsibility to reveal that secret which had been concealed from the world for eighty years?

Alison must have noticed my unspoken inner turmoil. She reached over and grasped my hand. "Hey," she said, giving me a smile, "we'll figure this out. We don't have to come up with all the answers in just one night. OK?"

I smiled tiredly back. "OK. Thank you." I stood up and went to the bedside table between the two beds to plug in my iPad and my phone. "So," I said, "which bed do you want to take?"

Alison got out of her chair and shrugged. "Which one do you want?"

I shrugged back. "I'll take this one," I said, nodding at the one with the better view of the TV.

Alison looked at me. "I want that one, too," she said quietly.

"All right," I said, "I'll take the other one, then."

"Then I want that one, too," Alison replied, not taking her eyes from me.

"Look," I said, "I really don't care which one I get, whichever one you want, I'll take the other one."

Alison moved towards me, shaking her head slowly. "What was that award you said you won, anyway, 'Most Oblivious Reporter'?"

"What do you mean?" I said, confused. Maybe I was just tired from the long day, but she wasn't making any sense to me just then.

Placing her hands on my chest, Alison pushed me very firmly down onto one of the beds. "They're both big enough for two," she whispered as she leaned down towards me.

She was quite right.

***

Our departure the next morning was somewhat later than we'd originally planned. And that was all right. We'd earned our little sleeping-in reward. Eventually, however, we did get up, get ourselves ready, packed, checked out, and headed for Alison's car. Soon we were back on the road, with Alison at the wheel, heading south out of San Francisco on the more scenic Pacific Coast Highway. With no pressing appointments to speed us on our journey, we took our time and just enjoyed the ride, and enjoyed our time together. We took turns driving, giving the other a chance to relax. The 80s channel was once again our soundtrack, and we enjoyed the gorgeous views of the ocean as we listened to the Pet Shop Boys, Phil Collins, Duran Duran, and such cheesy one-hit wonders like Baltimora's "Tarzan Boy", Peter Schilling's "Major Tom (Coming Home)", and "The Captain of Her Heart" by Double (pronounced "Doo-blay", of course).

It was a beautiful, crisp day, the sun bright overhead and sparkling off the waves of the Pacific, and my traveling companion seeming more beautiful and wonderful than ever. Looking at her, I could almost forget the difficult story I'd been working on for over a week. Almost, but not quite.

During our trek we did do a bit of work, eventually, working on Alison's timeline spreadsheet, slotting in some of the new information as best we could. There were still gaps, but overall the picture was really starting to come together. With that in mind, during my non-driving shifts, I tried to work on the actual article I was intending to publish. I didn't get very far, as I was still feeling it wasn't ready to be put down in black and white just yet. Eventually I just put the article away for another time when I could focus better on it.

Towards the end of our trip, when I happened to look up and see a road sign which mentioned Santa Babrbara, I made an excruciatingly lame reference to the wonderfully goofy TV show *Psych*, a very unfunny reference which I will not inflict upon you here. Alison's reaction to it was probably better than it deserved, but even she knew it was a dumb reference, too.

By the time we reached the outskirts of Los Angeles, the sun had already set. Alison weaved us through the traffic back to her apartment. She unlocked her door and let me in. I hauled my luggage over to the sofa in the living room, while Alison hurried down the short hallway leading from the living room.

The sofa wasn't big, but I figured I could curl up on it comfortably enough. I started arranging the pillows and cushions when Alison returned. She stared at me.

"What are you doing?" she asked, quirking an eyebrow.

"Just adjusting things a bit to make it comfortable for tonight," I said.

Alison threw up her hands. "It *was* 'Most Oblivious Reporter', wasn't it?" she said with mock (at least I thought it was mock) exasperation. She grabbed my hand and dragged me down the hallway and into her bedroom.

"Well, I didn't want to be presumptuous," I said meekly, somewhat embarrassed.

"Forget about it," Alison said with a gorgeous smile. She headed off to the bathroom with a quick "Be right back" over her shoulder.

I sat down gingerly on the edge of the bed. Had Alison retired to the bathroom to, well, use the bathroom? I wondered. Or was she perhaps going to, in the words of Lili Von Shtupp, "slip into something a little bit more… comfortable"? I didn't know. I hoped it was the latter, but I couldn't be sure, so I didn't quite know what to do with myself in the meantime. I glanced around the room. It was nice, comfortable, felt surprisingly spacious for an LA apartment of a non-movie star. A matching set of queen bed, beside table and dresser, a shelving unit, a closet, a curtained window. It was all tastefully done in an elegant, simple white-and-gray theme. My nervous eyes landed back on the beside table. Somehow, as tired as they were, my eyes noted next to the alarm clock a pair of faint, straight lines in the light dust, a longer, thicker line with a shorter, thinner line behind it set off somewhat at an angle. All at once, the reason why Alison had hurried in here after we'd gotten back and before she'd brought me into her bedroom struck me. She'd hidden away a framed photo, the lines in the dust from the bottom edge of the frame and the little kickstand behind it. "Most Oblivious Reporter", my ass, I thought smugly to myself. And then immediately I realized the photo Alison had hidden was probably a picture of her late fiance. A guilty feeling replaced the smug pride.

A sound in the doorway caused me to turn and see — Alison, standing there, wearing nothing but a very clingy, and very revealing pink teddy. She smiled demurely at me as I struggled to lift my jaw from the floor and put my eyeballs back in their sockets. She looked amazing. Yes, I'd just seen her naked the night before, but even so, she was a vision. Like they say, sometimes leaving something to the imagination can be just, if not more exciting as showing everything. Boy, did Alison prove that.

"Wow," I somehow managed to get out.

Alison hurried over to the bed and quickly slipped under the covers. "Sorry," she said, "it's just a little chilly."

I could tell, I thought to myself as I chuckled lightly and stripped down to my boxers and joined Alison under the covers. Alison snuggled right up against me, her right arm across my chest, her right leg hooked around mine.

"Can we just cuddle tonight?" Alison asked quietly. "I just feel so worn out from all the driving this weekend."

"Of course," I said. She handed me her glasses and I set them down gently on the bedside table. Then I wrapped my arm around her as she laid her head on my shoulder.

We just held each other quietly for a time. Her body next to mine felt so wonderful at that moment, so I was content just to hold her. Eventually I broke the silence. "It was for Excellence in Journalism, Small Market."

"Huh?"

"My award," I said. "It was from the Northern California Press Association a few years ago, for a series of articles I did on the troubles the local fishing industry had been dealing with at the time."

"Oh."

"So there," I teased.

"Got it," Alison said.

Comfortable silence returned. A little while later, I broke the quiet once more. "You don't have to hide him from me."

I felt Alison tense slightly. "What?"

"I assume that's who the photo was of," I said.

Alison didn't say anything for a bit. Then she shifted to reach across me, which felt *very* nice, let me tell you, and opened the little drawer of the bedside table. She slid back to my side holding a 4" x 6" photo which she then handed to me.

It was a picture of the two of them, both looking fantastically happy. Alison looked almost exactly the same, her hair perhaps just a bit longer. The blond man next to her was a good few inches taller than her, with a pleasant face, a somewhat receding hairline and a slightly weak chin. He was in his Army dress uniform and stood erect and proud.

"He looks like a good man," I said quietly, truthfully.

"He was," Alison whispered.

And she went on to tell me a bit more about him, and about them. She told me about how she'd met Matthew Calais through a convoluted connection of mutual friends who'd set them up, how they'd fallen for each other not quite immediately but fairly quickly, how they'd gotten engaged just before his deployment to Afghanistan, and how she'd gotten the news he'd been killed. When she'd finished, Alison snuggled a bit closer. "I think maybe me coming on too strong sometimes is a kind of defense mechanism, in a weird way, you know?" she said softly "Like I do it to distract myself from him, or his memory. If I focus all my energy and attention on someone else it pushes the pain away, at least for a little while. So I guess maybe that's why I seem kind of pushy and bold sometimes."

"I get that," I said sympathetically, giving her a gentle hug. "And I think my rather stand-offish, or I guess it's more just not paying attention to such things as potential romantic relationships, is a reaction to my own history, trying to avoid getting hurt again like I had been."

I went on to tell Alison a bit more about my relationship with Sarah, which I felt was only fair in view of how open she'd been about her Matthew. I told her of how we'd met bumping carts in a grocery store (God, how annoyingly cheesy!), the high highs we'd enjoyed, followed by the slippery slope of arguments and resentment, and the way I'd been treated, and how things ultimately led to our final ugly breakup. When I was finished, we lay quietly for a time.

Eventually Alison reached across me again (oh, how wonderful that felt) to put the photo back in the drawer.

"I said you didn't have to hide him," I said gently.

"I know," Alison said as she slid back across me to cuddle up against me once more. "It's just... I think that part of my life is over now."

I didn't know what to say, so I just held her. And that's what we did the rest of the night, just held each other, until we both finally fell asleep.

CHAPTER EIGHTEEN

Hide

The next morning found us performing the old hide-the-investigative-reporter-in-the-trunk-of-the-employee's-car-to-sneak-him-onto-the-lot-he's-been-banned-from trick. We were starting to get pretty good at it. Shortly after eight a.m., I was back in my little screened off chain link cage at the back of the Universal Studios Archive building. Well, temporary building, that is.

Now that I had more of the Broderick Carlsen story filled in, I had a much better idea of what to look for in the boxes of archive material I had before me. It wasn't long before I started to find some relevant items. I found contracts, invoices, check register memos, and various other items I duly imaged with my iPad. I found an invoice for a Dr. Frederick Powell, with the simple description "For services rendered". Plastic surgery services, perhaps? I needed to check that later. Also of note was a contract with Los Angeles Steel Crafters for manufacture and delivery of a large steel box, six feet by six feet by six feet, with supplementary chains and shackles. Since I didn't recall any big steel box on screen in *Frankenstein*, I figured that had to be the box Karloff said Whale had had Carlsen sealed up and taken away in after wrapping Carlsen's scenes. There was also an invoice from Hollywood Waste Haulers for "special pickup and delivery to dump". Disposal of Carlsen in his box, presumably.

It was while I was glancing through James Whale's contract to direct *Frankenstein* that something kicked at me in my brain. There was something about Whale's signature on the contract that scratched at my memory. And then I had it. Or at least I thought I did. I scrolled back through the images on my iPad and finally found—

I jerked my head up as I heard the main door at the far end of the storage area creak open. Footsteps approached, getting nearer and nearer. My heart was pounding until Alison peeked her head round the corner of the shelves which blocked the inside of my cage from view. She smiled as she slipped inside my little workplace, her purse slung over her arm.

"Find anything?" Alison whispered.

"Oh, yes," I said excitedly. "Look at this. This is James Whale's contract to direct the original *Frankenstein*. Look at his signature." I pointed at the scrawl at the bottom of the sheet of paper.

"OK," Alison said.

"Now," I went on, "look at this." I showed her the image I'd just searched for.

"It's the same signature," Alison said. "What's this one?"

"It's the release form from the Los Angeles County Coroner's Office, turning Broderick Carlsen's body over to a representative of the Heavenly Rest Funeral Parlor."

Alison looked at me, then looked back down, comparing the two signatures. "That means… that Whale picked up the body himself!" she breathed.

"It makes sense, doesn't it?" I said, snapping an image of Whale's contract to direct the film. "I don't think he was actually moonlighting as a funeral parlor employee. But this whole 'let's reanimate a dead body for our movie' plan strikes me as a need-to-know kind of thing."

"Yeah," Alison said. "Well, this strikes me as some pretty good corroborating evidence. What else have you found?"

"Well, I—" I broke off and we both froze as we heard the main door to the storage area creak open once again. This time there was the sound of more than one set of footsteps, and the increase in their volume indicated they were headed our way. We crept over to the edge of the racks of boxes screening my cage and peeked out. Approaching us down the long walkway was Mr. Suit, aka Adam, and a stout woman I didn't recall ever seeing before.

As the pair stopped before a storage rack, Alison whispered in my ear. "That's Sonia, my supervisor. They're probably just grabbing a file and should be gone in a minute or so."

I could just make out what Sonia was saying to Mr. Suit, some remark about not knowing why anyone would possibly want to look up something about "Jaws: The Revenge". I silently agreed with her. She pulled out a large box from a shelf near the floor. Mr. Suit just grunted in reply, then took the box from Sonia. As he turned to go, he glanced over in our direction, his eyes sliding past us, and then pausing, narrowing as he stared off to our left.

At the door of my little hiding place, which Alison had left slightly ajar.

"Oh, shit, I'm sorry," Alison barely whispered.

"Never mind that, run!" I hissed at her.

We ran. I grabbed my shoulder bag off the floor, Alison grabbed her purse. I swung open the rear exit, grabbed Alison's hand, and we burst outside into the harsh midday sunlight. We raced to Alison's car. Letting go of Alison's hand I fished out the spare set of keys she'd given me, unlocked the doors, remote started the engine, and headed for the driver's seat.

"I'm driving," I said as we bumped, Alison having assumed she'd be driving her own car.

"But you don't know this area like I do," Alison protested as she nevertheless rerouted to the passenger side.

"Just get in!"

CHAPTER NINETEEN

The Chase

We got in Alison's car. As I shifted into drive, I glanced in the rear view mirror. Mr. Suit was racing towards us. I floored the gas and we peeled away from the pursuing goon.

"Get me out of here," I said. Alison directed me quickly to the main gate. As we crashed through the striped barrier arm, I caught a quick glimpse of Arthur, the kind gatekeeper, staring at us with his mouth agape. Alison gave the old man a sheepish apologetic wave as we went by.

We bounced out onto the main road that passed in front of the main gate, and I swung the car to the right and hit the gas again. When I checked the mirror I saw a black SUV come barreling off the lot and swerving violently to follow us.

"Find us someplace we can lose him!" I barked.

After a quick glance back to see the pursuing SUV, Alison pulled out her phone and brought up its map app. Then she started giving me directions as fast as she could. Left. Right. Right again. Down that alley. Left. Through that intersection then next left. And so on, until I abandoned any thought of trying to keep myself oriented as to where we were. I just let myself be guided by Alison's instructions. Meanwhile the SUV, while still a ways back from us, was slowly but surely making up ground and gaining on us.

Eventually we reached a much more industrialized area of the city. Off in the distance I noted a large railroad area, and the fact that the road we were currently on was paralleling a twin set of railroad tracks.

"Keep going," Alison ordered.

I did as she told me. Soon I spied a train on one of the nearby tracks, far in the distance ahead of us but approaching steadily.

"I've got an idea," I said.

"I'm not gonna like it, am I?" Alison asked.

"It's probably not one of my smartest ideas," I said, "so, no, probably not. Just hold tight."

Keeping an eye on the gaining SUV as well as the approaching train, I tightened my grip on the steering wheel. This could go well, or it could go spectacularly wrong, I thought worriedly to myself. At least they're not shooting at us or anything, I also thought, then tensed in anticipation that I'd just jinxed ourselves. But thankfully no shots came, though I was still worried by the implacable determination of our pursuers.

I drove on, waiting for my moment. Our car and the oncoming train sped steadily closer and closer like a high school math problem. Alison kept checking behind us, ahead of us, down at her phone. I knew she was worried, but I needed to focus. The train loomed larger and larger. The SUV drew closer and closer.

Suddenly I yanked the wheel to the left, and time seemed to slow to a crawl like "bullet time" in a video game. Our rear tires slewed briefly then caught the pavement again and we shot across a railroad crossing, crashing through the lowered barrier arms.

"Too soon, too soon," I heard Alison hiss anxiously.

Safe on the other side of the train tracks, I swung right again and continued to parallel the railroad tracks, this time on the opposite side. I glanced back and saw the SUV had also crossed over the tracks and was now speeding towards us again. I stomped the brakes and swung the steering wheel. The train was nearly upon us. Accelerator to the floor, we shot through the railroad crossing again, this time with seconds to spare as the train sped through the crossing, cutting the SUV off from us.

I took a deep breath but kept driving. Why did people in movies and TV always stop to look back when they did the old cut-them-off-with-a-train schtick? Just keep going, put as much distance between them and you as fast as you can, was my way of thinking.

"No, I didn't like that idea," Alison gasped, collecting herself. "You could've at least warned me."

"Sorry," I said as I sped from the railroad crossing. "I didn't want to lose focus."

Looking out the rear window, Alison said, "I think I can see them driving towards the end of the train."

"Then let's find someplace to hid so we lose them for good," I said.

We both started scanning the area ahead of us, Alison also checking her map. It was even more densely cluttered than the railroad area we'd left behind. Then Alison pointed off to the right. "How about there?"

I looked where she'd pointed. "Yeah," I said, feeling vaguely like Han Solo in *The Empire Strikes Back*. "That'll do nicely."

I turned off the road and swung around to the rear of a large multi-stall automated car wash facility. Once I'd maneuvered the car all the way into one of the stalls, I cut the enging. I hadn't purchsed a car wash, so we were able to just sit inside amongst the apparatus and wait it out. Fortunately it wasn't a very busy day at the car wash, so we were thankfully undisturbed by any customers hoping for a wash.

Once we were parked and quiet, Alison and I looked at each other and heaved huge relieved sighs. The danger, we hoped, was over, for the moment.

"Now what?" Alison asked.

"Now we sit and wait, and hope we lost them," I said. "We'll wait in here long enough to give them time to give up and get out of this area."

"And then?"

I looked at her. "Fancy a trip to Arbor Harbor?"

Alison's eyes lit up. "Are you sure?"

I nodded. "I think I've exhausted pretty much everything I can think of at the moment down here. I doubt we'll be able to get back inside Universal now."

"That's true." Then Alison's face fell. "Oh, God," she breathed. "I've probably lost my job, haven't I? Dammit!" She thumped the passenger side door in frustration. "What the hell do I do now?" She looked at me. "What can I do?"

"I don't know yet," I said, placing a comforting hand on hers and giving a gentle squeeze. "But we'll figure something out, I promise."

"Thanks," Alison said quietly. We sat quietly for a time, just holding onto each other. Then Alison said, "Well, on the bright side, I won't have to pack much for the trip, since I never unpacked from San Fran."

"Honey," I said gently, "I don't think we can go back to your apartment right now."

"Why not?"

"They know where you live. They'll probably have it watched, at the very least. I don't think they'd break in, but I can't be sure. I can't be sure of anything anymore."

"Can we go to the cops?"

"I don't think so," I said. "Not with our crazy story. Maybe if we'd gotten the story published first, perhaps. But right now they'd never believe us."

Alison was quiet for a moment. "Will *they* go to the cops?" she asked eventually.

"Shit, I didn't think of that," I said. "But I doubt it. I don't think they'd take the risk of bringing anyone into this thing, however tangentially, not if they can help it."

Suddenly Alison clutched my arm. "What about your things?" she said worriedly. "At my apartment, what if they do break in and—"

"Hey, it's OK," I said soothingly. "I've got all my work stuff in my shoulder bag right here." I pointed at my bag in the floor well by Alison's feet. "And all I really need is right here next to me." I smiled.

Alison smiled back, then pretended to look around the driver's seat. "Where is it?"

"Stop it," I mock-scolded. "Anyway, the only stuff left at your place is clothes and such."

Alison sighed, nodding. "OK, good."

"And speaking of work," I said, "this would be a good time to go over some of the new info from today. Since we'll just be sitting here for a while yet. Mind handing me my laptop, please?"

"Sure," Alison said, handing it over. Then she reopened the iPad and started studying my most recent images from the morning's search. "Looks like you've got some good stuff here," she said as she scrolled. "Do you think—" She broke off and stared at the screen.

"What?" I said, looking down at the tablet. It was the invoice from Los Angeles Steel Crafters for the big box used to throw Broderick Carlsen away after filming.

"A big box," Alison said, frowning. "Hang on…" She scrolled further back in the photo collection, and eventually stopped, having found what she'd been looking for. It was a photo from the LAPD, from their crime scene photos from Joseph Holland's murder. Specifically, it was a photo of a huge mound of garbage at the north end of the fenced-in area of the Hollywood City Dump. "See it?" Alison said.

I looked. I didn't notice anything. "What am I looking for?" I asked.

Muttering "Most Oblivious Reporter, indeed," Alison zoomed in on the photo, and now I saw it. Fuzzy, but distinct, it was definitely a large-ish shape, with unnaturally straight edges and sides.

"Is that the box?" I said, peering closer at the image. It looked about right, though scale was hard to judge from just the one picture.

"I think so," Alison said. "I thought that box thing sounded vaguely familiar. And look." She zoomed in further. There was a dark area, not quite circular, on the top side of the box. "Think that's how he got out?"

"Sure could be," I said. "Amazing that it was still there after, what, thirty-eight years?"

"Think it's still there now?"

I shook my head. "I doubt it. But I think I'd still like to drop by that dump before we head north."

"Eww," Alison said, crinkling her cute nose.

"We won't stay long, I promise," I said with a grin. "You can even stay in the car if you want. Meanwhile I still want to give that SUV time to get far away from here. Let's keep at it, shall we?"

So we set to work once again, Alison on the iPad, me on my laptop. After shooting me the batch of images from the tablet, she started updating her timeline spreadsheet, while I tried to organize the dozens of images and documents I'd collected over the course of the last week or so, tagging and labeling, setting up folders, and what not. Together we put the investigation in fairly good, yet still rough, order.

Eventually I decided we'd waited long enough. It had been about two hours since we'd pulled into the car wash. "I think it should be safe to head out now," I said.

"Just a second," Alison said as we put away our tech.

"What's wrong?" I asked.

Alison just leaned over towards me, and kissed me smack dab on the lips. Of course, it felt glorious.

"What was that for?" I asked once she pulled back.

Alison gave a tiny laugh. "I'm in a world of shit, but I don't think there's anyone else I'd rather be in it with than you."

"I said you didn't have to get out of the car at the dump."

"Shut up," Alison said with a playful slap on my arm. "You know what I mean."

I backed us out of the stall, then stopped. We looked all around, very carefully, but there was no sign of the black SUV.

"Ready for a trip to the dump?" I asked Alison.

"Such wonderful places you take me," she replied with a wry smile.

***

The place was a dump. Officially, figuratively, and literally. It was an ugly sight, an expanse of garbage surrounded by tall chain-link fencing topped with razor wire. The dump backed up against the wooded foothills where Joseph Holland's body had been found all those years ago.

I drove up to the dump's gated entrance, where a short young man in grubby overalls slouched out of a tiny hut and leaned down as I lowered my car window.

"Resident or non-resident?" the man asked with absolutely zero enthusiasm.

"Press, actually," I replied, proffering my credentials.

The man peered at them. "So, non-resident, then?"

"Well, I guess…"

"Dumping fee for non-residents is—"

"No, no, hold on," I said. "Look, I'm just here on a story, I'm not here to drop off any garbage."

The man's eyes narrowed suspiciously. "What story?"

"I'm looking into the 1969 murder of Joseph Holland."

The man rolled his eyes and heaved a huge sigh, then straightened and shoved his hands in his overall pockets. "Joseph Holland died *outside* the dump," he said mechanically as if learned by rote. "If you care to—"

"No, look," I interrupted again. "I know that. But he did spend some time *inside* the dump before he went up into the hills. So if you could *please* be so kind as to let me in for a short while just to investigate the area, I would be *most* grateful."

The man stared at me. Then he said, "You'll still have to pay the non-resident fee if—"

"Oh, for crying out loud," Alison growled as she leaned over me and thrust her driver's license at the man and shoved some cash at him. "Resident! Let's go, Harry," she said as the man took her money.

The man pocketed the cash and lifted the barrier arm for us, and we drove inside the dump.

"Sheesh!" I grumbled.

"Don't let it get to you," Alison said. "People is people."

I laughed. "I guess so."

I took a right and headed counter-clockwise on the ring road around the massive heaps of garbage. "You know, you didn't have to do that," I said, "I would've convinced him to let us in."

Alison gave me a look that said she wasn't nearly as convinced of that as I was, and said a tad grumpily, "Well, he was getting on my nerves."

The enormous collection of waste on our left was gigantic, at least several football fields in area, climbing to a peak in numerous places of what I estimated to be twenty-or-so feet in height. It was difficult to say for certain, as everything was so jumbled it was hard to get any sense of scale, as with the picture from 1969. When we finally reached the far north end of the dump, I pulled off the road and parked.

Alison and I looked over at the garbage heap. "Well, here we are," I said, "where Joseph Holland spent most of his time inside the fence that day."

I opened the door and got out, as did Alison. We'd barely taken two steps when the smell hit us, and hit us hard. A rotten, putrid stench, the most horrible odor I have ever encountered, assaulted our senses.

"Holy shit, that's awful!" Alison exclaimed, pinching her nose shut.

We quickly got back inside the car. I started the engine to get the air conditioning going, using internal circulation, hoping that would help with the stench.

"I don't see any sign of the box," I said as we stared again at the mass of garbage.

"Me neither," said Alison.

"I think that box is what kept Holland here for so long," I said, "it almost has to be. If he spotted the big steel box that James Whale had crated Broderick Carlsen up in, he probably would have gone over and checked it out. It looked like it was still pretty accessible in the police photos."

"Brave man, to put up with that horrific smell," Alison said with a wrinkled nose.

"Yeah," I said. I sighed. "It would have been nice if it had still been here. More proof for our story." I hadn't consciously used "our" instead of "my", but truth be told I was starting to consider it our story, mine and Alison's. I wondered if she'd picked up my word usage.

Maybe she had, and maybe she'd turned away as I looked at her to hide a blush, for she gazed out her passenger side window. I followed her gaze as she looked up the hillside outside the fence. I couldn't make out the scene of Holland's death, nor could I spot the cave in which Carlsen had presumably been living for some time. All I could see was the hillside, trees, brush, rocks.

"What brought Holland up there, do you suppose?" Alison asked thoughtfully.

"I'm not sure," I said. "Maybe instinct? Maybe he happened to spot Carlsen moving up there? I don't know if we'll ever know for sure." I touched Alison's hand and she looked back at me. "Shall we go take a look up there?" I asked.

She hesitated, then nodded. "OK."

"What is it?" I asked, having noted her reluctance.

"I've never been to the scene of a murder before," she said as I pulled the car back onto the ring road.

"You'll be fine," I said. "It all happened decades ago, anyway."

"I know, it's just… creepy."

"Maybe so," I said. "But I'll be right there beside you."

Once outside the fenced-in dump, we parked in the adjacent parking lot. There were no public access roads back to the hills behind the dump, only a few "authorized vehicles only" paths, and, judging by our reception at the main entrance, I was not enthusiastic about having to deal with more of the same to get authorization to drive there. So we got out and walked.

After only a few steps away from Alison's car, however, I stopped. A sudden thought had struck me. Might we have parked in the very same stall that Joseph Holland had used in 1969? Could that be the exact same spot where Holland left his car, never to return? And might we, too, be on a similar path to destiny, fated never to return to our car from our trek up into the hills?

I shook myself back to my senses. That was silly, I told myself. I knew very well that Broderick Carlsen, Holland's likely killer, was safely tucked away, unconscious in a coma, hours north of where we were at that moment, back in Arbor Harbor. There were no killers awaiting us up in the hills behind the dump, I said to myself.

I caught up with Alison, who had kept on going when I'd paused. Just to check in with the doctor looking after Carlsen, and not, repeat, *not* in any way to reassure myself that anyone might be lurking in a nearby cave, I made a quick call to Sacred Family Hospital in Arbor Harbor and was put through to Dr. Ashraf.

"Hello, Harry," the cheery voice of David Ashraf crackled through the speaker of my phone. "What can I do for you?"

"Oh," I said casually, "just checking in on the status of your patient."

"The John Doe."

"That's the one."

"No change whatsoever. Vitals have remained consistent and steady. He has not regained consciousness. Basically he's the same as the last time you saw him."

"You sure?"

"Absolutely. Just checked in on him myself less than an hour ago."

"OK, thanks, Doctor," I said.

After I hung up, we continued walking. After a moment, Alison asked, "What was that about?"

"What was what about?" I said.

"That phone call."

"Oh, that." I shrugged. "Just checking in on Carlsen."

"Uh-huh," Alison said. "Because…"

I looked at her and knew I wouldn't be able to bluff my way through. I sighed. "I had a stupid thought. What if what happened to Holland happened to us?"

"Oh," Alison said. "I get that. But we really don't have to be afraid of that."

"I know, it was just something silly that struck me at the moment. Forget about it."

"Hey," Alison said with a smile as she linked her arm in mine was we walked, "I thought *I* was supposed to be the worrywart here."

I laughed, and felt a trillion times better.

We kept trudging on.

By the time we reached the scene of the crime up in the hills, the noises from the dump had faded. A hush was over the small clearing we were in, a hush that reminded me of my visit to the Vietnam Memorial Wall, years ago on a high school summer marching band trip to Washington, D.C. The memory of that had stayed with me ever since. Commemorating a tragedy, it felt as though such casual noise as human speech would befoul the sacredness and solemnity of the place.

I stood quietly and oriented myself. Over there was the bean-bag-shaped and -sized stone next to which Joseph Holland's body had been found. Behind that bush over there was the narrow entrance to the cave in which police presumed the killer had been living.

I looked at Alison, but she shook her head. I crawled through the small cave entrance alone, then took the quick sharp left into the main chamber. It was definitely small and cramped, but one could sense that a person could manage to survive in that place. The light from my phone showed nothing but the rock and hard-packed earth, no piles of animal remains, no prints or marks, no evidence that anyone had, indeed, spent any time there, be it hours, days, weeks, months, or even years, as I presumed was the case with Broderick Carlsen. It was almost like even the animals in the woods knew something unnatural had been in here, and avoided it.

I did not enjoy being in that cave, even for the scant few minutes I spent inside. Even without any tangible, physical proof Carlsen had been there, I knew he'd been there. I *knew* it. Just as I knew he'd killed Holland. For what reason he'd killed the reporter, I still did not know. The cave held no helpful clues in that direction.

Why had I come here, then? I asked myself in the tight confines of the cave. Following up any and all leads in a story, of course, I responded to myself. A crime connected to the tale I was unraveling had occured up here and I had a duty to check the place out.

Why had *Carlsen* come here? I also asked myself. And again, I didn't have a good answer.

The creepiness of the cave started to get to me, and I quickly scrambled through the narrow opening back into open air and the welcome company of Alison. She smiled at me as I stood up, brushed myself down, and went over to her. She didn't say anything, and neither did I. But together we turned and headed back down the hillside.

We got back into Alison's car, with Alison at the wheel this time at her insistence. As she stared the engine, she asked me, "Was there anything up there?"

I shook my head. "No," I said wearily. "I'd hoped that maybe there would have been some sort of clue or evidence left behind to positively place Carlsen at the scene of the Holland murder. But there was nothing."

"I'm sorry," Alison said quietly as she drove us away from the dump and the nearby hillside.

Shrugging, I said, "It's OK. I think there's nothing left for me to look into here in LA anymore, now that we can't get back into Universal." I looked over at Alison. "Ready to head up to Arbor Harbor?"

"Uh-uh," Alison said firmly.

"What?" I said. "Why not?"

"We just came from a huge garbage dump," Alison said. "I'm not going to be stuck inside this car with this stink for God knows how many hours. I want a shower first, and I'm gonna need fresh clothes, too."

"I still don't think we can go back to your apartment."

"I know," Alison said. "But there's somewhere else we can stop."

***

Freshly showered and wearing a new set of nice, clean, slightly baggy clothes, I sat across the kitchen table from Melissa Gorman, Alison's older sister, her steady gaze making me shift a bit uncomfortably in the hard wooden chair. Alison was in the shower at the moment, having insisted I go first, as I'd been the one who'd been "on hands and knees crawling around a lousy cave", as she'd put it. The shower had felt wonderful, and the jeans and t-shirt which belonged to Melissa's husband Tom had been laid out for me on the bathroom's wicker laundry hamper.

Melissa looked quite a bit like her younger sister, though her hair was more brown than black, and she wore it longer than Alison. She didn't wear glasses, and there was a distinct, Kirk Douglas-y dimple on her chin. Apart from these slight differences, they were very much alike in appearance.

Also, Alison didn't usually glare at me like Melissa was doing at the moment. At least, not in the cool, appraising manner I was currently being subjected to. Which was understandable, in the circumstances, I supposed. I doubted Alison was in the habit of dropping by her sister's place unannounced, smelling of garbage, with a strange man in tow and needing showers and changes of clothes. At least, I sure hoped she wasn't in the habit of doing that.

"So," I said, smiling politely, "what line of work are you and your husband in?"

Melissa waited a moment before speaking. "I'm Director of Marketing at a local fashion house. Tom is a computer programmer for a videogame company."

"Wow," I said, "very nice."

Melissa did not reply.

"I'm a journalist," I said to fill the silence, not quite sure why I felt somewhat embarrassed by saying that.

"So Aly said," Melissa replied evenly.

"Oh, OK," I said. "Um… How much did she tell you while I was in the shower?"

"Enough," Melissa said coolly. "She's helping you on a big important story. Then you got in trouble and now she's lost her job because of you."

Ouch. I nodded slowly. "Basically correct," I admitted.

Melissa's eyes bored into me as she leaned forward in her chair. "I know I don't know you," she said quietly but quite firmly, "and you don't know me. But you should know this. I don't like anything that hurts Aly or gets her into trouble."

"I understand," I said. "I don't either. I promise you, I will do everything in my power to protect her and keep her safe."

"Bit late for that," Melissa said sharply. "What with losing her job for her."

I winced. "I know. I'll find some way of fixing that, however I can. I swear. Believe me, she means a lot to me."

Melissa held my gaze. Finally she leaned back and said, "I believe you. Is your story that important?"

"It very well could be," I said. "And Alison's help has been crucial. I owe her a lot."

"Damn right you do."

"That's why I'm determined to protect her and repay her however I can."

Narrowing her eyes, Melissa muttered, "I'll bet you are."

"Look," I said, not caring for the insinuation, "I never meant for her to get in trouble. Me, sure, yeah, I get in trouble plenty…" Melissa's eyes narrowed even further. "…But I can take care of myself. This story we're working on, yes, it's important. But Alison has become important to me, too. Maybe even more important. I don't know, I'm still trying to figure things out. But make no mistake." I leaned over towards her now. "I am not simply using Alison only to discard her later when I'm done. She's too important to me now. And what develops between us, well, we'll figure that out as we go along. But she *is* a grown woman, you know."

Maybe that last remark was a bit too harsh, but there it was. Melissa stared at me silently. Then her eyes softened somewhat and she said, "Just don't hurt her. She's been hurt bad once. I don't think she can take that kind of hurt again."

"I think she's stronger than you give her credit for," I said quietly. "But I understand. And I won't. I swear."

The running water in the shower stopped. Melissa glanced toward the hallway leading to the bathroom, then looked back at me and whispered, "Just take care of her."

"I will," I whispered back.

Alison appeared a few moments later, clean and fresh in a new top and jeans, her hair still somewhat damp as it hung around her pretty face. "Oh, my God, that is *so* much better," she said. "Thank you *so* much for this, Mel."

"Hey, no problem," Melissa said. "Are you sure you won't stay for a bit?"

"Sorry," Alison said as she hefted a duffle bag over her shoulder, "I wish we could but we have a super long drive ahead of us."

"Is there anything else I can do for you before you go?" Melissa said as we all headed for the back door.

"Just say 'hi' to Tom for me," Alison said.

"Will do," Melissa replied with a smile. The two sisters hugged. "Be careful, you two, OK?" I noticed she'd said the "you two" part with her eyes locked on me and adding silently with a look, "Remember what I said."

I nodded. "We will," I said, adding with my own eyes, "I promise."

CHAPTER TWENTY

The Return

It was a long, long drive back to Arbor Harbor. Night fell. We took turns driving, switching off more often than we'd had on our San Francisco venture. To keep our minds alert and functional, we eschewed our usual 80s pop music soundtrack, instead turning to spoken word stations. We listened to some news, some sports, some comedy, but mostly we listened to old-time radio shows. The likes of *The Lone Ranger, The Shadow, Sgt. Preston of the Yukon, X Minus One, The Great Gildersleeve, Fibber McGee and Molly, Yours Truly, Johnny Dollar* and more kept us entertained and awake in the seemingly neverending drive. We made the occasional food and/or bathroom stop, but mainly we just drove and drove.

At long last, we took the lone exit from the interstate that connected to Arbor Harbor. The sun was just starting to give hints that it was threatening to rise when I finally pulled up in front of my house and parked. On the drive north, we'd reasoned that my home should be safe enough, because even though Universal CEO Roger Ahrens might know my name and where I worked, my home address was private and unlisted.

I let us in the back door which led into the kitchen. At once I head the familiar sound of my beloved dog Sonny jumping down from the bed onto the floor and scurrying down the hall, barking his, "Hey, you stranger, what do you think you're doing here?!?" not-very-threatening bark-growl. Once he turned the corner and caught sight of me, however, the barking stopped, he started squeaking, his tail started wagging a billion miles per second, and he scampered excitedly over to me. I crouched down and gave him a massive hug. "Hey, buddy," I said, "good to see you."

Another figure appeared from the hall leading to the bedrooms, and it wasn't who I'd been expecting to see. Jerry Willems strolled into the kitchen, clad, thankfully, in a robe. Sometimes you never quite knew what you were going to get with Jerry, but thankfully that morning no awkward embarrassment ensued. "Hey, Harry," he said.

Sonny, meanwhile, had gone over to sniff at Alison, who knelt down to pet the black-and-white bundle of energy.

"Oh, hey, Jerry," I said. "I wasn't expecting you."

"Well, yeah," Jerry said, scratching his head. "I guess Rachel had a family emergency so she and Johnny asked if I could pinch-hit for them since they had to go to Eureka, and I said 'Sure'."

"Thanks," I said.

"No prob." Jerry looked pointedly at Alison.

"Oh, I'm sorry," I said. "Jerry, this is Alison. She's been helping me out on my story. Alison, this is Jerry, one of my best friends."

"'One of'?" Jerry said as he shook hands with Alison.

"Pleasure to meet you," Alison smiled.

"The pleasure is all mine," the yet-again bachelor Jerry smiled back. He threw me a "Nice work, pal" waggle of his eyebrows when Alison wasn't looking.

I shot him back a "Be cool, man," furrowed brow.

"Sorry we didn't call ahead," I said aloud.

"No prob," Jerry grinned as he absently patted the hyper Sonny. "Just give me a few minutes and I'll be out of your hair."

"You don't have to—" I began.

"No worries," Jerry cut in smoothly. "Ive got an early meeting up in Blue Cove anyway. I'll be gone in a flash," he finished as he headed back down the hall.

My cat Sam chose that moment to put his little black head around the corner from the stairway to the basement.

"Well, there you are," I said as I scooped him up into my arms.

Immediately I felt and heard his powerful contented purring as he pressed his face against mine in a kitty hug. "You're warm," I said. "Been sleeping on the heating duct again?"

"Heating duct?" Alison said as she scratched the appreciative Sam behind his ears.

"Yeah, he sometimes sleeps on a little section of the ducting down in the basement. Found a nice little comfy warm spot he likes to curl up on."

True to his word, Jerry left a few minutes later. A few minutes after that, Alison and I were in the master bedroom, having shut the door on a disappointed Sonny and an supposedly disinterested Sam. Sonny started squeaking sadly.

"No, Sonny," I called as I slipped my shoes off, "not right now. Go sleep in the guest bed, you were just there, it's probably still warm." He was a furnace, was my sweet dog.

The squeaking stopped, and I heard Sonny plop himself down dejectedly on the floor in front of the door. Just before I turned the light off, I spied the tip of a white paw poking under the door and just resting there, as if being even that tiny bit in the room with me was all he was going to get, by golly he would do it.

"Poor doggy," Alison said as she slipped under the covers. "He really missed you, didn't he?"

"Yeah," I said, getting into bed next to Alison. "Apparently Springers can have severe separation issues."

"You don't say?" Alison chuckled.

"He'll be fine, though." In the meantime, I couldn't help but notice how quickly I'd gotten comfortable again with having a woman in my bed. I gave Alison a quick peck on the cheek, but she was already asleep.

Less than a minute later, so was I.

***

By the time I woke up it was almost noon. I gently nudged Alison awake. Neither of us particularly wanted to get out of bed, but we did. After our morning rituals and a quick breakfast, we headed out.

At the offices of the *Arbor Harbor Coast Post*, I wanted to update my boss. I looked for Lisa, but her office was empty. So we went to my cubicle and went to work on the Broderick Carlsen article I'd been struggling to find time to work on over the past several days. With Alison at my side, at long last I finally finished a very rough bare bones draft. It needed a lot of work, but it covered everything. It covered Broderick Carlsen's birth in 1887, his life of crime, his death at the hands of his partner, the director of *Frankenstein* and his plan to replace a hospitalized and out-of-action Boris Karloff in order to reanimate a corpse for real on film, Carlsen's being used as a tool on the film and being thrown out with the garbage when they were finished with him, his escape from the steel box and his living in the hills behind the garbage dump, Joseph Holland's phone interview with Karloff in 1969 which led to Holland's investigation and subsequent death at Carlsen's hands, Carlsen's reappearance in 2011 in Theodore P. Judah County Forest, his fall, and finally his current comatose state in Sacred Family Memorial Hospital.

By the time the article was done, at least in draft form, Alison and I were both itching to check in on Carlsen in person. Lisa still wasn't back from wherever she'd gone, so Alison and I headed over to Sacred Family.

I introduced Alison to Dr. Ashraf when he arrived at the hospital's reception area in response to being paged. Together we rode the elevator up to the second floor. Dr. Ashraf told us there had still been no change in Carlsen's condition as he led us to the patient's room.

Inside the hushed room, Dr. Ashraf went to check on the various pieces of medical equipment and appliances Carlsen was hooked up to. I couldn't help but think of the fantastic electric devices used in the *Frankenstein* movies, some of which had apparently been instrumental in Carlsen's resurrection, as far-fetched as that seemed.

Alison took my hand as we stood together at the side of the unconscious man before us. His head was still partially bandaged, as part of Dr. Ashraf's attempts to keep a lid on the unusual aspects of the patient. Even so, we could still discern the distinct head shape and portions of the face still visible, the factors which were what had sent me on my journey to unravel this whole crazy story. It was inescapable. This John Doe, aka Broderick Carlsen, really and truly did look exactly like the Frankenstein Monster from the original 1931 movie.

"His heart rate, his blood pressure, everything is still as abnormal as when he first arrived," Dr. Ashraf said quietly. "And we still can't explain it, much less how he's still alive with those extreme numbers."

I looked at Alison. She was gazing at Carlsen with curiosity mixed with awe mixed with sympathy. She must have felt me staring at her, as she turned to look at me. She gave a little smile and squeezed my hand quickly.

"I'll give you a few minutes," Dr. Ashraf said tactfully.

After the door had shut again, Alison said, "Do you think you should tell him?"

"Who, Dr. Ashraf?" I asked. "Maybe. Would it make a difference, or do any good, do you think?"

"I dunno," Alison admitted. She sighed and looked down at Carlsen again. "God, what kind of horrible existence he must have had since he… came back."

"Yeah," I said softly, placing my arm around Alison's shoulders. "To be brought to life like that, to be treated like he was, just for the sake of a movie. A fucking *movie*, for crying out loud. Used like a puppet, then thrown away like garbage once they were done playing with their toy. Having to break out of that steel box, then living like an animal up in the hills for who knows how long. Then someone finds him, something upsets him enough that he kills that someone. Then on the run, hiding ever since."

"What must he have felt?" Alison said. "Does he even *have* feelings, or emotions? Can you have emotions after you die? And his soul, what about his soul? Did it come back from… from wherever it had gone when he died?"

"I don't know," I whispered sadly. "I wish we could talk to him."

"What can we do for him?" Alison said. "He looks so… so sad. So hopeless."

"I wish I knew," I answered lamely, shaking my head.

A few minutes later Dr. Ashraf returned.

"Is there any chance he can recover and be able to talk with us?" I asked the doctor, not expecting a favorable response.

"Unlikely," Dr. Ashraf replied. "It's difficult to say for certain in a case such as this. I can't entirely rule out the possibility of recovery, but I wouldn't pin my hopes on it."

"I understand," I said.

"Did you..." Dr. Ashraf began hesitantly. "Did you find out anything useful in your investigation yet?"

I glanced uncertainly at Alison. She nodded, so I said, "Well, we're pretty certain that he really is Broderick Carlsen, like the fingerprint records say he is."

"But that would mean he's well over a century old, if I remember correctly," the doctor said, puzzlement and confusion etched on his well-worn face.

"One hundred and twenty-four years old, to be exact," I said.

"But... but he doesn't look anywhere *near* that."

"We also believe we've found evidence that Carlsen had undergone some special, um, medical procedures to... prolong his life." There, that covered things nicely, without revealing too much of the insane truth.

Dr. Ashraf frowned. "What sort of procedures?"

"That we don't know, not specifics, anyway," I said. "But we believe it did involve electricity."

"Like in the movie?"

"Yes," I said, "quite a bit like in the movie."

Dr. Ashraf gazed down at his comatose patient. "Hmm. Well, that *might* account for his condition and some of his unusual readings."

"That'd be my guess," I said, nodding.

"What else did you find out, if I may ask?"

"We learned some other things, but nothing else directly relevant to the medical aspect, I don't think. I will say he's had a very rough life for quite a long time."

"That doesn't surprise me," the doctor said. "I do respect your right to not reveal everything you don't have to at this point. But I would urge you to let me know if you learn anything else that might have a bearing on my treatment of this patient, whom I will continue referring to as 'John Doe' for official purposes."

"I will, I promise," I said. "Thank you, Doctor."

Alison and I headed back to the newspaper offices. I saw that Lisa was in her office, so, after setting Alison up at my cubicle again, I headed to my boss's office. I tapped on the open door.

Lisa Takagi looked up from her desk. "Harry, welcome back," she said. "What've you got?"

I entered, shutting the door behind me, which earned me a narrowed gaze from Lisa. I sat down across from her at her desk and pulled out my iPad. "I think I've cracked it," I said quietly. "Pretty much the whole story, from beginning to end."

Lisa's gaze did not alter. "'Pretty much'?" she said. "This is that John Doe story we're talking about, correct?"

"Right," I said. "And from everything I've gathered and looked at —"

At that point my phone went off in my pocket. "Sorry," I said to Lisa as I took it out to check the caller ID. It was from Sacred Family Memorial Hospital. "Excuse me," I said to Lisa as I hit "Answer".

"Hello?" I said nervously, afraid of what I might be about to learn.

"Roger? It's Dr. Ashraf. You may want to get back over here."

"What? Why? What's happened?"

"Your John Doe was just attacked, and now he's gone."

"The attacker's gone?"

"No, my patient is gone.. The attacker is here, but he won't talk, apart from insisting on seeing you."

"We'll be right there." I hung up. To Lisa I said, "I'm sorry, I gotta go." I rushed out of her office and collected Alison.

"What's wrong?" Alison asked as I hustled her to my car. "What's going on?"

"Carlsen was attacked," I said, jumping in my car. "I think our old friend Roger Ahrens might just have showed his face."

CHAPTER TWENTY-ONE

Escape to Danger

As the sun dipped towards the horizon, darkness encroaching, we sped the short distance over to the hospital. Two police cars were outside the entrance to the building. Inside we bypassed the elevator and charged up the stairs.

The second floor was, well, controlled confusion, if that makes any sense. Nurses hustled about, intent on their duties. Policemen were performing their tasks as well, interviewing potential witnesses to whatever had happened. An officer stood parked outside the slightly ajar door to Broderick Carlsen's room.

"Sorry, sir," the tall, slightly pudgy policeman said as Alison and I approached the door. "No one's allowed in."

I thrust my press ID at him and said curtly, "Dr. Ashraf called me."

"It's all right, let them in," Dr. Ashraf's voice barked out from inside the room. The officer stepped aside.

I quickly took in the state of the room. The bed was empty, the sheets and pillows tossed haphazardly. The window was shattered, the drab curtains billowing around the jagged remains of the glass. A policeman stood over Dr. Ashraf and a male nurse who were kneeling by a man sitting in one of the visitor's chairs. The nurse shifted position slightly, and I saw that the man was —

— *Not* Roger Ahrens.

"Josiah!" Alison gasped.

"What the hell is going on?" I said somewhat angrily, partly at Josiah.

"You do know him, then?" Dr. Ashraf said.

"Yeah, we know him," I said evenly. "Josiah, what the hell are you doing here?"

"He killed my father!" Josiah snarled, looking up at me, wincing as the nurse attended to the back of his head.

"Who killed who?" said another voice. We turned to see Police Chief Ray Packer standing in the doorway.

Oh, Lord, where to begin with that one, I thought wearily to myself. "Any chance we could have a bit of privacy," I said as politely as I could manage at the moment.

Chief Packer jerked his thumb, and his officer left the room. The nurse left as well, shutting the door behind him.

"All right," Packer said. "Now, what the heck is going on here? Who's been killed?"

"That was years ago, down in LA," I said, hoping to keep Chief Packer's temper from flaring up too strongly. I had a feeling he wasn't going to like what he was about to hear. I turned back to Josiah in his chair. "What *are* you doing here, Josiah?" I asked the old man.

Josiah looked at us with an expression that encompassed rage, shame, prideful defiance. "I came here to kill Broderick Carlsen."

"Who?" Chief Packer said, somehow frowning deeper than he had been.

"The John Doe who fell off the cliff and went into a coma—" I began.

"Not that shit again!" the chief growled, rubbing his eyes. "Are you still on that ridiculous idea that he's that hundred-year-old guy or whatever?"

"Yeah, I am," I replied, clamping down on my own anger at Packer's stubbornness. "I've investigated this since he showed up, and I've got all sorts of proof that that 'John Doe' is who the fingerprint record says he is. Now will you please let us talk to this man and figure out what's going on?"

Packer threw up his arms in frustration. "Fine," he grumbled angrily. "You do that. Meantime I've got a missing person to locate. I'll be back to get a statement from this man later," he said, throwing a nod at Josiah.

"Hey, ease up, Chief," I said, "he's hurt, angry, scare, confused—"

At that Chief Packer stormed out, slamming the door shut behind him.

I turned back to Josiah Holland. "All right," I said, forcing myself to calm down. "Tell us what is going on. How did you find out about Carlsen? And what happened here?"

"Wasn't too hard to find him," Josiah said with a shrug. "After you guys left, I drove up here and camped out near the newspaper offices and waited for you. Took you a while, but my patience paid off. A short time sitting in my car waiting was nothing compared to the years I've spent not knowing who killed my dad.

"Finally, you showed up this afternoon. I waited, hoping you'd lead me to the guy. I knew from the way you two guys had spoken that day at my house, I knew he was alive, and I knew you knew where he was. And you led me right to him. The hospital was rather obvious, but I wasn't sure I could find him inside all by myself. I followed you here, I saw the doctor take you up in the elevator, so I went up the stairs as quick as I could. I got to the floor in time to see you go into the room. I made my way over to it as casually as I could, hopping no one would get suspicious of me. Eventually I heard you refer to the patient in the room as Broderick Carlsen, and I knew what I had to do. I hid and waited til you guys left the guy alone, made sure no one was paying attention, and snuck into the room.

"And there he was. The fucker who killed my dad. And I hated him. I hated how peaceful he looked lying there so quiet on his bed. I hated him for taking my dad away from me too damn early. So I took one of the pillows and put it right over his damn face. I held it down as hard as I could, but he started to struggle and the next thing I knew I was lying on the floor across the room and the back of my head hurt like hell. And the damn bed was empty, the damn window was smashed, so I figured the guy had jumped out."

"The nurses heard the commotion," Dr. Ashraf said, taking up the story, "and came to see what was going on. They called me immediately so I ran here. I found this man here who started demanding to talk to a reporter he knew named Edwards. So I called you, hoping you could shed some light."

I knew what I had to do, I thought, unconsciously echoing Josiah Holland's words from a few short minutes before. Or, at least, I knew what I *wanted* to do. Carlsen was out there, somewhere. God only knew what would happen if the police found him first. I had to get to him before anyone else did. I knew his sad story, and I figured I was the only one who had any chance of getting through to him and ending this peacefully. I turned to Alison. "Do you mind staying here with Josiah for a bit?" I asked her.

She frowned slightly. "All right," she said. I could hear the reluctance. "Where are you going?" I had a feeling she knew exactly where I was going.

Heading for the door, I said, "I'm going to find Broderick Carlsen."

***

Outside the sun had set by now, and darkness was all around. I stood near the hospital entrance and looked around. To the west was the harbor and the ocean. Not a likely escape route for Carlsen there. North and east of the hospital lay the bulk of the village of Arbor Harbor. Not a huge metropolis by any means, but an inhabited area that a person on the run would likely want to avoid. South of where I stood were a few more buildings, but beyond the outskirts loomed the towering and densely-packed trees of Theodore P. Judah County Forest, where this whole crazy thing began nearly two weeks ago. My gut told me that Carlsen would head there. He knew how to survive in the woods, and these woods were the nearest available refuge for him. Once again, I went with my gut. I was beginning to regain some of my faith in my gut. Failing to see Sarah for what she really was, that had been a blow to my faith in my instincts, to be sure. But apart from that nightmare situation, I told myself, my gut had been a *lot* more reliable than ever. (Sorry for all the "gut"s. This paragraph has had more guts than an 80s slasher film.)

I hopped in my car and drove the short distance over to the main north entrance of the forest. I went past the little ranger station-slash-welcome center and drove on. Once inside the grounds a short way I pulled over to the side of the road and parked. I dug out a flashlight from the glove box of my car. A cold wind was whipping up, so I pulled my jacket tighter as I headed into the woods, flicking on the light. Far off in the distance, off to my left, I could see the tell-tale glow of the newly-resurgent forest fire which had flared up again while I'd been out of town. We'd caught a brief news report on the radio on our drive back home the previous night, and I prayed again that the town and its residents be kept safe. Now I added myself and Broderick Carlsen to the list. I knew Chief Brewer and his men were good, and I knew the area's firejumper crews were fantastic. Still, it wasn't exactly fun tramping through a forest that was on fire, however distant the actual blaze might have been. I'd never liked fire, not at all. But I had to find Carlsen if at all possible.

The strangely-pleasing-to-a-person-afraid-of fire scent of burning wood grew as I went further and further into the forest. I started calling out Carlsen's name, until it hit me that Carlsen might not recognize his name anymore.

After a good amount of hiking, having penetrated what I thought was quite a fair distance into the woods, I was jolted by the shock of hearing a nearby voice.

"Will you slow down, dammit, I can't keep up!"

I spun around and found Roger Ahrens, CEO of Universal Studios, leaning against a tree and gasping for breath. And of course, next to him loomed the imposing figure of his henchman Adam, aka Mr. Suit, looking much more fit than his superior. The two men trained their flashlights on me as I trained mine on them.

"What the hell are you doing here?" I cried, confused and irritated and exasperated.

"Following orders," Ahrens said.

"What? What orders?"

Having mostly caught his breath, Ahrens said, "Standing orders for every Universal CEO. If someone starts asking about Broderick Carlsen, they are to be shut down immediately and heavily warned off. There's even a neat computer thing that sends me an alert if someone runs a search on that name in the Archives database. That's how I found out about you, of course."

"Of course," I said drily. "But why?"

Ahrens shrugged. "Tradition? It's been part of our marching orders since the early 1930s. I just do what I'm supposed to do."

"Which is, what, to keep the secret about Carlsen from getting out to the public? That might not reflect well on your company, I would guess."

Ahrens narrowed his eyes. "Do you know the secret?"

Uh-oh. "Maybe," I said cautiously.

Ahrens nodded at Adam. The big man pulled out a gun and pointed it at me.

"Whoa, whoa, whoa, hang on!" I sputtered anxiously, automatically raising my hands. This was not going well so far.

"Tell me what Carlsen's secret is," Ahrens barked.

Eyeing Mr. Suit's gun nervously, I said, "Why the hell should I tell you?" Probably stupid of me to try to brazen it out at gunpoint, but there you go.

Sighing, Ahrens said, "Because I want to know what it is."

It took me a second to process and comprehend what he'd actually said. Having a gun pointed at you tended to mess with your thinking. "Are you actually telling me you don't know what it is? What this is all about?"

Ahrens shook his head. "No, I don't."

"So you and your fellow CEOs have been protecting this secret for years and years, and you don't even know what the hell it is you're protecting?"

"When you put it like that," Ahrens conceded, "it does seem rather improbable. But it's the truth. I would have to assume whomever created the original orders knew. And maybe the man after him. I don't know. But you will tell me what you know. Now."

I hesitated. I didn't think it was a good idea to tell Roger Ahrens about the possibility of mankind having the ability to resurrect the dead.

"I presume our friend Alison Whatever-her-name-is knows the secret, too?" Ahrens said calmly. "Maybe she'll be more willing to tell me."

Shit. Well, there was no way I was about to let *that* happen. So I told Roger Ahrens the story of Broderick Carlsen, the whole damn thing, start to finish.

When I'd finished, Ahrens started at me. "That's insane," he finally said.

"It's the truth, however insane it may sound," I said. "It's up to you whether you believe it or not. And based on everything I've seen, I'd say your standing orders probably came from Whale and Laemmle Jr. to cover the thing up to protect their careers, and also due to their regret and shame, but probably also to prevent anyone else from ever trying something like this again."

"Can you prove any of this?"

"A hell of a lot of it, yeah," I said.

"And what sort of proof do you have, exactly?" Ahrens asked. I told him about the various documentation and proof we'd found during the course of the investigation. "I'm going to want all of that," Ahrens said smoothly once I'd finished.

I shook my head. "Hell, no."

"Adam?" Ahrens said quietly.

Adam stepped forward, focusing the barrel of his gun squarely at my chest. We were still separated by several yards, but I could tell he wouldn't miss if he really wanted to shoot me. I didn't know what to say, and I didn't dare move.

Suddenly, as if from nowhere, out of the darkness came a strangled, anguished cry. It echoed amongst the towering trees as the three of us looked about us for the source. Just as suddenly, a huge dark shape came charging at us from the black. Our flashlights had just enough time to reveal the hospital-robed shape of Broderick Carlsen. He charged at Adam, who fired his gun wildly.

Carlsen screamed, then smashed into Adam. The henchman crashed to the ground, his gun flying away as he fell.

And just as suddenly as he'd arrived, Carlsen was gone, racing into the dark forest and out of the range of our flashlights.

Thinking fast, I searched for and quickly spotted Adam's gun. I ran over and scooped it up. I had zero experience with firearms, everything I knew about them came mostly from TV or movies or books. I couldn't have told you what make or model or whatever Adam's gun actually was. But one thing I did know for sure about firearms. They could be very dangerous, even to the persons wielding them. So I grasped Adam's gun carefully but firmly, pointing the barrel in the general direction of Roger Ahrens, but towards the ground in front of him.

Ahrens knelt by Adam, checking him over. The big man appeared to be out cold. Ahrens looked up, saw me holding the gun, then stood up slowly and carefully. "What are you going to do to me?" he asked nervously.

"Dunno," I said, trying to remain cool and calm. "Behave yourself and, well, we'll see."

"Was that…?"

"It was."

"Damn. He really *does* look like Frankenstein."

Once again I bit my tongue, saying simply, "Yeah."

I could almost see the gears working inside Ahrens' head as he struggled to come to grips with the situation. Eventually he said, "So what you told me, it's actually true?"

"Yeah," I said again. Now I was getting impatient to go after Carlsen. I started to head off into the trees after him.

"Hey, where are you going?" Ahrens cried plaintively.

"After Carlsen," I replied, glancing back at the studio executive.

Ahrens bent down and placed Adam's flashlight by the unconscious man's head, pointing it in the direction I was heading. Then he actually hurried to catch up with me. "Are you going to kill him?" he asked as we pushed on through the forest, the glow from the fire still distant to the southeast of us.

"No," I said, "I'm going to help him."

"Killing him would be the best solution, I think," Ahrens said. "It gets rid of the problem and keeps the secret a secret. Without him, even if you did publish your story, no one would believe it. And isn't it better that way?"

"What are you talking about?" I said in a disgusted growl.

"Do you honestly believe that the world could handle this?" Ahrens went on. "That there actually is a way to bring back the dead? The secret of eternal life? And that it actually worked?"

I didn't respond. Because, as much as it galled me to admit it, even to myself, the man had a point. The world would go mad over the secret. It would be utter chaos. Rich people living forever, poor people never having that chance. Overpopulation. And on top of that, the resurrection of the dead just seemed to me to be against the natural order of the universe, against the way of God's creation. No, this selfish, petty world couldn't possibly handle such a thing. And yet I could not bring myself to believe that killing Carlsen was the right thing to do.

We hurried on. The darkness felt thick. All we had were the beams of our two flashlights, and the dim glow on the horizon. After a period of trudging through the trees and brush, the ground suddenly disappeared from before us. We stopped just in time to prevent ourselves from falling over the edge. Instead, we cautiously peered over, aiming our flashlights down below.

It was a deep gully of some sort, possibly a dried-up riverbed, running in front of us from left to right. The sides of the little valley were steep, and I could spy no easy way down or across in our vicinity. Then we spied a movement down below, and we fixed our lights on it. The beams barely reached, but we saw that it was Carlsen, on the ground in the center of the gully, his left leg covered by a dark stain, presumably blood, likely from Adam's gunshot. His right leg was bent at a horribly wrong angle. We could hear a pitiful moan echoing up from the riverbed as Carlsen clutched at his bleeding wound.

"Broderick Carlsen!" I called out.

The whimpering stopped, and Carlsen looked up. He just stared at us.

"Mr. Carlsen," I said, feeling a bit silly, "I'm not here to hurt you, I'm here to help you, I promise."

Carlsen stared, making no sound.

"Does he even understand what you're saying?" Ahrens murmured quietly out of the side of his mouth.

I didn't know. I thought he did. But I didn't bother to answer Ahrens. "I know that you're frightened and confused. I know you've had a terrible life. I know what happened to you. And I know that you probably aren't very fond of people anymore. But not everyone is evil. I don't believe you're evil. I try to be a good person myself. You don't need to be afraid of me. Will you let me help you?" I called down to Carlsen.

"What's that noise?" Ahrens said, interrupting me.

Getting even more irritated at Ahrens, I hissed, "What noise?"

"That kind of rumbling, don't you hear it?"

I did hear it then. It was a sort of roaring rumbling sound, getting louder. I looked about for the source. And then I spotted it. Far off, I saw the forest fire, still safely distant, I thought. But there was something else, some movement or other. A thin finger of light was snaking its way in our general direction, getting closer and closer. As it approached, I could see from its glow that it was some sort of rogue offshoot of the main blaze, and it was racing its way towards us down the deep, dry riverbed in front of us.

The riverbed in which sat Broderick Carlsen, wounded and injured and unable to move.

And there was no way down to him from where we stood at the lip of the gully.

"We've got to help him!" I said over the crescendoing noise from the approaching finger of flame.

"Are you fucking kidding me?" Ahrens yelled back.

"He's a human being, for God's sake!"

"Are you sure about that?"

I'd had just about enough of Roger Ahrens and his attitude. I was starting to lift my right hand to gesture with the gun when Ahrens said, "Screw this!" and charged me. I had no time to react before he barreled into me. The impact itself didn't hurt, but the man's momentum threw me backwards. My head hit a very solid tree trunk, and I slid woozily to the ground, still somehow clutching the gun.

When I managed to struggle to my feet, on very wobbly legs, Ahrens was gone, and the fire in the riverbed was close. With a ringing in my ears, with a spinning and aching head, with fuzzy eyes, I edged my way to the lip of the precipice. Carlsen was still down there, unmoving. I looked around desperately, but could still see no way down to him. And even if there had been, I wasn't sure I could get him out of there in time all by myself.

The fire roared ever closer. Carlsen turned his head to see the approaching inferno. Then he looked back up at me. And he spoke.

"Help… me!" Broderick Carlsen howled.

Oh, God, I wished I could. His plea nearly broke my heart. But there was nothing I could do.

And then the blaze reached him, enveloped him, continued running on. As I watched, horrified, I could see the poor man literally catch on fire. Dear Lord, it was terrible. I turned, no longer able to watch.

"Kill... me!" Carlsen screamed pitifully.

I turned back. Lifted my hand. Pointed the gun. Finger on the trigger. It would only take one squeeze —

CHAPTER TWENTY-TWO

Remembrance

Pain! So much pain! Oh God, the pain! Everything hurts so much I want to scream but I can't. I try to move but I can't. It feels like I'm lying down. I try to look around but I can't see. It feels like something is covering my face. The pain won't stop, it hurts so much.

Then the pain hurts a bit less. I try to move, and I think my hand moved a little.

"It's alive!" I hear someone cry out. I don't know who it is. I don't know who I am. I don't remember anything, and I still can't see anything.

…Later, the pain is much less but I still feel it always. But I can move now and they took off whatever it was that was covering my face. Now a man is talking to me. He had sent everyone in the room away and now it's just us. I see some machines and lights and things all around us. The man, who says his name is James, says I've been chosen for an experiment. We're going to do some pretending, he says, some make-believe. All I have to do is behave and do exactly what James tells me to do, and he'll take care of me, give me food and a place to sleep when I'm not pretending. It sounds all right, I don't know what else to do.

…The next day for our pretending I'm told to walk into a room backwards, then turn around slowly. I do it. Some men are pointing machines at me. James tells me I will see those a lot. Then I'm told to sit in a chair. I sit. Suddenly there is light coming in from above me. It feels nice and warm, and I can almost see the light dance as I reach out to touch it. But then the light goes away suddenly. I am

sad. I liked the light.

...I pretend a lot. A lot of the time I pretend with a thin man with slicked-back hair and really intense eyebrows who looks at me almost with... disgust? An older man is with us a lot, too. And a shorter man, who is sometimes mean to me but then he's really nice to me and says he's sorry for being mean. I guess he's pretending, too.

...I'm playing by some water with a little girl. We're throwing flowers into the water and watching them float. Then we run out of flowers. But the girl's yellow hair kind of looks like the flowers we'd been playing with. I wonder if she'll float, too, like the flowers did, so I toss her in the water to find out. Then everyone starts screaming and yelling at me, some of the people behind the lights and the big machines rush to the water as I run away, I'm scared, I'm confused. We were just playing, what did I do wrong?

James finds me and talks to me alone. He says the girl is all right but that I did a bad thing. He says he told me just to reach towards the girl when the flowers were gone, not to actually throw her in. I don't remember that. I want to say I'm sorry but I still can't talk, and I don't know why. I feel so bad. James says I am only supposed to do exactly what he tells me when it's pretend-time.

...Fire! I don't like fire. James says it'll be all right, that the fire won't actually get close to me or hurt me. But I don't like fire, it really scares me. Are they mad at me because of the little girl? I didn't mean to hurt her, they said she was all right. I'm so confused.

And still the pain, the pain never stops...

...The thin man with the smooth hair, Colin, is with me on top of a mill. But the mill is inside a building. I don't understand that. Maybe the mill is pretending, too, like I am, like Colin is. And why are the people down below yelling so much at us? What is "Frankenstein"? They keep yelling that. Are they yelling at Colin? I thought his name was Colin. Is it my name? Maybe. I don't know my name. Some people have called me Boris but I don't think that's my name.

We finish the pretending on top of the mill, then James yells, "Cut!" like he does a lot, then the people down below start clapping their hands. I'm not sure why. After everyone else leaves and it is just me and James, James tells me he needs me to do one more thing and then we're done with pretending. I feel glad about that, but sad, too, because I don't know what I will do after that.

James tells me to go up on top of the mill again, then tells me to walk to a specific spot. I do. When I get there, the floor breaks and I fall...

...I wake up and it's dark, I can't see anything, it hurts to move. Oh, no, is it starting all over again? No, it's different this time. I think I'm stuck in a big pile of *junk, wood mostly but metal things, too. I try to get out of the pile and stand but I hit my head on something. I think it's a metal ceiling. I'm very cramped with all this junk in here. And I still can't see. I feel around for a door or a way out but there's nothing.*

Eventually I see a few tiny dots of light in the wall. So small. But the light is still beautiful to me. Like when I was in the chair. I touch the light but it doesn't feel like the warm light from when I was in that chair. Is the light from outside? Is it the sun? I want to get out. How do I get out? I want to get out of here so bad.

I get mad. I get so mad I start hitting and punching the wall near the dots of light. I hit it again, and again, and again. I punch and punch and punch and punch. It hurts my hands but I don't care, I want to get out of this metal dark thing so bad…

…I don't know how long I've been punching the wall. A long time, I think. I keep punching until finally I make a hole in the wall. I can see that it's dark outside now. The light from the tiny holes kept going from light to dark so I guessed it was light from the sun outside coming in. From what little I can see through the small hole I made, I think I was right.

I keep punching and punching, I pull and pull at the opening. I have to make it bigger. I have to get out.

…Finally the hole is big enough for me. I pull myself out from under all the junk inside the box and I crawl outside. I'm in a bigger pile of even more junk and garbage. Nearby, I see a fence. I run over and climb up and drop down the other side and keep going, up into the hills. Then I find a little cave, so I go inside and lie down and fall asleep…

…I spend a long time living in the hills, living in my little cave. I like it. No people ever come around to bother me. Once in a while I go out and get some plants to eat or catch some small animals to eat whenever I start to feel hungry, which isn't very often. When I go outside my cave, I usually go out at night so no one sees me. But since I never see anyone during the day either as I look out the front of my cave, eventually I start hunting during the day, too. Eating feels like something I should do. James always gave me things to eat even though I was never really hungry then, either.

…One day I hear something outside my cave. I was just back from hunting a rabbit. It's day time. I think it's a person out there, he's saying something, really loud, but I can't understand it. I hear the man get closer and closer, talking as he comes closer.

Then the man says something I recognize. "Frankenstein." I still don't know what that means, but the angry people were yelling it that last time I was pretending. But they weren't really angry, were they? It's so confusing. But that word was what they were yelling that time, that time just before I was trapped in the box. Are they here to take me back there? To make me pretend again? No! I won't go back and do that again! Not after what they did to me!

I rush outside my cave so angry and see the man who'd been calling out that word. I'm not going to let them take me back. I grab the man by the neck and squeeze and squeeze. I am so angry. Then I let go and he falls to the ground. I look around. I don't know how the man found me, but if he found me, other men might find me, might try to take me back to pretend. I won't go back!

So I run away…

…I run and hide, run and hide, for a long time. A really long time. I try to stay away from people but sometimes I can't. I see some people shooting guns at each other in an alley in a city. I see people playing in parks. I see people driving cars, hiking in the woods. Sometimes people see me. Sometimes they scream. Sometimes they say, "Is it Halloween already?" Whatever that means. But when I know I've been seen I have to go. I keep running and hiding…

…Eventually I find a really big forest, and I find a nice cave in it like the one in the hills. I hope I can stay here a while. I'm so tired of running and hiding…

…I've been in my new cave for a long while. Then one day I start smelling something, hearing something. I leave my cave to go look. It's night but there is light in the distance, getting brighter and closer as I watch. The forest is on fire! No! Just when I'd finally found a place to stay for a while with no one around at all to bother me! It's not fair!

The fire keeps getting closer, so I run. I run away from the fire, all the way to the end of the woods. Then I stop at the edge of a cliff. I can see the water down below, stretching away. It's so pretty, even in the dark. I look behind me. The fire is still there, still burning. But not as bright now. I think I've run far enough away to maybe be safe from it. Maybe I can—

Someone down below and behind me yells something. I spin around, startled, and lose my balance, and I fall—

…I wake up. I can't see. Again. Why does this keep happening to me? Except this time I can't breathe. But I can move. I reach up, feel a pillow on my face, it's being held there by someone. I thrash out, angry again, hear a big thud, and the pillow flops off my face.

I'm in a bed in a room. There's an old man on the floor across the room. And there are weird machines and lights all around me. No! Not again! I won't go through that again! I have to get out of here!

I hear people outside the door to the room. The only other way out is the window. I can't figure out how to open it, so I just jump through it, and land on some bushes. Then I run. I see tall trees in one direction, so I head that way, hoping to find safety in the woods, where I've always found safety, at least for a while. I can hide there, I can be alone there again.

My body hurts and my head feels funny, but I keep running. Then I stop to rest, because the hurt and the funny feeling in my head get worse. A lot worse. It's so bad. I rest by a big tree trunk, as it gets dark.

...I hear voices now, people arguing. I find them. In the light they're carrying I can see one of the men pointing a gun at another man. No! I hate guns! I hate how they hurt people! I rush at the man with the gun. Just before I run into him and knock him down, I feel an even worse pain in my leg. But I keep going. I have to get away from these people.

I run, limping with my hurt leg, which gets worse and worse as I run. Then I fall and tumble down a very steep, very tall slope, and come to rest. Now my other leg hurts bad, too. So bad that I can't move when I try. It hurts so much. So much pain...

I don't know what to do anymore.

I hear something, a roar. I see light up above me. Did those men find me? Now what do I do?

What's that other noise?

I hurt so bad.

Oh, no, I see fire heading towards me. And I still can't move, no matter what I do, no matter what I try. I'm stuck.

I look up, and for the first time I can remember, I force myself to speak. I scream up at the men at the top of the slope. "Help...me!"

But it's too late. The fire reaches me. And I burn. It hurts, it hurts so much! Worse than ever! I cannot stand this pain, it hurts so much, I want it to end, I want the pain to go away, go away forever, but it doesn't.

I remember one of the men had a gun. Do they still have it? I can't see. But I scream at them anyway, hoping. "Kill...me!"

I can't tell if they're still up there now. Dear God, it hurts so much! Please make it stop! Please make it st—

CHAPTER TWENTY-THREE

Journey's End

By the time I made it back to my car on the entrance road, I was feeling rather sick. Partly from the smoke I'd inhaled from the fire as it roared past me, which thankfully hadn't climbed the banks of the riverbed, and partly because of what I'd done. But I tried not to dwell on that. I trudged on, pausing to let the fire trucks rumble past on the road with their blaring sirens. Well, they should have that offshoot taken care of fairly quickly, I thought.

I noticed a vehicle parked by mine. A black SUV. Uh-oh. I wished for just a second I hadn't tossed Adam's gun away into the fire after I'd... used it. Sure enough, as I approached my car, Roger Ahrens and Adam stepped from their SUV and headed over to me. To my surprise, Ahrens actually appeared... contrite? Concerned, even? Adam looked rather apologetic, too.

"Well?" Ahrens asked.

"I'm fine, thanks," I coughed out, still not feeling very cooperative towards these men.

"Sorry," Ahrens said. "And, um, what about..."

"It's over," I said icily.

Ahrens nodded. "And it's over as far as I'm concerned, too. Done. Finished. No more standing orders, no more bullying people into forgetting about Broderick Carlsen. I'll get that computer alert thing deleted, too. Now that there's no Carlsen anymore, it's all academic, anyway, isn't it?"

I wasn't sure he was using that phrase in quite the right way. But I didn't reply.

Ahrens went on. "And no newspaper story, right? I mean, we both know that's not a very good idea, right?"

I folded my arms and stared at him. "You're right. There will be no story about this. But not for your sake, that's for damn sure."

Ahrens had the decency to look humbled as he nodded and said, "I understand." He turned to Adam. "I think we should go."

"I agree," I muttered wearily, coughing up a lung again.

"Oh, one last thing," Ahrens said, pausing on his way back to the SUV. "You can tell Miss Alison…" He hesitated, obviously hoping I'd supply her last name, which he could never seem to remember, if he even ever knew it in the first place. I didn't oblige him. He continued. "Well, she can have her old job back if she wants. No strings, no recriminations, nothing. Just business as usual."

"Business as usual, huh?" I croaked. "Right. I'll tell her." But she'll tell you to shove it up your ass, I wanted to add but didn't. Truth was, I wasn't sure she would. Maybe she would go back to Universal. I didn't know what Alison's plans were. Though I knew what I hoped they might be. "Oh, by the way," I added, looking at Adam. "I lost your gun. Sorry." I wasn't sorry.

Adam shrugged, then hopped into the SUV with his boss. A minute and a U-turn later and they were out of sight.

I got in my car and headed back to Sacred Family Memorial Hospital. On the short drive over, I called the police chief and let him know he could call off the search for Carlsen. Or John Doe. Or whatever the hell he wanted to call him. I also told him I'd been completely mistaken about the man's identity. He seemed smugly pleased by that, but I didn't care. I also convinced him not to press any charges against Josiah Holland. It took some arguing, but eventually Chief Packer grudgingly agreed, then told me I owed him one now. I didn't care.

***

* * *

Alison was curled up and asleep on a sofa in the hospital lobby. I wanted so much to go over to her, but I had a few things I had to do first.

I found Dr. Ashraf and told him that Carlsen was dead. He understood, and didn't question me further. Then I had him lead me to the room they'd put Josiah Holland in.

Inside the dimly-lit room, it was just me and Josiah. The old man was asleep in the bed. I went over to him and gently woke him up. "Josiah," I said quietly.

Josiah's eyes squinted open as he looked at me. He looked so tired. God only knew how *I* looked. "Huh?" the old man murmured.

"It's over," I told him. "Carlsen's dead."

Josiah smiled weakly and nodded. "Good," he whispered. "Thank you." Then he fell asleep once more.

I didn't particularly feel like I'd earned anyone's gratitude. But I didn't say anything. Instead, I left Josiah a note on the bedside table with Betty Reynolds' phone number at the *Los Angeles Daily Record*.

Returning to the lobby, I went right over to the still-sleeping form of Alison Perry and knelt down beside her. I touched her shoulder, and she awoke. I must have looked terrible, because she immediately looked concerned.

I reached out and pulled her to me in a tight embrace and clung to her as I told her what had happened. By the end of it I was crying, I was sobbing. Alison just held me. It was exactly what I needed.

CHAPTER TWENTY-FOUR

Closing Time

I woke up the next morning and dressed quietly, so as not to wake Alison. She looked so… right, lying there in my bed. I didn't want to think about what little time we probably had left together before she headed back to her life in LA. I hadn't told her about Ahrens' offer yet, nor had we discussed it, but I had a resigned feeling that she would go. So I wanted to enjoy what I had while I still had it.

I stepped out of the bedroom, blocking Sam and Sonny from charging in to say good morning to their new friend. A few minutes later, I was off to work.

The newspaper offices seemed so incredibly normal to me that morning. And so small. Everything was in its proper place, and I felt myself start to, not exactly relax, but something close to it, like I hadn't for quite some time. Getting back into my routine would be good, would help ground me back in the real world. But I couldn't help but feel that even this normality was, for lack of a better word, insignificant. I'd learned more than anyone should know about matters of life and death, and writing newspaper stories felt inconsequential now.

I shook my head. Forget it, Harry, I told myself. It's over and done, it's all in the past, no one needs to know anything about it, just let it go. Easy for me to say. But it was true. And shortly Alison would probably be gone, too, and then things really would be back to their small-town normality I'd become so accustomed to.

My first order of business at the office was to stop by my boss's office. Lisa was typing away at her computer when I tapped on her open door.

"Come on in," she said without looking up.

I went in and sat down across from her.

Lisa looked up and immediately looked shocked. Which was rare for her. "You look like hell, Harry, what the fuck happened to you?" So much for hoping a quick shower and fresh clothes would mask my fatigue and sadness.

"That John Doe I was doing the story on," I said, choosing my words carefully for this conversation. "Well, he woke up last night and ran off into the county forest and got caught in the fire."

"He died?"

I nodded.

"And did you figure out who he was, exactly?"

"No."

"No? I thought you were on to something."

"I thought I was too, but…Well, for one thing, the fingerprint match was an error in the records, just like everyone told me. And when I was digging around down in LA, I… Well, I screwed up. I misread something and ran with it and ended up on a wild goose chase. Long story short, I've got nothing."

"Nothing, huh?" Lisa frowned, narrowing her eyes.

"'Fraid so," I said with an embarrassed shrug. "I'm sorry."

It was true, I really did have nothing to publish. And I was sorry for wasting Lisa's time.

Lisa stared at me for a minute. "Uh-huh," she said eventually. "Well, if that's how it is, that's how it is. Write up a brief summary with the bare bones of John Doe's story and send it my way. Then go home and get some rest. You look like shit."

"Will do," I said. "Thank you." I got up to leave and had just gotten to the doorway when Lisa's voice stopped me.

"Harry," she said. I looked back at her. "Good work," she said very quietly, then turned back to her computer.

Lisa Takagi. Smart woman.

Back at my desk, I sent an email to Fire Chief Brewer. I told him basically the same thing I'd told my boss, that I'd screwed up and that there was no information as to who the John Doe had been. I thanked him for the help he'd given. He sent me a quick email back thanking me for the update. I didn't know if he'd read between the lines or not, but I really didn't want to find out. He also let me know the rogue trail of fire from last night had been extinguished safely. Thank goodness.

Then I turned to the task of writing up the John Doe story for publication. It would have been easy just to ignore it and never publish anything, but general word about the mystery man had gotten around town, so ignoring it might make the public suspicious. And oh my God we did *not* need that.

So I stuck to the truth as much as possible as I wrote. It went somewhat against the grain in terms of my journalistic ethics, but deep down I knew it was for the best.

***

UNIDENTIFIED MAN DIES IN FOREST FIRE

An unidentified man died in the recently resurgent forest fire in Theodore P. Judah County Forest, the same forest in which he was first discovered by authorities.

On Saturday, March 12, the John Doe was spotted by Arbor Harbor Fire Chief Henry Brewer, apparently fleeing from the forest fire then raging in another part of the county forest. Mr. Doe fell from one of the cliffs near the North Shore Beach area, receiving a head injury from the fall. He was then taken to Sacred Family Memorial Hospital, where he remained stable but in a coma for the next ten days.

Last evening, Mr. Doe woke from his coma. He apparently panicked, jumped out of the window of his second-story hospital room, and fled into the county forest, where he was caught in the blaze and died.

Police were unable to identify the man. A check on his fingerprints returned no valid matches, he matched no descriptions of known missing persons, and his face was in any event too disfigured for authorities to circulate a photograph of the man for identification inquiries.

Our condolences go out to the deceased's loved ones, whomever and wherever they may be.

* * *

***

I sat back, reread the article, tweaked a few things, then gave up. I just couldn't face it any longer. I hit "Send" and it was on its way to my boss.

Then I deleted every bit of documentation I had collected in the Broderick Carlsen story. Every scanned document, every photo, every note, every printout, right down to the audio file of the Holland-Karloff interview, all that I had on the story was deleted. From my phone, my tablet, my notebook, the cloud, everywhere. At last, it was all gone.

I knew Josiah Holland still had the original audiotape of the interview with Boris Karloff, but I trusted the old man to either keep it secret or to destroy it himself. Either way was fine with me.

And finally the sad saga of Broderick Carlsen was over.

***

Alison and I went out for dinner that night at the Earl of Essex. Just as we sat down at our table, Jerry walked in. I waved him over and he sat down with us. We had just placed our drinks order when Johnny and Rachel strolled in. They spotted us and came over to join us.

"We thought you might be here," Rachel said as she and her husband took their seats.

"How is everything?" I asked.

"Mother is doing so much better, thank you," Rachel said.

"We're sorry we weren't able to stay until you got back—" Johnny began.

I cut him off with a polite dismissive wave. "Don't worry about it," I said. "That's what we keep Jerry around for." I clapped a companionable hand on Jerry's shoulder. "Our permanent understudy."

"Ha, ha," Jerry grumbled good-naturedly.

"By the way," I said. "Johnny, Rachel, this is Alison. She helped me out a great deal on my story while I was in LA. Alison, these are the Goldschmidts, Johnny and Rachel. They were house-sitting for me while I was away."

"Hey, I helped, too," Jerry added.

"How is that story coming along?" Johnny asked.

"It's not," I said, trying to be casual. I hated lying to my friends, but once again, I felt I had to. "Turns out it was just a complete waste of time. I screwed some stuff up and it all just went to pot."

"I'm sorry to hear that," Johnny said kindly.

"So, what do you do, Alison?" Rachel asked politely.

"Well," Alison said shyly, "I used to be an archivist at a major motion picture studio."

"'Used to'?" Johnny asked.

"Oh, hey, I keep forgetting to tell you," I said, turning to Alison. "Your old boss said you could have your old job back no strings, nothing. If you wanted it." Okay, so maybe I hadn't exactly been "forgetting" to tell her.

Alison looked at me. "I really don't think I want to work there anymore."

I noticed Johnny and Rachel exchange a glance.

"What?" I asked them.

"Well," Johnny said, "one of my full-timers at the bookshop jut put in his notice. I'm not sure how well an archivist's job would correlate to a bookseller's job, but…"

I held my breath. This was going so fast. I'd been afraid of what would happen when Alison decided to return to LA, Universal Studios job or no. I'd desperately wanted her to stay, but I didn't want to influence her decision. It was her career, after all. It had to be up to her. So I just smiled encouragingly when she looked at me before replying to Johnny.

"Well, I'd need someplace to stay…" Alison said quietly.

"That's not a problem," I said just as quietly, feeling my heart thump faster and stronger.

Alison smiled her beautiful, warm smile at me, I felt my spirit soar. She turned back to Johnny. "Tell me more," she said happily.

"It would involve much more than just selling books," Johnny explained. "Though that is a large component of what we do. We also deal in rare books, book repair, rebinding, things of that nature. The position also involves some accounting, bookkeeping, inventory…"

I felt a jab in my ribs. I turned to see Jerry grinning at me, his eyes glinting over the top of his John Lennon glasses. "I'd say that story of yours wasn't a total waste of time, wouldn't you?" he whispered with a wink.

I looked back at the beautiful, smart, strong, brave Alison as she talked with my friend Johnny. She glanced at me and gave me another heartwarming smile.

"No," I whispered back to Jerry. "Not a waste of time at all."

EPILOGUE

And there you have it. How I met your mother. Yes, I know that's a TV show. But it really is how we met. And we've had a wonderful life ever since. Especially since the day you came into our lives. What a gift from heaven you have been, peanut!

You might be asking yourself why I told you all of those secret things about Frankenstein and Carlsen and resurrection and such. Well, I'm pretty sure between your mother and I, onc of us was bound to slip up at some point and say something we shouldn't. (Your mother says it'd be me. Who am I to argue?)

Not only that, you are our child. To give you this story without all of the details would do you a disservice. You deserve the truth. And you're finally at the age where we trust you to understand the story, and understand why no one else should ever know the full truth.

Out of tragedy, out of one man's sad life, such happiness as your mother and I have can spring. And our love for you.

So be a good kid and don't blab about this, OK?

Now go help your mother with your little brother's bedtime.

Catch ya later, peanut.

Author's Afterword

Thank you so very much for making it all the way through the book! If you did, that is. If you didn't, and jumped ahead to here, how dare you! Go read the whole thing! Right now! I'll wait.

First and foremost, thank you to everyone who has helped, encouraged, edited, beta-ed, published, hosted, read, reviewed, and anything else on my previous projects. I could never have gotten this far without your help and support. I am eternally grateful to you all.

Second, this story is in no way intended to besmirch, belittle, smear, mudsling, libel, or do anything else negative to the names, persons, reputations etc of any real persons, in particular those I've included as being in on the plan: Boris Karloff, Carl Laemmle Jr., Colin Clive, Dwight Frye, Edward Van Sloan, Jack Pierce, and anyone else who might be inferred as being involved. I hold the work of all of these people in very much high esteem. The sentiments of the protagonist in this book regarding his appreciation of the original 1931 Frankenstein are pretty much mine. Big respect to all, and apologies if I've wronged any of you. This is a work of fiction, and not intended to be negative to anyone. (Well, maybe one person, who knows who they are, if they even ever read this. In which case... No, I'll bite my tongue.)

Third, no negative connotations are intended to be placed against the originator of the Frankenstein story, Ms. Mary Wollstonecraft Shelley, way back in 1818. Over 200 years ago! Much kudos to you, for making such a success of your work in an extremely chauvinistic world. (Not that we're much better now, but...)

Finally, thank you to my mother, Kay, who has supported me through thick and thin, my entire life, and always encouraged me to use my imagination. It's not

250

often said, but imagination is so important, in so many ways, not just for making silly stories like this one. Keep imagining, people!

Good night!

Kevin Schultz
Appleton, Wisconsin
April 2024